THE STRUGGL

The determination to be a great scientist burned up with a bright flame in Albert Woods's boyish heart and it never dimmed. It is the story of his career as a scientist that I propose to tell. And at the same time honesty compels me to add that this was not the only flame of greatness that burned up in Albert's heart.

As life rolled on all sort of flames of greatness burned up with varying degrees of impressiveness or absurdity. In his different phases Albert Woods was a great psychologist – this with considerable success; a great literary man – he was too busy to write anything; a great man of refinement – I let this pass for the time being; and – you may as well face it now – a great amorist. And that is not the sum total by any means. Enveloping them all was the concept of himself as a great everyman.

Nevertheless they were all great. All had the glow of Napoleonic inflation. And all of them in due course received that last touch of the little man.

Works by the same author

WILLIAM COOPER

THE
STRUGGLES OF
ALBERT WOODS

METHUEN

First published in Great Britain 1952
by Jonathan Cape
Copyright © 1952 by William Cooper
Published 1966 by Penguin Books
This edition published 1985
by Methuen London Ltd
11 New Fetter Lane, London EC4P 4EE

Reproduced, printed and bound in Great Britain by
Hazell Watson & Viney Limited,
Member of the BPCC Group,
Aylesbury, Bucks

ISBN 0 413 56820 2 (hardback)
0 413 56830 X (paperback)

This Book is Dedicated
to My Mother and Father

CONTENTS

As for myself, I take a great displeasure
In tales of those who once knew wealth and leisure
And then are felled by some unlucky hit.
But it's a joy to hear the opposite,
For instance tales of men of low estate
Who climb aloft and growing fortunate
Remain secure in their prosperity;
That is delightful as it seems to me
And is a proper sort of tale to tell.

From *The Canterbury Tales* –
Words of the Knight to the Host

PART ONE

World of Promise

CHAPTER ONE

NAPOLEON WITH A DIFFERENCE

Wherever he was, whatever he did, there was always something of the little man about Albert Woods. I might have said wherever he is, whatever he does – he is still alive in 1952 – there still is something of the little man about him. For although many of his dreams of glory have come true, you can just as easily see him manfully fighting a brute three times his own size when suddenly his braces burst, or impetuously diving head first into a lake to save a drowning baby when the water happens to be only a foot deep. Some things about a man never change.

I doubt if people would have noticed his touch of the little man so quickly if it had not been that really Albert Woods was made on the grand scale. True he was a small man physically, small and sturdy; but his temperament was wondrously grand: it was broad, it was deep and above all it was expansive – so expansive that he often had the air of its having blown him up like a balloon.

Albert Woods's temperament was compounded of intelligence, gusto and absurdity, of warm-heartedness, cunning and uninhibited imagination, of bombinating passion and sustained pervading will. And the whole shoot was grandiosely inflatable.

He was aware of his rich and varied endowment. Albert Woods may have taken most of his life to see that he had a touch of the little man, but he recognized at the age of fourteen that he had more than a streak of Napoleon. He felt like Napoleon.

Unfortunately a temperament that is grandiosely inflatable lays its possessor wide open to deflation. Hopefulness was Albert Woods's greatest single inflating agent, and in this world one's hopes are only too often pricked. So Albert Woods was constantly being deflated. His army got lost in the snow time after time in spite of all his efforts. And he responded to the loss almost physically. Having given the impression of being slightly larger

3

than life despite his stature, he suddenly looked much smaller: having moved with an energetic bustling gait he suddenly began to trail his feet miserably as if they were too loose at the ankles.

And then in a few hours, a few days perhaps, what happened? His hopefulness returned just as fresh and as inflating as ever before. Life was strong in him.

Albert Woods was born in 1900. He came from the lower middle class, that great reservoir of English energy, ability and talent, which has provided in the last hundred years our most creative artists, scientists and founders of industries. You had only to take one look at Albert Woods, no matter how far he had got on in the social world, to see that he could have been born nowhere else: it was written all over him. He was the youngest and cleverest of three children born to Arthur Woods, who was a compositor, and his wife May, who had originally been in service with the Duke of ——. They lived in a respectable side-street, two-thirds of the way out from the centre of a big industrial provincial city.

Mr Woods was employed in a largish press; and in case anyone should happen not to know, I may say the job of a compositor requires skill amounting to craft and carries high prestige in the printing world. Albert Woods's father was a clever man, though at first sight rather unobtrusive – not so Albert's mother, who was portly, authoritative and rather stupid. There was not much to be said for Albert's elder brother and sister, but in Albert it appeared that Providence had seen fit to combine the more admirable features of both parents.

The Woods family was embedded in the heart of the lower middle class and the atmosphere of their home was permeated with a strong air of social independence. Mrs Woods in her argumentative way would have liked to be something of a Tory, but she made no impression apart from noise. The tone was firmly and unobtrusively set by Mr Woods, and it was common to that of millions of other English lower middle-class homes at that period. It was a tone of unabashed radicalism.

For Albert it was just right. The world was filled with promise for any man of gifts, glory was to be had from the struggle, hopefulness was the source of all good – if you were truly convinced of the dignity of man. That is the point, the dignity of man.

Albert Woods forgot his own dignity only too frequently, but he never, never forgot the dignity of man. More power to his elbow, say I.

The consequence was that from as early as he began to think about such things Albert was passionately anti-bourgeois, anti-clerical, anti-military, anti-anything that he fancied held a man down.

At the age of nineteen he looked up from reading the Communist Manifesto and said across the kitchen to his father:

'Men have got to hold their heads up!'

Goodness knows what visions were inflaming his mind. His manner to his father was hot and hortatory – becoming to a youth who in the moment of revelation has forgotten that his father is one of the leaders of a branch of his own Trade Union.

Quite early in his boyhood Albert Woods had fixed on becoming a scientist. You may think there is nothing Napoleonic about that. Albert Woods had fixed on becoming a great scientist. He declared the fact to his family and his schoolmates without delay, let alone choice of occasion. His father received the news cheerfully, his schoolmates with idiot rebellion.

'Yah – look at Woods the great scientist!' they chanted.

Albert stood in their midst, with his small face turning red.

'You shut up!' he shouted: 'How can you be a great scientist if you don't think you're going to be one?' His was a loud cry, but as if lacking heads the other boys did not hear it.

It was a serious cry, and a true one. If there is an answer I do not know what it is.

The determination to be a great scientist burned up with a bright flame in Albert Woods's boyish heart and it never dimmed. It is the story of his career as a scientist that I propose to tell. And at the same time honesty compels me to add that this was not the only flame of greatness that burned up in Albert's heart.

As life rolled on all sort of flames of greatness burned up with varying degrees of impressiveness or absurdity. In his different phases Albert Woods was a great psychologist – this with consider-able success; a great literary man – he was too busy to write anything; a great man of refinement – I let this pass for the time being; and – you may as well face it now – a great amorist. And that is not the sum total by any means. Enveloping them all was the concept of himself as a great everyman.

5

Nevertheless they were all great. All had the glow of Napoleonic inflation. And all of them in due course received that last touch of the little man.

Can you be a great man if you have a touch of the little man?

That was Albert Woods's life problem. 'How can you be a great man if you don't think you're going to be one?' I have already observed that if there is an answer I do not know what it is. 'How can you be a great man if other people don't think you're going to be one?' is another question, and a very tiresome one. If there is an answer to that I do not know what it is either.

The immortal gift of Albert Woods was his capacity for answering both questions with a glorious hot-headed '*Somehow!*'

And it is because of that that I am writing down his story. I do not imagine that the whole of the story will please everybody. Certain passages will not be found to be entirely edifying. Yet perhaps something may be learnt from them. Others will not be found to be entirely comforting. That cannot be helped – I have to admit that in the long run I am telling the story to please myself.

You, whom I must assume to be everyman, may stop before deciding to turn over the page. 'Why may they not be entirely comforting?'

Albert Woods often thought of himself as a great everyman. There was something in it.

CHAPTER TWO

A NEW LIGHT IN THE WINDOW

By the time he was twenty-one Albert Woods had reached his full stature physically, that is to say five feet six inches. He was a sturdy young man, inclined to be plump. He had a fair amount of muscle sleeked over by a thin layer of fat that gave his body a faintly pneumatic look. He had a hefty chest and buttocks and a high waist. His body was strongly made, tough and resilient, but there was nothing of the cart-horse about it. He had a certain fineness and grace. The flick of his eyelids was rapid, the movement of his hands was delicate.

His head was round like a ball and he had long dark silky hair. His face was small and broader than it was long. His big grey eyes protruded so far that he swore his eyeballs got sunburnt in summertime – he was short-sighted and wore spectacles. His nose was short and rather stubby, his mouth wide with red slightly pouting lips. It was a good, clever, homely, sensitive, pleasing, English lower middle class face – not specially beautiful.

I call this a somewhat detailed picture of what he looked like: the trouble with pictorial representation as an art-form is that the subject cannot move, and the chief impression Albert Woods gave was that he was always moving. Even when he was sitting down relaxed there was usually a hot restless look in his eye as if he would very shortly be off again. And when he did get up to go he moved with every particle of his body albeit with considerable grace. His walk was characterized by a mixture of bustle and bounce. (I say characterized because inflation was his vastly predominant state – deflation, as I have already mentioned, produced his alternative of feet-trailing.)

With one vastly predominant state there were two vastly predominant emotions which transformed Albert Woods's face. Both had the same effect. His face appeared to swell up. His eyes bulged still

7

further and his fine skin changed colour – 'red as a turkey-cock' his mother described it and I cannot do better. His voice thickened and his hair fell over his spectacles. The two emotions which wrought the transformation were enthusiasm and rage. (He would have liked to think sexual desire did the same but it did not.) Enthusiasm, rage, and of course a mixture of both.

For the rest he could look mild, sagacious, tender or lewd as the occasion stirred him. And he was an excellent mimic.

In the autumn of 1922 Albert Woods had been engaged in original research for just over a year.

While he was at school Albert had announced his ambition to get a scholarship to Oxford. It was the smallest and poorest secondary school in the city and he was the only boy in his year to have such an idea. 'Too big for his boots' was the comment in the staff-room. Albert took the college entrance scholarship examinations at both Oxford and Cambridge and failed to get any kind of offer from either. Perhaps it gave some satisfaction to his masters to see him temporarily too small for his boots.

But Albert Woods was not lacking in intelligence. From the start I want to record that quite apart from anything else he was a man of high intelligence. It could have been demonstrated by any means you like – a series of examination questions set by teachers, a battery of tests by psychologists or a short conversation with someone of equally high intelligence.

Albert Woods failed to get a scholarship to Oxford because he had been inadequately taught at school. As soon as he saw the question papers he was sharp enough to recognize it, and furthermore to see that he would do no good by staying at school another year and taking the examination again. So he left school in a fit of desolation and bad temper at the age of eighteen and went to the local university instead.

Three years later, in the summer of 1921, he took a first class honours degree in chemistry. He deserved it. All the same it was something of a feat because the night before the theoretical examination began he went out with his friends and rashly got drunk. They had decided it was fatal to their chances to swot the night before an examination. That it was also fatal to get drunk did not dawn on them till it was much too late. They assembled in their favourite public house and, toasting their hopes of success, they drank pint after pint of beer. Albert was thoroughly uplifted by the evening. Clairvoyantly he realized that he was a certain first. He was beginning to get drunk, of course. And oh yes – I almost forgot this – clairvoyantly he realized that he was remarkable also as a great roysterer.

In fact he did not do as well as all that in his theoretical papers. It was in the practical examinations about three weeks later that he scored heavily. He happened to be an unusually good experimenter. When the result of his examination came out the university offered him a scholarship to remain and do research.

At about half past six one November evening Albert came home from working in the university chemistry laboratory. He swung off the tramcar as it passed the end of the street where he lived, and walked springily along in the gas-light. The houses cluttered the street on both sides in bow-fronted rows of red brick. Each had a little front garden that contained a privet hedge or a laburnum tree and two or three decrepit hardy plants. Few of them were illuminated because the occupants spent most of their time in the kitchens which were at the back. The night air smelt of fog and the wilting leaves of chrysanthemums together with an occasional gust from a nearby fish-and-chip shop.

When he came to his home Albert exclaimed with pleasure. Every window was brightly lit, the sitting-room, the hall, the front bedroom and his own little bedroom above the hall. His Uncle Fred must have just finished wiring the house for electricity. Before he had turned his key in the front door his mother opened it. In the passage he saw her shining face, beyond it his father's and his Uncle Fred's, and above them a dangling electric bulb incandescent.

All the houses in the street had originally been lit by gas. The Woods's was only the third to have electric light put in.

'What do you think of it, our Albert?' his mother cried. Her finger was on the switch of the hall light. She switched it off and on again.

Albert's eyes were shining. 'Lovely,' he said. He began to untie his scarf. 'Now I'll be able to see to read at night.'

'We have to thank your Uncle Fred for this.' Fred was her brother. He was a bigger, less portly, more authoritative, much stupider version of herself.

Albert caught his father's eye. It was at Mrs Woods's insistence

9

that Fred had been called in to wire the house. He was not an electrician by trade, and did this kind of job in his spare time for people who were incautious enough to try and get their houses wired on the cheap.

'And look,' Mrs Woods went on. 'Your Uncle Fred's put a light on the landing with two switches, so that we can put it on at the bottom and switch it off at the top.'

'Or vice-versa,' Fred enunciated pridefully. He was the sort of man whose face always looked rigid, whatever he was saying.

The switch in question was beside the one Mrs Woods had been using. Albert stretched out his arm past her. They all looked up at the landing light. Albert flicked the switch. The light shone down on them just the same.

'Here, let me,' said Fred, pushing them both out of the way. Masterfully he worked the switch up and down. There was no result.

'You've wired it up wrong,' said Albert.

'Don't be rude to your uncle.'

'Of course he has.'

'No I haven't,' said Fred, his face as rigid as his mistake.

Their voices were rising. (The whole conversation was being conducted in broad flat singularly unbeautiful midland accents.)

Mr Woods intervened. 'See if it'll go from upstairs, Albert lad.'

Albert ran upstairs. The light went off. 'Try it down there, now,' he shouted.

Fred tried and the light remained inexorably off.

Albert was coming down again: in the darkness at the top of the stairs he missed his footing, and let out a word Mrs Woods had never thought to hear cross her son's lips. The flat 'u' and the soggy 'g's' resounded in the passage. Mrs Woods screamed. Albert arrived at the bottom, furious. He and Fred stared at each other.

'You've done it wrong!'

'No I haven't.'

'Yes you have.'

'No I haven't.'

'Try the switches then.'

'I've told you it isn't wrong. I've told you, see!'

'Draw the circuit then.'

Fred scarcely blinked. He looked like a mesmerized ox. He spoke. 'You don't draw it,' he said. 'You keep it in your head.'

'You can't if your head's made of teak!'

Mr Woods turned his face away. 'Albert!' cried his mother.

Albert had forgotten himself altogether by now. He took out a pencil and drew the circuit on the wall. His mother screamed with dismay at the marks on the wallpaper. Uncle Fred's stare changed to a glare.

'See there,' said Albert. 'That's how it ought to be done. I'll alter it myself.'

'That you can't.'

'Yes he can,' said Mr Woods. 'He's a scientist.'

'I say he can't.'

'Why not?' cried Albert.

'You can't open the junction boxes.'

'Why not?'

'I've soldered them up.'

'You stupid ——!' the same word crossed Albert's lips again. Mrs Woods screamed again.

Fred towered in a rage over Albert's head.

'I've a good mind to punch your nose.'

'I'll punch yours if you do.'

'If it weren't for your specs . . .'

'If it weren't for your false teeth!'

Their fists were clenching when Mrs Woods suddenly interposed her portly person: it pushed them both backwards.

'Now then, will you stop it?' she began, and shortly worked up into a clattering tirade. The upshot was that she threatened to leave the house if Albert did not apologize to his uncle.

Albert refused to apologize.

She had to go. She decided to go and eat her supper at Fred's house. Albert and his father were left alone.

It was a lot of trouble to do the re-wiring, but nothing would deter Albert. The electricity had to be switched off at the mains and he worked by candlelight. His father held the candle and went to and fro to the gas stove in the scullery to heat the soldering-iron.

At one point Mr Woods was kneeling down where they had taken up the floorboards on the landing. He was holding a candle while Albert manipulated a pair of pliers. The house was so quiet that they could only hear each other's breathing.

'I suppose you know,' said Mr Woods, 'it wouldn't have cost a penny more to let the Sapcote Electrical Company do it?'

Father and son glanced at each other. No word passed.

In a little while Mr Woods spoke again. 'You were very rude to your Uncle Fred.'

'He asked for it.'

'That's not the point. He can't help it.'

Albert looked up from what he was doing and grinned at his father.

'Do you agree, his head's made of teak?'

'Perhaps.'

Conversation lapsed again. Albert got on with the job speedily. The light from the candle gleamed on his silky hair and on the gold rims of his spectacles. His father watched him.

'You oughtn't to have quarrelled with him, Albert.'

'I enjoyed it.'

Mr Woods sounded firmer. 'Above all I'd have thought you'd have had the sense not to threaten to fight him.'

'He threatened me.'

Another pause.

'You're very mad-headed.' (Mr Woods pronounced it 'mad-'eaded'.)

'I know.'

'You'll have to learn to control it.' He was thoughtful. 'If you want to get on.'

That was about all they said that evening before Mrs Woods came back.

Late that night Albert sat up in bed, wearing his dressing-gown, reading. He was comfortable. A bright new light glowed on the· pages of Cohen's *Organic Chemistry*. He had completely forgotten his quarrel with his uncle, he had completely forgotten being advised by his father. On his bedside table lay an apple, an orange, a bar of chocolate, a glass of milk and a fountain-pen. He was happy.

He was reading easily with a delightful freedom of attention. The chapter he was reading did not bear directly on the research he was doing, and he had read it before. It was interesting sheerly for its own sake. As he came to the end of a long paragraph he stretched out his arm half-absentmindedly and picked up the apple. He began to chew it.

Half-way through the next paragraph he paused. Quite irrelevantly a name came into his mind. F. R. Dibdin. It was the name of the reader in experimental chemistry at the university of Oxford. Albert's thoughts played round the name while at the same time he started to read his book again.

The name was not new to Albert – Dibdin was one of the most distinguished researchers in the branch of organic chemistry in which Albert had chosen to begin his own research: he was some fifteen years older than Albert and had published in the journals of learned societies several papers which Albert had studied.

Albert gave up reading. The new thought that had come into his head kept sweeping his attention away from the printed lines.

During the last few weeks Albert had been turning over the prospect of writing up his own experiments in a publishable form. He was not certain what to do when it was written, and he had no faith in his professor's advice. The idea which had just come to him was to send the paper to F. R. Dibdin and ask him which was the best journal to try and get it published in.

The idea was neither very new nor very original: it would have come to any young chemist in Albert's position. But that did not affect the impression it made on him. F. R. Dibdin. In Oxford. The fact that Albert's paper was not written, his experiments not finished, could not prevent his imagination swelling with a golden dream. It was a dream of F. R. Dibdin reading his, Albert Woods's paper and seeing the truth about certain kinds of chemical reaction dazzlingly revealed.

It was impossible for Albert to go on reading. He glanced at his wrist-watch that he was still wearing in bed. It was time to switch out the light. But the reverie had taken too firm a hold of him. The light went on casting down its glow on the crumpled white linen pillows and the bottle-green quilted eiderdown.

Because reverie had taken a firm hold of Albert Woods he did not lie back on the pillows in a state of trance. He pulled his dressing-gown round him, got out of bed, and took his diary out of his dressing-table drawer.

Everyone noticed the tremendous energy Albert Woods threw into exhorting other people to greater efforts. He was given to throwing equal energy into exhorting himself. To this end he had the habit of apostrophizing himself in the third person in his diary.

'Today read 100 pages of *War and Peace*. Not enough, Woods. You must read and read and read.'

'My new stirrer works beautifully. Well done, Woods!'

And now, with his dream touching the pages with gilt, he picked up the bar of chocolate in his left hand and the fountain-pen in his right. He wrote. The idea no longer floated out of reach. It was set down in glowing black and white. He read it and re-read it, his eyes bulging brightly and his skin turning pink. He grasped his pen again.

The room seemed brighter than it had ever been before.

'Forward, Woods! Let your light shine!'

Then he drank his glass of milk, lay down in bed and fell sound asleep.

CHAPTER THREE

EXPERIMENTAL CHEMISTRY

FR. Dibdin in 1923 was thirty-seven years old. He had held the readership in experimental chemistry for nearly five years, during which time he had published an unusually large number of papers.

The status of reader is a degree lower than that of professor; as a rule a reader comes for administrative purposes under a professor, though as far as research is concerned he is entirely autonomous. He has research students working under him and in Oxford may have access to university funds: he often has the advantage of not being compelled to lecture. The thing he has not got is the status conferred by a professorial chair. You can therefore take it that most readers at some time or other conceive of their readership being transformed into a professorship – not, as they will invariably hasten to say, because they want status for themselves, but because they want status for their subject.

Now scientists are by definition completely disinterested persons, but the definition appears to be relaxed at just one point: just one trait of un-disinterestedness is permitted – loyalty to one's subject. That is to say if one is for example an abracadabralogical scholar it is permissible, nay proper, to feel that abracadabralogy ought to receive greater recognition.

Consequently a reader may very properly feel he owes it to his subject that it should claim a separate department of its own instead of being an offshoot of another.

Above Dibdin there was the professor of one of the main departments of chemistry. He was always referred to as The Professor or The Prof. His name, like that of certain tribal deities, was never uttered. He was rather like a tribal deity if it comes to that.

Below Dibdin were seven or eight research students – men

who had already taken their degrees – with varying aptitude for experimental investigation. They were more numerous than one would have expected, considering that the particular field of research was new at the time. This was a tribute to Dibdin's enthusiasm.

Nobody could deny Dibdin's enthusiasm. The quality of the papers he published was judged in some quarters of the university to be subject to fluctuation, but there was no doubt at all about the constancy of his enthusiasm. He had overwhelming enthusiasm for research, for publishing papers, and for acquiring research students. He was a remarkable man. In the university of Oxford the department of experimental chemistry hummed.

It was at this period that many chemists became particularly interested in the mechanism of certain reactions which were known as Wurmer-Klaus reactions. One cannot pretend that the scientists' research had any special practical end, such as enabling them to blow up a lot of people, but they got an enormous amount of excitement out of it. For the last thirty years organic chemists all over the world had been making use of Wurmer–Klaus reactions without really knowing why they worked at all: the first shafts of insight thrown into their mechanism by Dibdin's school gave promise of fascinating and fundamental discoveries.

In his provincial university, with very little help or advice from his professor, Albert Woods was working independently on Wurmer–Klaus reactions. He had chosen a different set from Dibdin's. At that time Dibdin's and his pupils' sets of reactions were regarded as typical, Albert's as untypical. Though Dibdin was not to know it, Albert's choice had been made not because he deduced in advance that untypical reactions would be the more interesting, but because he did not fully comprehend when he embarked on his research which reactions were typical and which were not.

Albert had some luck at the start. Luck plays as big a part in scientific research as in any other human activity. His post-graduate scholarship was for two years, and in that time he did a notable first piece of work: it covered only a detailed bit of the terrain which Dibdin regarded by now as his own province, but it covered it with something of a bang.

Out of the blue, in the spring of 1923, Dibdin received a paper from Albert Woods asking his advice on the best place to get it published. He read it through and felt for a moment as if the bang were on his own ears.

It takes a man of sublime confidence, when he sees a youngster solving a problem that he had been thinking was his own property, not to feel momentarily shaken – or if not momentarily shaken at least to feel he ought to find out exactly what the youngster is like and be quick about it.

Dibdin sent Albert his first invitation to spend an evening in college with him.

In the summer of 1923 Albert had pushed on farther and collected enough material to put in his thesis for an M.Sc. His luck had been to light on a problem which, with the talents he had available, he could just solve completely in the nick of time. His thesis showed a combination of insight and ordered conduct. It would have appealed to any scientist. Albert was awarded a valuable scholarship to enable him to continue his research at any university in the United Kingdom.

There was no need for Albert to write and tell Dibdin he had been awarded the scholarship. Dibdin happened to have been privately co-opted as a member of the committee which awarded it.

The issue was never in doubt. Albert received an invitation to go to Oxford and work in the department of experimental chemistry.

This is not the moment for me to go into Dibdin's motives. All I will observe in passing is that if you feel a young man is likely to be a rival in your own line it is not a bad idea to send for him to work with you.

Albert paid his first formal visit to Dibdin's laboratory one morning in the following August. The High Street and the Broad were as crowded as ever with townspeople, but in Parks Road, where most of the laboratories lay, the somnolent air of the Long Vacation was apparent. There was not an undergraduate in sight. The trees along the sides of the road stirred leafily in the morning sunshine, and the air was fresh with the scent of buddleias and dust. Albert turned into South Parks Road and saw the two domes of the observatory rising above the trees like breasts, one black and one white. 'Ah!' he murmured, and listened to the birds twittering.

Outside the entrance to one of the chemical laboratories Albert saw a milk-cart drawn, even at this stage in the history of transport, by an elderly horse. The milkman was running milk out of a big can into a little one while a laboratory attendant stood waiting. Albert patted the horse's nose as he bustled past. He was feeling light-hearted, excited and awed. He turned back and asked the laboratory attendant which was the entrance to the experimental chemistry department.

The boy answered in a pert nasal tone. He stared at Albert. Albert's flat midland accent was not the sort he was used to in his masters. He made some impudent comment to the milkman as Albert walked away, but the horse scraped its foot on the ground and prevented Albert's catching it.

The entrance to the department of experimental chemistry was through an archway. Albert opened the door and went up some stone steps. On the wall immediately opposite him was an indicator-board with a list of names on it. The name at the top of the list was DR F. R. DIBDIN – OUT.

There was nothing to indicate which was Dibdin's room, and no sound came from any of the corridors. From a nearby room there was a faint hissing. Albert looked in. From the amount of glass tubing and sheet metal about the place he took it to be a mechanic's room. The noise came from a kettle boiling on a gas ring. The room smelt warmly of gas, turpentine and methylated spirit. Albert heard footsteps on the floor above. They ceased. It was the Long Vacation. The hum of Dibdin's department was temporarily stilled.

Wandering down the corridor Albert identified Dibdin's room by a visiting card stuck to the pitchpine door by a drawing-pin. He decided to go in and wait.

The room was neither large nor impressive. It was rather dark because the building opposite was near. In front of the window was a desk covered with papers, and along two of the walls were glass-fronted bookcases with cupboards below them. The shelves were filled with books, journals and pamphlets in no obvious order. The sliding doors of the cupboards were open – clearly one of them could never close, since what looked like a spectometer case projected out of it. The fourth wall was decorated with the framed annual photographs of Dibdin and his team of co-workers. Albert looked at them. Dibdin always sat cheerfully smiling in the centre, but Albert was struck by frequent changes in the faces of the team.

When he sat down Albert noticed that high up on the wall above the photographs there hung a small wooden shield with a college crest painted on it, the crest of Dibdin's college. It was almost out of sight. Albert recognized it at once. And his heart swelled with pleasure and pride. Thanks to Dibdin he was now a member of that college himself. He studied the crest fondly, and the thought fascinated him of how it had persisted for five hundred years. And it was his crest now. The past gripped his imagination – five hundred years of it. And then suddenly it switched to the future – to ten, twenty years hence, when his five hundred year old college might be proud of him, Albert Woods.

Dibdin came in.

A bright light of recognition lit up Dibdin's eye as he held out his hand warmly to Albert. 'Good morning, Mr Bowls.'

Albert blushed as he shook hands. 'My name's Woods,' he said abruptly.

'Of course, Mr Woods, I beg your pardon.' On his way to sit down he took his pipe out of his mouth and glanced back at Albert with a sly friendly smile. 'I expect we shall be calling you Dr Woods in due course.' He sat down. 'Ah well,' he said with conviction, 'the labourer is worthy of his hire.'

Albert Woods was not exactly mystified because everything Dibdin said appeared to him to be true.

'If you'll excuse me for a moment,' Dibdin said, 'I'll sort out one or two of our recent papers that I want you to cast your eye over. Never hesitate to cast your eye over papers.'

Albert was flattered. 'Of course,' he said respectfully.

Dibdin sorted out his papers. Albert sat silently waiting.

Dibdin was a biggish, comfortably-built man, with heavily slumping shoulders and a shapeless rear. He had a big rather flat squarish face. His forehead was broad, his jaw was heavy and rounded, and his nose must have been broken at some time or other. It was not the face of a tribal deity. Somehow it was a very human face. What gave Dibdin's face its particularly human quality were his eyes – they were big, sad and wily.

Dibdin's hair was the colour that is first called sandy and later pepper-and-salty: it was curly and looked as if he had not brushed it. His collar was clean but had obviously been rumpled when he tied his tie. His tie was black with narrow stripes of light blue, and it looked as if he had been wearing it for the last fifteen years – he had: it was an old Etonian tie bought when he came up to Oxford. His hands, even first thing in the morning, hardly looked as if he had scrubbed them. Altogether it did not look as if F. R. Dibdin took much care of his personal appearance.

Yet the carelessness of Dibdin's physical appearance was deceptive. Behind it there was a shrewd, child-like, astute mind at work.

Dibdin was still busy. Among the pamphlets were tobacco-tin lids which had been used as ashtrays, an old pipe with a broken stem, some bits of glass tube, an empty match box and a half-eaten chelsea bun. Albert noticed the long galley-proofs of a new scientific paper.

'My wife would say I don't know exactly where everything is,' Dibdin said. His mouth relaxed though he did not look up. 'Sometimes I don't.'

He opened a drawer and pulled out what he had apparently been looking for.

'And now, Mr Woods . . .' Dibdin gave Albert a smile so friendly and spontaneous that in spite of his awe Albert's heart warmed to him. 'Let's talk about your ideas for research.' Before Albert could speak he held up a finger. 'I must warn you not to hope for too much. You've made a very good start, Mr Woods, but that doesn't mean you're bound to make a good finish.'

Albert was dashed.

Dibdin's hazel eyes looked sad and meditative. 'I was a very slow starter myself.' He paused. Then he said: 'But my duty's not to discourage you. It's to encourage you.' He laughed. 'You'll find we've no room for discouragement here, Mr Woods.'

Albert mumbled something.

'Now,' said Dibdin, 'after that little sermon, let's talk about your ideas for research.' His pipe must have gone out. He pressed the tobacco down, lit it, and blew out clouds of smoke.

Albert began to talk about the research he had already done, and Dibdin discussed it interestedly. Albert's nervousness wore off. He began to enjoy himself.

There was a pause.

'That all sounds satisfactory, Mr Woods,' Dibdin said. 'I'm glad you've come to work with us. There's nothing like the experimental chemistry department for giving fresh talent a chance.' He puffed his pipe with a cheerful expression. Then he looked sideways at Albert. 'I suppose we must think about what you're going to do next.'

'Yes,' Albert said.

Dibdin nodded wisely and thoughtfully. 'We must put you one or two irons in the fire.'

Albert was so astonished that he said loudly: 'But I've already got some irons in the fire!' His face turned pink.

Albert apologized.

'It's nothing,' said Dibdin, smiling again. 'We like youthful enthusiasm.'

Albert was contrite and tried to get the conversation back to where it had been before. Dibdin took the lead this time. He made a long speech composed of reflections, observations, suggestions and guesses. Albert listened with increasing interest. Some of the observations struck him in passing as inaccurate, but the total effect on him was hypnotic. He was carried along. Suddenly among the suggestions he heard one that was completely unexpected and original. The hypnosis vanished. He exclaimed with excitement.

'Say that again!'

Dibdin repeated it. As he saw the look of wonderment on Albert's face a look of naïve pride and pleasure appeared on his own.

Albert declared his wonderment.

Dibdin burst into a merry laugh. 'It takes an old hand to bring something out of the hat,' he said happily and with a faint air of relief as well. His hazel eyes looked big and luminous for a moment. Then his glance altered. 'You'll hear lots of ideas thrown out,' he said with a gesture of his hand. 'No one can say you won't hear lots of ideas thrown out here. It's up to you to pick up any that are useful. All ideas are common property here. So don't hesitate, Mr Woods.'

'Thank you very much, Dr Dibdin,' Albert said warmly. He wanted to get to work immediately.

There was a pause.

Albert was simmering with enthusiasm. Dibdin's idea was wonderful. He felt he was afloat on real scientific research at last. And this man was his captain.

Dibdin blew out a few more clouds of smoke. Then he stood up to indicate that it was time for Albert to go.

They exchanged expressions of goodwill. Albert was small and Dibdin was looking down on him.

As they shook hands Dibdin appeared to be amused by something in Albert's manner. They walked to the door and suddenly Dibdin put his hand on Albert's shoulder. 'You and I have got something in common, Mr Woods,' he said.

'Have we?' Albert looked at him.

'We're both lucky,' said Dibdin. His voice was momentarily mysterious and solemn. Albert could not imagine what he was going to say. 'You know I got away to a quick start in my research, just like you.' Then he turned thoughtfully to look over Albert's head. 'You'll find it was a great advantage.'

By evening that day Albert's awe was expanded if anything. And the effect of awe on men's judgement of each other is unfortunately about as reliable as that of alcohol. Albert wrote in his diary:

'I am truly lucky to have got the chance to work under Dr Dibdin. I can see already that he is a wonderfully inspiring leader. While he was talking to me I thought what a strong face he had got. He will give Woods the discipline he needs.'

CHAPTER FOUR
STABLE-COMPANIONS

Next morning Albert went along to instal himself in his new laboratory. It was a room near the flight of stone steps inside the entrance – Dibdin had pointed it out to him when they were leaving the building on the previous day.

Albert had brought up to Oxford a certain amount of apparatus and a lot of books. They were packed in the back of a little second-hand motor-car he had bought with thirty-five pounds borrowed from his father. It was a Morris-Cowley open two-seater with a high body and a low blunt-nosed brass radiator: the door beside the driver was permanently jammed fast while the other uncontrollably swung open. Albert picked a load of books out of the motor-car and went into the building, pushed open the door of his new room and walked in.

He found himself face to face with another young man. The other young man was wearing a white lab-coat and was standing in front of a bench piled high with apparatus. A tap was running. Water was pulsing through an elaborate maze of glass-work. Heaters were going and stirrers were stirring. An experiment was clearly in progress.

The man said curtly: 'I beg your pardon.' He was the same height as Albert, had a round head and a chest as broad and deep as a barrel.

'Sorry,' Albert muttered over the top of his books.

'You've got the wrong room.'

'I don't think I have.'

The other man stared. He had full heavy-lidded eyes and a beaky nose. His stare was calm and piercing. 'What were you proposing to do here?'

'Work, of course – research.' Albert was thoroughly flustered. 'Dr

Dibdin told me this was to be my room.' He tried to smile with extreme politeness. 'There must be some mistake.'

'I should put the books down if I were you.' The other man stood perfectly still.

Albert put his books on a small table. His hair had fallen over his spectacles. He brushed it back and looked round him. 'Excuse me.' He bustled outside, looked at the number on the door, related the position of the room to the stairs. He was sure he was right. He went in again. The other man had turned back to his apparatus, but he swivelled round.

'Well?'

'This is the room all right. The one Dr Dibdin told me I could have.'

'I've been here two years.'

Pause.

'I'm a new research student. My name's Albert Woods.'

'Mine's Smith. Clinton Smith.'

Albert held out his hand nervously yet in a friendly fashion. The other man shook it.

'There must be some mistake,' Albert said.

'Agreed.'

'He must have some other room for me.'

'He hasn't.'

'What?'

'The place is full. He can't take any more research students.'

Albert's face turned pink. 'But he's taken me!'

'We heard that.' The other man's calm piercing look did not waver. 'We wondered where he'd put you.'

'Do you mean to say – ' Albert began.

'Yes.'

'But it's impossible. It's ridiculous.' Albert looked round the room again, this time with his eyes beginning to bulge. 'He can't do that. I mean – '

'He has.'

'Then I shall go and see him. I'll go and see him now. I intend to get it straight.'

Smith nodded.

Albert bounced out of the door into the corridor. At that moment he saw Dibdin come out of his door at the far end. 'Dr Dibdin!' Albert was too late. Dibdin promptly sidled through the next door.

Albert raced down the corridor and tried to open the door. It was locked. Judged by the sounds from inside, it was a lavatory. Albert decided to stand outside and wait.

Minutes passed. Five. Albert began to pace up and down. Ten minutes. Dibdin was still inside.

At last the lock turned. Dibdin came out and began to walk past as if Albert were a stranger.

'Dr Dibdin!'

Dibdin glanced back. 'Oh good morning, Mr Bowls.'

'Woods.'

'Mr Woods.'

'I want to speak to you.'

'Perhaps if you could call back later, Mr Woods. . . .'

'I'm afraid I've got to speak to you now.'

'Come into my room, then.' Dibdin walked in and Albert followed him. Dibdin stood beside his desk. His big sad hazel eyes had a badgered expression. He began to light his pipe.

'There's been a mistake over my room,' Albert said.

'I'm sorry, Mr Woods. Can I help you?'

'You promised me a room to work in.'

'You're quite right, of course. You'll need a room to work in.'

'You showed me which one was mine, yesterday.'

'Oh?' said Dibdin innocently. 'Which was it, Mr Woods?'

Albert told him.

Dibdin suddenly gave Albert a knowing grin. 'Ah,' he said. 'You'll find Mr Clinton in that room.'

'Mr Smith.'

'Quite right. Mr. Smith.'

There was a pause.

'What am I going to do about it?' said Albert.

'Would you mind talking it over with Mr Smith?'

'What? Isn't there a room for me?'

'We're very congested here, I'm afraid. It's an old university.' Dibdin was pleased with the idea. 'You've come to one of the old universities now, Mr Woods.'

Albert looked at him directly. 'Do you mean,' he said, 'I've got to share a room?'

'That's right – that's an excellent suggestion, Mr Woods,' said Dibdin. 'I always felt you and Smith would get on well together.'

'Well!' said Albert.

'Yes,' said Dibdin. 'I was thinking about you last night, Mr Bowls. And again this morning. To get the best out of yourself you need . . .' He paused, obviously at a loss. Suddenly a remarkable inspiration came to save him. 'You need a stable-mate.' A broad smile came over his face. 'That's right. Stable-mates for all!'

Albert stood still. Then he turned away and went down the corridor to break the news to Clinton Smith.

At luncheon the following day Albert Woods and Clinton Smith were sitting in the snack-bar of a public house not far from the laboratory. Albert was studying his stable-mate, and Clinton Smith was studying him.

Clinton Smith was aged twenty-seven, four years older than Albert and about fourteen years maturer in appearance. He was stocky, powerful and strongly masculine. His hair and moustache were clipped short, his complexion was tanned to a leathery brown, his nose was like a beak. The way his eyelids descended gave him a hooded look: his smile, when it came, was fixed and mechanical and showed glittering gold fillings in his teeth. He was a dominating man. And yet he was humble.

Clinton Smith was one of the young ex-soldiers who had come up to Oxford after the 1914–18 war. He had been a captain in the Duke of Cornwall's Light Infantry. The atmosphere of living in command of men had suited him as perfectly as that of living in the hurly-burly of a radical lower middle class home had suited Albert. And he no more forgot the savour of the experience than Albert forgot his.

The public house was a regular meeting-place of Dibdin's research students. It was old-fashioned, dark and uncomfortable. It had ancient beams across the ceiling, leaded window panes, and blackened oak tables and settles that were all false.

Albert and Clinton Smith were sitting at a little table by a window. Their surreptitious studies of each other had already gone some distance, Clinton's with restraint, Albert's without. Yet in spite of his restraint it was Clinton Smith who had parted with the more factual information. For one thing, Albert's curiosity and inquisitiveness knew no restraint; for another, he could be an unusually sympathetic listener.

From the beginning Albert's instinct had told him Clinton Smith was a formidable man. When Albert had first read the list of names on the department indicator-board, the name stood out because he had seen it associated with Dibdin's on several important papers. And then they had spent Albert's first afternoon in the laboratory discussing Dibdin's research. Clinton Smith had shown Albert that he was able, direct, capable of sustained and concentrated thought. Dibdin had a couple of men in his team who were older than Clinton Smith but they had not done very much: the rest were as yet unknown. Clinton Smith was Dibdin's best man.

Now they were half-way through Clinton's experiences in the war. Albert, seeing himself as a soldier, was leading him on.

'I expect you got a decoration.' Albert's eyes were bright behind his spectacles.

The other man stared at him with his hooded look. 'Yes.'

'What was it?'

'An O.B.E.'

'What's that?' Albert genuinely did not know – in any case the order had only been instituted in 1917.

Clinton Smith's brown face suddenly, surprisingly, reddened. He could not force himself to pretend it was awarded for gallantry in the field.

'What did you get it for?' Albert asked.

'It came up with the rations.'

Albert was snubbed but not put off.

There was a pause. Clinton Smith looked out of the window – he grasped Albert's forearm as he said:

'Look! The Professor.'

Albert followed his glance. A tall cadaverous elderly man was passing with a curious loping stride. He was hatless and he had shaggy grey curly hair.

Out of sudden curiosity Albert glanced at Clinton. He was watching the professor till he was out of sight. His leathery face was glowing with unashamed hero-worship.

'There's a great man, Woods.' His voice was harsh. 'A very great man.'

It touched Albert's own enthusiasm. For a moment dreams claimed them both.

Albert was thinking of the colleges, the laboratories, the cultivated life of Oxford that could give freedom to a man's greatest aspirations. 'How I envy you being here always,' he said.

There was a very slight pause. Clinton Smith looked at him with a piercing glance.

'Do you want to stay in Oxford indefinitely?'

The conversation was transformed. Instantly Albert was on his guard – the conversation meant something quite different. To stay in Oxford – it meant to do his research there, to get a fellowship of a college and an appointment on the staff of the university. There were only a limited number of fellowships and university appointments going at any one time, and they both knew it.

'Of course I do.'

It came out at that moment: they were going to be rivals.

They looked at each other, Smith with his full-eyed stare, Woods with his lips pursed in a friendly smile.

'It's time to get back to the lab.'

'Not yet.' Albert smiled imperturbably.

Clinton hesitated. Neither of them could quit mutual exploration. Neither of them felt he dare.

Clinton took out a silver cigarette case and offered Albert a cigarette. 'After this I'm going.'

Albert struck a match. 'So am I.'

They began to talk about their work, but gradually Albert brought the subject of their conversation round again to people.

From their research it went to Dibdin and the other members of the laboratory. Albert would have liked to know Clinton's opinion of Dibdin as a man but Clinton was wary.

'Anyway,' Albert said stoutly, 'you can't deny he's got a very fine team.'

'I don't deny it.'

Albert smiled. 'It's an excellent stable.'

Clinton's lip stiffened.

'I hope you don't mind me being forced on you as a stable-mate . . .' He made a gesture with his hand.

'That's all right, Woods.'

'Stable-mates for all,' Albert quoted, half in fun, half in annoyance. 'I wonder what races he's entering us for.' He glanced at Smith.

'Yes.' Clinton's gold fillings glittered in his mechanical smile. 'Very amusing.' A faintly contemptuous, faintly triumphant gleam showed in his eye. His rival was irreverent about his teacher and saw his career as a subject for joking.

'I'm going,' he said, and stood up.

They walked back to the laboratory side by side.

CHAPTER FIVE

IRONS IN THE FIRE

'We must put you one or two irons in the fire,' was one of Dibdin's favourite promises and nobody could say he did not fulfil it.

A combination of two things makes a great experimental scientist – an outstanding ability for doing experiments and a sure instinct for knowing which experiments to do.

Dibdin did not possess an outstanding ability for doing experiments. He lacked the quickness of eye, the delicacy of touch, the physical tirelessness that Albert Woods, for instance, was already showing signs of. His pupils tried to keep him away from their benches because ineptitude did not damp his enthusiasm for participating in their experiments.

As for a sure instinct for knowing which experiments to do – how can you judge a man who at one time or another suggests all experiments imaginable, from the inspired to the impossible?

Even Dibdin's enemies, who said he had no capacity at all for doing experiments, had to admit that he was most ingenious in inventing experiments for other people to do. Dibdin's school had more irons in the fire per man than any other school in the country. One of the things with which the department of experimental chemistry hummed was fertility. (To say it hummed a little with dizziness as well is neither here nor there.)

Dibdin had his enemies among the senior chemists of the day. They read with interest the stream of papers that came from his school: often they were impressed by the experiments that had been done. But obstinately they went on repeating that the experiments did not do very much towards elucidating scientific truth. This opinion they would give – justly, had they been correct – as a reason for not electing him to the Royal Society.

Election to a fellowship of the Royal Society is what every

research scientist looks on as the most desirable of all signs of recognition. The number of fellows of the society is about five hundred. The number of professional scientists in the country doing original research is of the order of ten thousand, possibly rather less. You may think these figures make the society sound less august than I made out, and the competition for getting into it less fearsome. But it is just this degree of competition that is the most fearsome. If the society were say one-tenth its present size, the odds against election would be so great that all but a few would feel they had not got a chance. But at twenty to one everyone feels he has got a chance: he enters the competition. And so at the age of thirty the thought of being elected is to men like Dibdin, Woods and Smith inspiring: at the age of forty-five the thought of not having been elected is agonizing.

Dibdin's research pupils were aware of his peculiar gifts. They were alternately illumined, hypnotized and maddened by them. They found it difficult to believe that a man they knew so well, whose weaknesses were so innocently paraded before them, was a great scientist. Yet at the bottom of their hearts, whether they liked to admit it or not, they all felt loyalty and a curious confidence in him.

Albert Woods, after a year in the laboratory, had not lost his enthusiastic respect for Dibdin. Refusing to have any irons put in the fire for him, he had obstinately gone on studying non-typical Wurmer–Klaus reactions: it gave a pleasant inflation to his pride to think that Dibdin had neither initiated his experiments nor taken any serious part in them. He felt freer than the others to recognize Dibdin's considerable if peculiar gifts.

'He brings things out of the hat,' Albert was wont to say loyally if he heard Dibdin being criticized. It was a curiously apt expression.

When in the following March Dibdin was not elected to the Royal Society in that year's list, Albert was indignant.

'He brings things out of the hat, and that's more than a lot of the old gentlemen do!'

His stable-mate took the irreverence of the remark ill.

On the whole Albert and Clinton shared their room amicably. Albert had now got an elaborate experiment going which involved working at low pressures: he spent hours pumping out his apparatus and sealing up leaks in the taps and joints with extraordinary care and patience. He was proud of his work, and Dibdin had several times complimented him on it.

One day Albert came back from luncheon rather later than usual. He went straight into his room because it was time to begin a new set of readings. The pump was whirring harmoniously. He was feeling excited and pleased with himself.

To his surprise one of the pressure gauges was giving a completely unexpected indication. He exclaimed in dismay, looked at another one. Also quite wrong. With his eyes popping he ran his fingers over the whole system.

Two of the taps were open and it was obvious that air had been let into the apparatus.

'Sabotage!' he cried.

At that moment Clinton came in.

'Somebody's sabotaged my experiment.'

'Don't look at me, Woods. I haven't been near it.'

Albert was making feverish adjustments. His hair fell over his spectacles as he bent down. 'Give me a hand.'

'What do you want me to do?'

Albert told him. Clinton did it.

'Five weeks' work gone up the spout,' Albert kept saying. His face was given up to expressing chagrin.

The immediate remedies had been administered. They faced each other.

'Who's done it?'

Silence for a moment. Then simultaneously they lifted their noses, Albert his stubby one, Clinton his beaky. They smelt the same thing – pipe-tobacco, fresh on the air, stale in the pipe, immediately identifiable.

'It's him,' Albert cried.

'Agreed,' said Clinton. His eye gleamed. 'He likes taking a hand in experiments.'

'But with my apparatus! Why in Heaven's name with my apparatus?'

'He does it to all of us.'

'Five weeks work up the spout!'

'He likes to come in and take readings.'

Albert was speechless.

In this silence they heard footsteps outside the door. Albert ran across the room. He saw Dibdin quietly padding up the corridor.

'Dr Dibdin!'

Dibdin turned round. 'Yes.' He took his pipe out of his mouth.

'Someone's interfered with my apparatus.'

'What apparatus?'

'My apparatus – the apparatus I'm working with.'

'When?'

'While I was out at lunch, of course.'

'I'm sorry to hear it, Mr Kelly.'

'My name's not Kelly, it's Woods!'

'I beg your pardon, Mr Woods.'

Albert was beside himself with fury.

Dibdin was recovering from his alarm. 'I know what we'll do,' he said.

'What?'

'I'll come back with you myself and help you to put it right again.'

'No!' burst out Albert. 'Please no! I mean, don't bother, Dr Dibdin.'

Dibdin had put his pipe back again in his mouth. He looked hurt when Albert turned his back on him and went down the corridor to his own room.

It was a bright summer morning. Dibdin was sitting in his room reading a small sheaf of typewritten pages. Sunlight was reflected into his window from the building opposite. Blue pipe-smoke rose into the air. As he read, Dibdin's big sad wily eyes were lit with mild pleasure. The pages were an account of Albert Woods's recent work.

There was a tap on the door and Albert came in.

'Thank you for coming, Mr Woods. Please sit down.'

Dibdin studied the papers for a moment longer. He blew out a cloud of smoke.

At first Albert glanced nervously at Dibdin's face. Dibdin's expression .reassured him. Albert settled himself comfortably in his chair and watched, his lips pursed in a smile.

'You know what I wanted to talk to you about, Mr Woods.'

'My paper.'

Dibdin quietly turned over the last page again.

He looked up. 'I think it's a very satisfactory piece of work.'

Albert blushed faintly.

'We've got some interesting irons in the fire here.' Dibdin tapped the page with a blunt not very clean finger. 'Very interesting.'

Albert did not speak but pride welled up in him.

'There are one or two points I want to discuss with you before we go on to publication.'

'Yes,' said Albert, confident they could not be serious.

'We mustn't rush into publication.' Dibdin smiled mischievously.

Albert nodded without much conviction.

'If you'll accept the guiding hand,' said Dibdin, 'of an old hand at the game.'

'Of course,' Albert said.

Dibdin put the papers down on the desk, took his pipe out of his mouth and examined the stem. The window was wide open and the sound of a lab-boy whistling down below came in. The fresh air was warm and summery. Albert was wearing an open-necked shirt with the collar pulled outside his tweed jacket. The gold rims of his spectacles gleamed.

'It's always my practice to go through any paper that one of my pupils is preparing, point by point first of all,' Dibdin said easily. 'It clears the air.' He glanced at Albert. 'You may have noticed that about our papers in this department. The air of them's always clear.' Before Albert could reply he went on: 'Now. Let's start with your preamble.' He smiled friendlily, almost affectionately. 'I think we can make the air of your preamble a little clearer.'

Dibdin was right. Albert's literary style was not sharp, in fact it was often rambling. But that it could be made sharper by Dibdin was a different matter entirely – a matter, one would have thought, for speculation.

Dibdin waved his pipe. 'Just a little, perhaps. But every little helps.'

Albert took Dibdin's first modest emendations quite humbly.

They passed on to the opening section, in which Albert outlined what the experiments were going to be and what his aim was in doing them.

Dibdin proposed to remodel one of the key sentences. At first Albert nodded as humbly as he had done earlier. Then, as Dibdin's voice moved on, it dawned on him that the sense had been changed.

'I beg your pardon, Dr Dibdin. I think we ought to think about the last change you were making. It makes it mean something really different.'

'Does it?' Dibdin looked up with innocent surprise.

Albert looked back with equal, if less innocent surprise.

'Of course it does.'

'You surprise me by saying that, Mr Woods.'

'Really?' Albert could scarcely believe him.

Dibdin looked first slightly taken aback and then shrewd.

Albert began: 'Don't you see that would imply that non-typical reactions don't all involve the same type of energy changes – '

'Don't they?'

'Don't they?' Albert's voice began to thicken: 'Of course they don't. That's the whole point – ' He broke off. It suddenly looked to him as if Dibdin could not have understood his work properly at all, in fact had possibly got the work on the whole subject muddled.

They embarked on a long discussion. It was soon heated on Albert's side, evasive on Dibdin's: on both sides, after twenty minutes, it was getting very involved as well.

Albert simply could not tell if Dibdin understood what he was talking about or not. At one moment Dibdin would be saying something penetrating – Albert felt he had learnt something: at the next moment Dibdin would be making a mistake that was childish.

However in the end they came back to Albert's original sentence. Albert sat back trying to conceal his triumph. And Dibdin said with satisfaction:

'You see, Mr Woods, what I mean about clearing the air.' He looked triumphant also. 'Don't be discouraged.' He began to puff his pipe. 'I think we shall make something out of you. That's one of our jobs here.'

Albert's mixture of emotions was almost too much for him to contain. All the same something in Dibdin's tone made Albert glance at him sharply. Dibdin now had a mysterious expression.

'We don't forget the labourer is worthy of his hire,' he said.

'Yes,' said Albert, feeling he was not a labourer and wondering what could be coming next.

'I've been thinking the time will soon be ripe for us to fix you up with a fellowship of a college.'

Albert's heart jumped. 'There's nothing I'd like more.'

'It's time you had a bit of home and beauty.'

Albert was momentarily incoherent with delight. Dibdin caught the word 'grateful'. Then Albert said: 'What do I have to do? Do I have to take any steps?'

'The prize,' said Dibdin.

Albert stopped.

'We'll enter you for the prize fellowship.' Dibdin explained that their college, the one of which he was a fellow and Albert nominally a B.A., awarded each year a prize and research fellowship. Albert had known about it for nearly two years already. The only thing Albert did not know was which year he should enter. The prize depended on the candidate's record of research, plus an essay, plus an interview. The former was the most important.

'Next year,' Dibdin said, cheerfully.

'Not this?' said Albert.

'We mustn't rush it, Mr Woods.'

Albert said nothing. He was compelled to take Dibdin's advice since Dibdin would be one of the judges.

Albert was not cast down. 'By next year my record of research will be more impressive.'

'That's the spirit,' said Dibdin. 'Every little helps.'

The interview had apparently come to an end. Dibdin's pipe had gone out and he was lighting it again. Albert stood up to go. He looked at the papers on Dibdin's desk. Dibdin put down his match in one of the tobacco-tin lids and picked up Albert's typewritten sheets.

'You'll be wanting to polish them, I expect,' he said. 'We're never too proud to polish.'

'Yes,' said Albert respectfully.

There was a hiatus while the papers passed from hand to hand. Albert glanced down – there was a nervous, faintly apprehensive look on Dibdin's face.

'There's one other little matter,' Dibdin said.

'Yes.'

'Just to clear things up.' The look of apprehensiveness vanished.

'Yes.'

Dibdin said: 'I see you've put your own name at the top of your paper, Mr Woods.' His eyes looked sad and thoughtful. 'I always make it a matter of principle to put my name as well on every paper that comes out of the department.'

'Yours?' Albert said incredulously.

'Yes,' said Dibdin, still sad and thoughtful. 'I make it a matter of principle, Mr Woods. And I like my name to come first – it makes it easier for purposes of identification.' He rounded it off. 'First come, first served.'

For a moment Albert could not speak. His face reddened, his eyes flickered behind his spectacles.

'I see.'

Albert took the papers from Dibdin's hand, and lest he should say anything more rushed out of the room.

Albert went straight to his own room. Clinton Smith looked up from his work. Albert's face was as red as a turkey-cock's. Clinton said:

'What's the matter with you?'

'The ——!' The word that made his mother scream burst out. The flat midland 'u' and the soggy 'g's' echoed round the Oxford laboratory. 'The ——! He's going to put his name on my paper. On my paper, I tell you.' Albert waved the paper in Clinton's face.

'It's perfectly in order if he wants to,' Clinton said. 'Most heads of department do it.'

'That's the way they make their reputations, I suppose.'

'I don't propose to give you my opinion on that.'

Albert sat down. 'But on my paper, Smith. Don't you understand? I'd started this work before I ever came here.'

'What's that got to do with it?'

'What that's got to do with it is that I doubt if he even understands it. He's going to put his name on it when he doesn't understand what the theory's about and when the only time he touches the apparatus it goes up the spout for a month!' He was breathless.

Clinton maintained his fixed look.

There was a pause.

Clinton said curtly: 'What else did he say?'

'He advised me to go in for the college's ruddy prize fellowship.'

'Did he?'

Albert started at the tone. He looked at Clinton. 'Did he advise you to go in for it, too?'

'Yes.'

'Which year?'

36

Clinton did not answer. He stared at Albert with bright eyes under hooded lids.

Albert said: 'He advised me to wait till next year.'

'That's the year he advised me to enter.'

CHAPTER SIX

A PRIZE

Throughout that year there were two possible theories about Wurmer–Klaus reactions in the air. Though experimental evidence was steadily accumulating nobody felt inclined yet to come down in favour of one or the other – or perhaps I ought to say several people felt inclined to come down but none of them dared. In the department of experimental chemistry several young scientists would have liked a lead from their director.

With the beginning of 1926 Clinton Smith and Albert Woods were thinking hard about the record of research they were going to present for the prize and research fellowship. To decide in favour of one theory or the other was in both their minds. Clinton spent many hours discussing it privately with Dibdin, in conversations that were amiable and interesting and illuminated by flashes of insight but left him no nearer to knowing what his master's choice was.

Dibdin smiled, puffed his pipe, looked intelligent, contradicted himself, muddled the facts, made a shrewd guess or two and then guilefully suggested he should take a hand with Clinton's experiment.

It would have been clear to an experienced eye that Clinton's thesis was going to be thoroughly competent, thoroughly orthodox, thoroughly sound.

Albert Woods's work was of a different kind.

Woods's work reflected his temperament very clearly. And in some ways there were strong affinities between his work and Dibdin's. Both of them had able astute minds but neither was greatly given to orderly intellectual processes. Albert's intellectual processes were powerful but disorderly: I do not think I am being unjust when I say Dibdin's proceeded largely by free association.

Now it does not for a moment follow that such minds cannot

arrive at the truth. Though their intellectual processes were disorderly both Dibdin and Woods possessed a gift which was often lacking in orderly thinkers. The best I can do by way of describing it is to call it an instinct for reality. Intellectual discipline did not keep their scientific imaginations in order but an instinct for reality did – do not forget that reality often is muddled and contradictory.

Though I personally do not doubt that an instinct for reality is the deeper and more valuable gift, I have to say that compared with intellectual order it is much less reliable. The flashes of inspiration that came to its possessors were divine or secular according to no particular rule – in Dibdin's case, to no rule whatsoever.

With the natural equipment he possessed Albert Woods had instinctively made the right choice in becoming an experimental chemist; the line of research he had taken was more empirical than theoretical. Had he chosen to become a physicist he would not have done half so well. Had mathematics been his only hope he would have been a non-starter.

Albert Woods's record of research reflected these things. It displayed his inexhaustible supplies of energy – he had done an enormous number of experiments. It displayed his instinct for reality – the experiments had a sort of relevance to what he was trying to find out. It displayed his courage in believing in the divineness of his own flashes of inspiration. He had come down in favour of one of the two theories.

It also displayed a strong touch of the slap-dash.

In Oxford at that time there was a small carefully-chosen group of chemists called the Willard Gibbs Society which met twice a term. It was composed of equal numbers of senior chemists and juniors. The Professor was president, Dibdin was a member. Clinton Smith had been invited to join the year after Albert came up to Oxford.

At the meetings a member or guest would read a short paper about his work and the others would criticize. Albert Woods had been invited to attend once already as a guest and he was hoping to be invited to become a member. About three weeks before Albert was due to add a paper about his most recent experiments to his collection for the prize fellowship, Dibdin suggested to Albert that he should try it out on the Willard Gibbs.

'I think that will do the trick,' Dibdin said.

Albert took it to mean that he would impress the Professor. Every high opinion he could win would improve his chances.

The meeting took place on a warm summer evening in the Professor's rooms in his college, which was a different one from Albert's and Dibdin's. The scientists assembled after dinner in Hall. The General Strike was on, but it was far from their thoughts – Clinton had once thought of driving a locomotive and Albert of doing a bit of picketing, but to most of the rest the strike meant nothing except irritation.

The Professor's rooms overlooked a small quadrangle with a fountain trickling in the centre. Through the windows shone a bright summer twilight that changed into dusk as the meeting went on. The sky was cloudless and the faint stirring of the air carried a flowery scent from the wistaria that grew over the Warden's Lodgings. Inside there was the smell of coffee sent up from the college kitchens and of the damp you get in rooms that have never been properly dried out for four hundred years. The Professor handed out cigarettes with formal politeness to the members as they arrived: they helped themselves to coffee.

Albert was nervous. Like Clinton Smith, he was awed by the Professor.

There were not many people in Oxford who failed to be awed by the Professor. He was a man of Jehovianic majesty. He was tall and cadaverous, and had a hollow chest over which he folded his arms. His manner was lofty and remote. He had a handsome face which looked as if it had been ravaged by intellectual torment. His cheeks were hollow and lined and worn: his eyes burned continually with suppressed fire from some region of the spirit. He spoke in short rapid bursts.

As a scientist the Professor was the antithesis of Dibdin and Albert Woods. He operated entirely in the realm of conceptual thought, and his rare papers in theoretical chemistry had the same quality of extraordinary distinction as his person. They were perfectly constructed, lucid, restrained: they had a highly refined penetration whose peculiar essence was aesthetic as much as scientific.

There were about fifteen people present when Albert began to read, stammering slightly at the start, in a throaty midland accent. Beside him there was a blackboard on which he could draw diagrams and copy out tables of results.

Throughout the whole paper there were only two interruptions – both characteristic of the somewhat unviscerotonic air of scientists' company. One voice said: 'What about having the lights on?' and the other: 'Isn't that 2 supposed to be a 4?'

Just as Albert was ending, a college servant in a white jacket brought in fresh supplies of coffee and milk. Albert had to wait while it was served before discussion of his work could begin.

Anyone not conversant with scientific society who entered the room would have been struck by the look of simmering excitement on a collection of extraordinarily lively intelligent faces. Albert's cheeks were pink with triumph. As his glance met the Professor's he looked down at the ground. The Professor was watching him acutely, with burning eyes.

The discussion began. Albert had committed himself to one of the two theories, and most of the men present felt a curious thrill. He found questions being thrust at him from all sides. He answered them, flustered with confidence.

The Professor did not say anything.

From time to time Albert glanced at Dibdin, and saw his broad flat face warmed with a smile of delight.

Most of the questions involved reconciling facts with his chosen theory, facts which had been thought to be explicable only in terms of the other one.

But a new element came into the discussion. Someone had discovered that he did not quite follow Albert's argument all the way through. At one point there appeared to be a gap.

For a moment everyone was silent. A pang of dismay suddenly shook Albert's triumphant mood. For the moment he could not see how to explain it.

'What does the Professor say?' It was Dibdin asking innocently from the depths of a big leather arm-chair.

The Professor instead of replying glanced across the room at a young man who was sitting opposite. It was one of the Professor's pupils, a young man who had collaborated with him.

In five simple pointed sentences the young man laid the break in Albert's chain of reasoning bare.

Immediately Albert plunged into argument without thought. His tone was truculent.

It was no use. There really was a gap.

Albert looked round the room, his eyes bulging behind his

spectacles. 'Rubbish!' he said. 'It would take just one afternoon's experimenting to show I'm right, which I should have thought anyone could see if he wasn't daft!'

Dibdin glanced slyly at the Professor.

'I doubt if anyone here is likely to be daft.' It was Clinton Smith. Everyone turned to look at him. He was wearing a pale-blue shirt, and in the light of parchment-shaded lamps his face looked deep brown by contrast. He smiled and his gold fillings gleamed. He appeared to be weighing his words with great care. 'I suspect that in the sober light of day Mr Woods will see that he's been a trifle hasty. Though I think he's right.' He paused with decision. 'I confess I hadn't seen the point we're discussing as clearly as I see it now that our friend has pointed it out. I'm worried.' Clinton addressed himself to the Professor. 'An afternoon's experimenting wouldn't settle the problem. I say this advisedly, sir. I see the kind of experiments Mr Woods has in mind.' He could not keep a brutal tone out of his voice. 'Unfortunately his imaginary experiments don't quite tie up with some results I've actually obtained.'

Albert was astounded. He did not doubt that it was a calculated piece of treachery.

'What results?' he cried.

Clinton did not reply.

'What results?' He did not believe they existed.

'I'm prepared to produce them as soon as I can get them from the lab.'

'Explain them.'

Clinton explained. They sounded reasonable enough.

The whole atmosphere of the meeting changed. The note of challenge rang through the air, and Albert lost his head. He was not above treachery himself, but Clinton's treachery threw him into violent rage. He blustered with generalizations, and bolstered them with details that were often patently inaccurate.

And yet he was sure he was right, sure, sure.

There was a gap in Albert Woods's argument. Had he been in the mood for reason he would have realized its existence was not the most important point at issue. Many of the world's greatest scientific discoveries – not that Albert's was one – have been made by jumping a gap. The question was – had Albert jumped the gap by scientific imagination or by sheer guesswork? Everything he said while he was inflamed with anger made it sound like the latter.

At the height of the discussion Clinton turned a dominating but respectful look on Dibdin.

'I would like to know what Dr Dibdin thinks.'

It was delivered in such a way that there was no getting out of it. Dibdin started. His smile vanished and he looked badgered. He blew a few puffs of smoke out of his pipe. Everybody was watching him expectantly. He had to make a speech.

Clinton got what he asked for. Dibdin made a speech of some ten minutes length in which he covered goodness knows how many theories without giving a single clue to his preference. It was like a wonderful intellectual smokescreen – certainly it set them all intellectually coughing. Dibdin sat back at the end of it with a seraphic air of triumph.

Arguments set up in all directions at cross-purposes.

The Professor sat through it unchanged. His attitude towards the divagations of his colleagues was like that of our Deity towards the divagations of Man.

The meeting adjourned well after midnight. The coffee dregs were cold, the ashtrays were full. The liveliness of the faces was diminished by about one per cent.

The Professor said good night to his guests with exactly the same formal politeness. They went away in twos and threes, disputing. Only Albert and Clinton went away without speaking to each other.

Dibdin was one of the last to leave.

The Professor stood up, tall and hollow-chested. He folded his arms and bent his head a little towards Dibdin. His eyes, though burning, did not appear to see much.

Dibdin's last observation, cheerful and sly and surprising, was aimed half at the Professor, half at nobody in particular. He said:

'We may not be good scientists. But we do have fun.'

Ten days later, on a damp cloudy evening, Albert Woods was walking solitarily across the Parks towards the river. He was pondering gloomily on the results of being what his father called mad-headed. He was trailing his feet as if misery had almost broken them at the ankles.

Clinton Smith had won the fellowship.

PART TWO

The Good Life Begins

CHAPTER ONE
THE VINEYARD

It always seems to me that the world in which scientists live, compared with other people's worlds, is a rather bleak one. But it has the rare compensation of at least being regulated by some kind of judicial fairness – though you may think judicial fairness is rather bleak too. Nowhere else is a man judged so closely and so impartially by his work, and nowhere else so closely and impartially esteemed accordingly. If he makes a fool of himself privately it matters not at all. If he makes a fool of himself professionally and then publishes a good piece of research his work brings in its reward just the same.

Albert Woods had temporarily lost the Professor's high opinion of his capabilities in research. The word had gone round, nobody knew exactly how, among those fellows of Dibdin's college who favoured Clinton Smith for the prize fellowship, 'Woods is not sound.' Albert's chances were dished.

Although Albert had lost his head when he was criticized, he recovered rapidly. The experiments that he had declared could be done in an afternoon took him a couple of weeks to perform and gave him a result slightly different from what he had expected. But in essence his work was sound and the gap in his argument was more a matter of words than of scientific reasoning. He rewrote part of his paper and discussed it with Dibdin who complimented him on it.

'I think it's watertight now.' He puffed his pipe. 'We learn by our mistakes, Mr Woods.'

Recollections of Clinton Smith's treachery surged up, and Albert said hotly, 'We lose fellowships by them.'

Dibdin stared at him with an innocent quizzical expression. Further recollections surged up, of Dibdin's failure to notice the

47

gap in his argument before the meeting of the Willard Gibbs, but Albert stared back and managed to hold his tongue.

'I expect something else will turn up, Mr Woods.'

'When?'

Dibdin looked badgered. 'We all have to toil in the vineyard for a spell,' he said with considerable absence of conviction.

Albert's work was both sound and promising. It was duly published as a paper to the Chemical Society by F. R. Dibdin and A. Woods. Albert thought he perceived the nature of the vineyard only too clearly.

One day in the following term Albert was summoned by the Professor. The meeting-place, to Albert's surprise, was in the Professor's rooms in college – not in the laboratory. Albert found himself waiting for the Professor in the room which had seen his humiliation. It looked different in morning light. The warmth of the parchment-shaded lamps had gone, and in the air clear of tobacco smoke everything looked shabbier.

Albert was standing looking through the window, at a shower of rain falling over the grassy quadrangle when the Professor entered behind him.

'I asked you to come and see me, Woods – I hope you didn't find it inconvenient to come this morning – to discuss a personal matter,' said the Professor – his name was Bunstone, Sir Norman Bunstone. 'Pray sit down.'

'Thank you.' Albert sat in the leather arm-chair again and faced the Professor with an eager expression. He looked younger than his age.

'As it's a matter of some importance I thought it would be best to discuss it here privately.'

Albert nodded. The Professor spoke in rapid nervous bursts which gave the impression that he was stammering slightly. One would have thought he was too nervous to come to the point immediately. He was sitting awkwardly with his long thin legs bent, one knee crossed over the other: his burning blue eyes were fixed on a point just behind Albert's left shoulder. As he uttered the word 'privately' he glanced round the room and then gave Albert a smile. The smile was encouraging, direct, almost sweet: it passed oddly over his ravaged face.

'I won't waste any time over preliminaries. This college have

48

recently decided the society of fellows needs another chemist, a junior person, of course.'

Albert blushed deeply.

'I've just been re-reading your paper to the Chemical Society. I congratulate you sincerely.' The Professor was leaning back: he folded his arms over his chest. 'I thought it was excellent.'

'But the fellowship?' Albert wanted to say. His lips moved but no sound came out.

'It was quite up to fellowship standard,' said the Professor. He said it in a congratulatory tone while still making it sound as if he did not want Albert to think he considered fellowship standard to be as high as all that.

'Do you think I was treated unjustly?' Albert wanted to ask, but he was too late.

'I understand your own college passed you over.' He was quite unaware of having hurt Albert's feelings. 'I wondered if you'd consider a fellowship here.' He paused.

Albert's tongue stammered its way into freedom. His voice sounded muffled and his accent uncontrollably flat, yet nobody could have missed the note of joy.

'Of course,' the Professor went on, 'you must understand that other names will be canvassed.'

Momentarily dashed but still greatly uplifted, Albert expressed his happiness in having the Professor appreciate his research.

'Unfortunately,' said the Professor, aiming at tact, 'if we do elect you it will be not so much for research – it will be chiefly to do some teaching, and to look after the undergraduates who are reading chemistry. We badly need someone on the experimental side – we recently elected one of my pupils but he's too much of a theoretician.'

Dashed even further, Albert was still dazzled by the prospect of becoming a fellow after all. The Professor stood up. 'I should like you to think it over, Woods.'

'I think I can tell you the answer now – that's if you . . .' Albert fumbled.

'Yes, I'm sure you can,' said the Professor, and fleetingly looked down on Albert from a great height.

Albert did not know whether he was supposed to say anything or not. The Professor was accompanying him to the door.

The Professor's college was a small one, so the election of a new fellow in chemistry was to a much greater extent within the Professor's nomination than it would have been at say Christ Church or Balliol.

Now it happened that Albert had done a fair amount of teaching in order to supplement the income from his scholarship. His pupils had been drawn from colleges other than his own and their success in Finals had been noted with favour by deans and tutors and by such people as Dibdin. Albert was good at teaching and had acquired something of a reputation for it.

It would have seemed to an outsider that Albert, having recouped himself in his reputation for doing good research, now had both qualifications the Professor's college demanded. Therefore they might elect him without delay. Affairs in Oxford did not move in that style. They moved with delay, with constant maddening delay.

Having lost a fellowship that was awarded sheerly for ability in research Albert would naturally have given anything to be offered another one of the same kind. To be offered another one chiefly, as it seemed to him, for his ability in teaching wounded his pride. And not to be offered it but to be kept waiting roused his rage.

Albert was in a constant state of agitation. He could not see what the barrier was between him and election. As he was not a member of the Professor's college he was not in a position to do any quizzing for himself. One day he found an opportunity to question the Professor about it.

'I have nothing to report, Woods,' said Sir Norman. There was a long bare pause, and that was the end of the exchanges.

'Does he think I have no feelings?' Albert asked himself angrily.

Dibdin, forgetting that he had previously discussed the matter with Albert, said: 'I hear you're still up for a fellowship of The Prof's college, Mr Woods.' A shrewd glance shone from his big hazel eyes.

'Have you heard anything?'

Dibdin shook his head. 'I should be confident if I were you.'

Albert could not help responding, even though he recalled Dibdin having used precisely the same expression when referring to his chances of winning the prize fellowship.

'I think our little paper may have done the trick for you, Mr Woods.'

'Our little paper' – Albert needed hope too much to argue about that. This part of the vineyard, if tricky underfoot, was less bleak than the Professor's, and at heart Albert preferred it.

'I've been dropping a word here and there,' Dibdin went on. A reminiscent smile lurked at the corners of his mouth. 'Into various ears.'

'Thank you, Dr Dibdin,' Albert mumbled.

Back in the room where he worked Albert was questioned by Clinton Smith about the state of his affairs. Albert shrugged his shoulders.

Clinton was fitting up a new piece of apparatus. 'I happen to know,' he said, looking at what he was doing, 'that Dibdin's pushing you.'

'So he tells me.' Albert had had time, while he walked down the corridor, to study the beauty of Dibdin's remarks. 'He says he's been dropping a word into various people's ears.' He paused. 'Like a combination of a busy bee and Hamlet's uncle.'

Clinton's lip curled to display a glimmer of gold fillings. 'That's very amusing, Woods.'

'The trouble with you, Smith, is that you've got no sense of humour.' Albert sat down on his stool and watched the operation of a new valve he had just installed.

Clinton did not reply. The pump made the only sound in the room.

The relationship between Clinton and Albert was more or less unchanged. Clinton's sense of his own rectitude was so strong that his intervention at the Willard Gibbs seemed to him to have been impelled by a need to ensure that the best man should win the prize. Albert had accepted Clinton's treachery because his instincts told him that treachery was an element in men's natures – to Albert treachery like loyalty, friendliness or anything else for that matter, was an element of all men's natures.

Clinton bore Albert no ill-will. Usually when you have done somebody down you bear him ill-will as a consequence for quite a long time. Clinton was as well disposed towards Albert as he had ever been.

The continuous small noise of the pump was broken. 'They ought to elect you soon,' Clinton said.

'Thanks,' said Albert. 'But I doubt if they're able.' His fury got the better of him. 'They're as impotent in their business as they are in their beds.'

The Michaelmas term ended without the election being made. Albert came up for the Hilary term in a pessimistic mood. For once quizzing brought some information to light. In the twenties it was still unusual for a man to be elected to a fellowship who had not received the whole of his education in the university. Though Albert was the only candidate, it appeared that two or three of the older fellows found it difficult to vote for his election because he had not been an undergraduate at Oxford.

'What good does that do?' Albert rounded on Clinton, as if Clinton were their spokesman.

Clinton's answer was unsatisfactory.

More weeks went by. Albert foresaw Easter passing without a decision being reached. The Professor suddenly informed him that the election was due to come up again at the next college meeting. Albert's anger now faded into unmixed anxiety. Sir Norman asked him to be available on the telephone on the day of the meeting: he did not deem it necessary to say why.

It was a Saturday and the meeting began at eleven-thirty and extended over luncheon. Clinton, as a fellow of Dibdin's college, now had a set of rooms there in which a telephone had just been installed. He invited Albert to have luncheon with him while he waited.

It was a rainy spring day. Clinton's room had been newly decorated with thick buff-coloured wallpaper and the warm humid atmosphere brought out a disagreeable smell of size. When his own interests were not at stake Clinton could be moved by a pleasing masculine concern for the well-being of other men. Instead of having his usual meal of cold meat and cheese he had ordered from the college kitchen some dishes he knew Albert liked. Yet although the mixed grill was excellent and the sweet made from tangerines delicious, the only thing about that day that Albert remembered beyond his anxiety was a rainy grey light and a smell of size, a faint pervasive disagreeable smell that still remained when all the doors and windows were open. He never smelt it again in his life without a pang reviving – 'today my fate is being decided'. The telephone rang. Clinton's tanned face lifted and his full grey eyes watched unwaveringly while Albert answered it.

'I'm in!' Albert put his hand over the mouthpiece while he

spoke, and then went on listening. Clinton rose and went across the room to him.

The Professor was speaking. 'Are you free to come along immediately?'

'Yes, yes, of course,' Albert stammered. 'What for, Professor?'

'It is usual to be admitted straight away. It's only quite a short ceremony, in the college chapel – not a religious ceremony, by the way. You should be wearing academic dress.' Statements and parentheses followed each other in characteristic bursts. Albert hardly mastered them. Truly he had never been in a college chapel since he came up, but this was no time to stand on ideology.

'I'll come round immediately.' He put the earpiece back on its hook and turned.

Clinton shook him by the hand. His grasp was strong and friendly. Albert's face was flushed: his own grasp was no less strong and friendly in return.

'You haven't got your gown and square here,' Clinton said. 'Take mine.'

A few minutes later Albert was trotting towards his new college. Normally he would have been carrying his academic dress under his arm. For this occasion he was wearing it through the streets. The black gown with its deep wide sleeves billowed round him, the square was tilted so that the long silk tassel hung down in front of his spectacles. He had a big umbrella which he let down as he entered the gateway. At the door of the porter's lodge he saw the Professor, tall, with his gown drawn round him like scraggy black wings, waiting for him.

They went straight to the chapel. There were two or three of the other fellows there whom Albert did not know. Albert was called upon to kneel before the Warden for the ceremony. It was short and Albert barely took it in. He noticed the large black and white stone flags of the door, the threadbare dark-red tapestry hassocks, the carved wood of the stalls touched here and there with gilt, and the sixteenth-century stained glass shining with splashes of brilliant yellow. The Warden was a very small man with a wizened child-like face, a drooping moustache and an Edwardian starched collar. The light from a side-window was constantly reflected in his spectacles so that Albert hardly saw his eyes.

A fellow of a college, a fellow of a society that had lived for nearly four hundred years – himself, Albert Woods. He was kneeling. The Warden's wheezy slightly irritable voice recited over his head. If there is such a thing as humble pride Albert's heart was filled with it at that moment. If there is such a thing as the force of destiny, Albert felt it at that moment almost hurting as it carried him aloft like a strong sustained kick up the seat. He knew that now he could stay in Oxford to research as long as he pleased. The vineyard – he had a place of his own in the vineyard now, and if it meant toiling he was ready to toil. He was filled with vigour. He was completely confident of his work. The Professor had judged him. The Chemical Society had judged him. The College had judged him. He was satisfied. He had intimations of great things to come, of the years in which his research would bear fruit and astonish the world.

'That's all, Mr Woods!' A sharp whisper from the Professor interrupted him.

He stumbled to his feet. His face was red with happiness and modesty.

In the quadrangle outside, Albert's modesty fell away and left him in a glow of unrestricted glory. The Professor invited him up to his rooms, but when they got there it was too early for tea and there seemed to be nothing for them to talk about. Albert wanted to get away. The Professor noticed his restlessness. He would have liked Albert to stay with him for a while.

'Would you like to leave before I order tea, Woods?'

Albert ought to have stayed. It was a reunion of allies after success. But his glorious mood claimed him. He could not bring himself to stay. He wanted to get out, to move. The dust of gold was shining on his bulging eyelids and his dark silky hair.

'If you don't mind, Professor, I would.' He stood up and thanked the Professor. A new slightly formal polite smile played fixedly round his pleasing blunt features.

He left. His expression was modified with a shade of anxiety. He strode hurrying through the quadrangle. He was making for the garage where he kept his little Morris Cowley two-seater. He knew with overriding desire what he wanted to do. When the motor-car started properly and he found himself driving steadily through the outskirts of Oxford the shade of anxiety disappeared, and the mixture of glory and wonderment reigned again now mixed with anticipation, delightful, swelling, compelling anticipation.

Albert was driving to the provincial town of his birth. He was driving fast and furiously to get to a young woman with whom he was conducting an amorous affair. That was what he had bought the motor-car for.

CHAPTER TWO

YOUNG LOVE

There is nothing for it now but to embark on describing some of the scenes about which I gave you warning at the start, the unedifying ones. I do not see how they can fail to be found unedifying; for the fact is that in his youth Albert Woods slept with young women – not many, I hasten to assure you – without offering them marriage. It will no doubt make some slight difference when I add that the young women whom he chose for the purpose would have been more likely than not to turn down a proposal of marriage had he seen fit to make one: it will no doubt make the scenes seem distinctly less unedifying – or else distinctly more.

In any case, may I point out that anyone who knows he or she is bound to be shocked can save us all embarrassment by the simplest manoeuvre – just skip. Albert's life becomes perfectly respectable a little later on, so if you feel the preliminary twinges of moral indignation, now is the time to take the remedy. It is better to skip than to burst.

A few months before he went to Oxford Albert Woods had begun an amorous affair with a girl called Thelma Mason; so that at the time he was elected to his fellowship, it had been going on for four years. Albert had been faithful to Thelma for all of this period, excepting two spells of a month each when he had been on holiday abroad, once in Brittany and once in Provence – on his other two annual holidays he had taken Thelma with him.

If you are inclined to carp you may say this does not sound like the performance of a great lover. Only one at a time, you may observe, thinking of say Casanova. I take the point. But I am not sure that I agree with it. Being a great lover is not necessarily a matter of sheer performance. Surely it can also be a matter of the imagination, the enthusiasm, the fervour with which you invest performance – of the imagination, or, in the opinion of Albert's less inflammable acquaintances, of the sheer palaver.

Nobody could ignore the imagination, enthusiasm, fervour and most of all, palaver, with which Albert conducted his affair with Thelma. The two-seater Morris Cowley was a symbol of them all. It swerved and dashed – Albert was short-sighted – along a road leading out of Oxford every Saturday morning and back again every Sunday night. On Saturday it might have been borne on the wings of anticipation, on Sunday propelled by the force of joy remembered. Its bull nose threw off glancing rays of light, its throttle was full out, it was like a chariot of desire.

It is all very well to reflect to Albert's disadvantage that Dante hung about statically for hours on a bridge. That was a long time ago. Can we be sure that if Dante were living now he would not appreciate the uses of a little motor-car? The reward Dante got for his pains would not have satisfied Albert, even if it would content you or me. Albert, when the need for Thelma was too much for man to bear, drove to see her in the middle of the week.

Thelma Mason was an engaging attractive young woman. She had a broad strong frame, but her flesh, of which there was a good deal, was light and plump. Her face was broad: she had a fine forehead, rather square jaws and a pointed chin. She had shining golden hair which she was always dressing in some new style advocated by women's magazines. Her eyes were big and blue, and their expression mingled frankness and evasion. She was a clever girl – she was a schoolteacher, the same age as Albert – and in a peculiar way it showed.

Thelma's face was constantly alight with a nervous flicker, as if she were being stirred by a succession of inward jokes. Was she beautiful? Alas no – fate had endowed her with a short upper lip which when she smiled gave a completely unjust impression that she was sneering. No girl could have been less given to sneering than Thelma. She was gay, lively, talkative, kind and friendly, completely democratic though extremely shy. She read a great deal, she had a passion for long hot baths and she could find something attractive in practically every man.

Thelma was an engaging person, but it is no use pretending that the concept of feminine chastity held a ruling place in her moral cosmos. Thelma's moral cosmos was such that it would have been difficult to say what concepts held a ruling place in it. I can only suggest that in action at least Thelma appeared to be ruled by the truly democratic concept that all men are equal. Being able to find something attractive in every man gave her a good start.

Confronted with men whose physical charms one would have thought were non-existent, Thelma would say enthusiastically of one: 'But look at his ears! They're sweet.' Of another, with surprising emphasis: 'His knees! Have you seen his knees?' At such times her face would be positively illumined by the nervous flickering smile that seemed to spring from inward jokes. Given goodwill of this kind, the men in question found something encouragingly attractive about Thelma. A woman's being essentially diffident or uncertain about her own charms, as Thelma was, tends to put a lot of men off: being essentially positive and certain about theirs, however, tends to bring them on. Thelma brought a lot of men on. In a particular sense Thelma Mason was a great democrat.

Albert arrived on the doorstep of Thelma's lodgings after his election. He was hot and inflamed with success. He wanted to make love to Thelma immediately. Her landlady opened the door.

'Is she in?' he demanded, his eyes popping.

She was: he made his way down the corridor, knocked on Thelma's door and flung it open.

Thelma was standing near the door. 'I've been elected!' Albert grasped her in his arms. Thelma's cry of delight was muffled as they kissed. Albert thrust his tongue between her lips and her body pressed against him. Triumph was surging through him.

Suddenly he noticed a noise in the room and looked. There was someone else there. Sitting on Thelma's divan in the corner beside the gas-fire was another young woman. Thelma ran her hand up the back of Albert's neck.

'That's Madge,' she said, and pressing his head down began kissing him again.

They went on kissing. Thelma was very fond of it and Albert in the rôle of great amorist had taught her how to incorporate little bites in her technique. But it was not long before Albert felt his surge of triumph turning into a surge of displeasure. It was all very well for Thelma to go on kissing in the presence of another girl, but that was as far as they could go and Albert was in a hurry to go further. He broke off their kissing.

'I'm terribly glad.' Thelma looked up into his face. 'I mean about the fellowship and all that. You deserve it, Albert ... you know what I mean, and all that.' She spoke rather rapidly, taking in her breath in gulps. 'I mean, you know.' She giggled and turned so that she and Albert were facing the other girl, who remained exactly where she was, smiling at them with a bright impersonal interest.

'This is Madge,' said Thelma. 'Be introduced. This is Albert – isn't he sweet?'

'Hello,' said Madge. She appeared to be only about nineteen and she was pretty. She still did not move. In spite of her bright smile there was something permeatingly remote about her.

'She's just come to teach at the school,' said Thelma. 'On supply.'

'Is she staying long?' said Albert.

'We hope so.'

While they were speaking Madge picked up a packet of cigarettes from beside her on the floor, took a cigarette out and lit it. She dropped the packet back where it was before.

'How long's she staying here?' Albert turned a goggling expression on Thelma.

'She lives here.'

'What? In this house?' Albert's tone of dismay suddenly changed to a falsely confident one. 'In another room, of course.'

'Not yet, Albert. But she's going to. She's sharing mine till there's one free.'

'Where does she sleep?' There was only one divan. Albert's eyes were fixed on it.

'We share the divan. Don't we, Madge?'

Madge gently blew out a cloud of smoke. 'It's got a broken spring,' she said.

Albert's face was red with agitation. 'I expect you're going out for the evening anyway,' he said.

'Oh!' Madge stood up, tremulous with alarm. She looked at Thelma. 'What shall I do?'

Thelma turned to Albert. 'We didn't know you were coming. You didn't tell me – I didn't know what time you'd be elected, I mean, how could I? ... Madge and I were going to wash our hair. The landlady's got the water hot for us and I've done mine but Madge hasn't. We were going to have an evening at home.' She giggled nervously. 'All girls together.'

Albert was hardly listening. 'She'll be washing her hair in the bathroom, won't she?'

'Yes.'

'How long does it take?' He turned an inflamed look on Madge.

'Oh,' she said. 'It sometimes takes half an hour.'

'Not long enough!'

Albert's cry burst out from his heart and they were all silent.

Albert turned to Thelma. 'You'll have to come out with me in the car.'

Thelma's face flickered mysteriously.

'Won't you?' he said.

'Oh, Albert. . . .'

'You must.'

'Yes, but . . .' She looked at him. 'I mean, I'd like to.'

Thelma's voice was hesitant: Albert's was not. 'I want you to.'

Thelma turned and looked at Madge, who was watching her.

'What about you, Madge?'

Madge did not reply. She looked nervous: she kept raising and lowering her eyebrows. Albert saw a look pass between the two girls, a peculiar secret look that he felt left out of. It was something to do with their sex being the same and his different – he wanted to break it up.

'What about it, Madge?' he said in a loud voice.

Madge waited for Thelma's decision. Thelma said evasively to Albert: 'Will it be comfortable?'

'You know it is.' His voice was breathy.

'I oughtn't to go out till my hair's set.'

He noticed that she was wearing a net over it. Her head looked smaller than usual.

'I've had my hair cut.' Thelma's voice regained its franker tone. 'Do you want to see it?'

She took off the net and Albert saw that her golden hair had been cut as short as a boy's.

'It's an Eton crop,' Thelma explained. 'Isn't it sweet?'

It was the first Eton crop Albert had seen. It made her face look bigger, the bone-structure stronger. Her head looked like a boy's. The difference to Albert at that moment was negligible.

'What about coming out?'

'You are persistent, Albert.'

'Of course I am.'

A pause.

'Well, what about it, Thelma?'

After a tiny hesitation, Thelma giggled. 'Oh, all right.'

'Come on.' Albert put his arm round her waist urgently. The scent of her setting-lotion was noticeable. She was wearing a yellow woollen jumper, and he saw her big light plump breasts swelling inside it.

He glanced at Madge and then whispered into Thelma's ear. 'Now.'

Thelma's glance met his for a moment. 'Give me three minutes.' She broke away from him and went out of the room.

Madge stooped and picked up the packet of cigarettes. 'Have a cig.' She offered him one and took another one for herself. Albert lit them. Madge smiled. 'Aren't you going to sit down?'

Albert glanced at his watch and accepted the offer, but he was in no mood for conversation.

'Shall I put the gramophone on?' said Madge. She crossed the room in a distant manner rather as if she were walking in her sleep.

The room was big and badly lit. It had a window that opened on to a paved yard. There was a table and a sideboard and a wardrobe and a bookshelf. The gramophone was on a small coffee-table in front of the fire: it looked as if the girls had been playing it just before Albert arrived.

A voice began to sing:

> *Just picture you upon my knee . . .*

Thelma came into the room again, wearing a long dark coat over her yellow jumper. She had tied a band of paisley silk round her head after the fashion of a woman tennis-player. She looked brisk and unconcerned.

Albert jumped to his feet. Thelma gave last instructions to Madge but Albert was not listening. They were off at last.

The little motor-car sped through the dusky streets and avenues on to a country road. Everything was still warm and wet from the afternoon's rain, and a sharp smell of fresh leaves and grass rose up into the air. When the motorcar turned into a side lane and drew in beside the gateway to a field, the first stars were showing. It was a spring night. Albert and Thelma, sitting where they were, turned quietly to each other and kissed.

The kiss lasted. Albert's anxiety vanished – the joyous moment was assured.

The grass was wet: they had to stay in the motor car.

Albert began to make love to Thelma. Their desire rose like the sweet smell from the earth. But anyone who has tried to make love in a two-seater knows that it is not easy. Albert and Thelma turned this way and that in their embrace. The manuals that tell young lovers how to go about these things always assume that they have unlimited space at their disposal. Thelma's arms were tight around Albert's neck. Albert pressed against her. Eagerness, desire and determination took hold of him. His feet were braced against the door of the motor car – the one that did not latch properly. 'Oh!' cried Thelma, with her eyes closed in excitement. The door of the motor car flew open and Albert fell on to the floor.

Hotly he picked himself up off the handbrake and gear-lever and got back again. He was rough and powerful in his haste. 'Oh,' cried Thelma, this time with her eyes open.

Albert felt her quivering beneath him and thought it was with passion. His face was close to hers, his voice thick and breathless as he said:

'Sometimes I'm terribly animal.'

Thelma did not speak. She was shaking with laughter.

The following Sunday evening Albert returned to Oxford a little earlier than usual. His enjoyment of Sunday afternoon with Thelma had been restricted by the presence of Madge. Thelma, on the other hand, seemed to Albert's eye positively infatuated with Madge's presence. At tea-time he left in a huff. Ah! love . . . Who, aprostrophizing thus, recalls the huffs of love?

And yet as evening came on, as the motor car rushed down steep country lanes and flew over hump-backed bridges, Albert's huff disappeared. He was filled with the sweet charity of satisfaction. The first stars came out, the trees were rustling, and Albert thought of Thelma's embrace. Another week to go! He pressed down his foot on the accelerator.

By the time he reached the outskirts of Oxford the sweet charity of satisfaction was overwhelming. Albert was so filled with the wonderment of love that he felt compelled to extend it to others. Instead of going straight to his college he turned off towards Islip. Clinton Smith's mother owned a cottage there. She was a widow –

Albert judged that she had a little money – and Clinton, aged thirty-one and still unmarried, spent all his weekends with her. As far as Albert could see Clinton never met any young women, let alone enjoyed the ecstasy of a love-affair.

It was the ensuing exaltation that gave Albert confidence when he was planning to help Clinton to find a similar experience. When Albert pointed his bull-nosed Morris Cowley in the direction of Islip it was with the zeal, the ardour of a missionary setting sail for China. The fact that he might get rebuffed never occurred to him. His soul was in a state of expansion.

And yet, as with a missionary, Albert's state of expansion did not lead him into excesses of spiritual proselytizing. What occurred to him, as the lights of Clinton's house came into view, was a simple practical plan. He was calculating that now he had a fellowship he could afford to invite the girls up to Oxford for the weekend. He would try to pair off Clinton with Madge.

Albert walked purposefully up the path to the cottage door. A lamp was shining softly from the window of Clinton's study. There was a damp leafy smell in the night air. Already Albert was seeing a succession of Saturday evenings in the rooms he would now be given in his college, of pleasing cosy little dinner parties – they could have candles on the table, they might drink wine. It would make Thelma happy, Madge happy, it could make Clinton happy – and not least of all it would make him happy, too.

CHAPTER THREE

TEA-PARTY IN A LABORATORY

In March of the following year, 1928, the efforts of the experimental chemistry department were crowned with success. F. R. Dibdin was elected a Fellow of the Royal Society. Dibdin was jubilant. He could not resist announcing that he was an F.R.S. before he began his lecture next morning.

'I'm glad it's come at last,' he said. His flat face beamed with child-like joy, his pepper-and-salt hair curled in all directions, and his bright hazel eyes were sparkling.

His audience were freshmen, innocent boys who just about knew what the Royal Society was.

Dibdin leaned forward against the bench and said confidentially: 'I expect it was my little idea about pseudo-Wurmer–Klaus reactions that really did the trick.' He looked round his audience with a friendly expression. 'If any of you ever come to work in my department you'll find we're never short of ideas. There are always plenty of them in the air.' He paused. 'That's how research is done.'

He was not trying to recruit new research assistants from this audience, and yet absurd though the speech was, there lurked in it an element of shrewdness and truth that stirred the imagination of at least one of his hearers. 'That's how research is done.'

Dibdin's voice became more confidential. 'And there are more surprises coming along,' he said and gave them a knowing look that meant he was going to be Professor Dibdin. Such of his audience as were interested were now completely mystified. 'Very soon,' Dibdin said, adding the effect of mystery at the expense of truth.

The news of Dibdin's election to the Royal Society was received by his research assistants with feelings surprisingly unmixed considering his relations with them.

'I'm glad the ——'s got in,' said Albert Woods, and in spite of the abusive name he was calling Dibdin, Albert's small round face was bright with pleasure and satisfaction.

'Good work,' said Clinton.

'We must give him a party in the lab.' As usual Albert's desire to share his pleasure took a practical form. 'Let's have a tea-party this afternoon.'

'Tea?' Clinton had still not lost the taste for spirits he had picked up as a subaltern in Flanders.

'What's wrong with that?'

Clinton said nothing.

'F. R. likes tea,' said Albert. 'We'll buy him some cream cakes.'

Clinton glanced at him. 'You're right, as usual, Woods.'

They decided not to do any work that afternoon. By teatime they had arranged a tea-party, too large to be accommodated in the library, so they decided to hold it in one of the big lecture theatres. They hired a tea-urn and ordered lavish quantities of cream cakes and ham sandwiches which they arranged on the lecture bench. One of the laboratory stewards conceived the idea of illuminating what he referred to as the festive board by training on it the light from the lantern projector which stood on the highest tier of seats. Against a back-cloth composed of a huge coloured wall-map of the Periodic Table the festive board looked theatrical, scientific and tempting to healthy appetites.

From the start the tea-party was a great success. The room was crowded. On the whole a good many people were well disposed towards Dibdin: and I may say that everybody was well disposed towards getting into the Royal Society.

Dibdin was in excellent form.

'My little idea about pseudo-Wurmer–Klaus reactions . . .' he was heard frequently to repeat with all the obvious naïve pride of a schoolboy.

There was a characteristic note in the observations made about their master by Woods, Smith and various other research assistants, a note often heard for that matter in all scientific circles with reference to all directors of research.

'He can't touch a piece of apparatus without breaking it.'

'He can't write down a formula without getting it wrong.'

'He doesn't know one end of a molecule from the other.'

65

And yet Dibdin's hold over his pupils was not diminished. His laboratory hummed as loud as ever. In his foggy disquisitions they still saw bright flashes.

Albert bustled to and fro, delighted with his rôle of impresario. The Professor arrived and bestowed a distinguished smile on him. Albert, feeling at his ease, tried to engage him in social conversation. It was unfortunate – and at the same time typical – that since his election to a fellowship of the college Albert had contrived to get on worse terms with the Professor, who had done most to support him, and on better terms with Dibdin, who had done least.

'I can't stand a man who behaves like Jehovah,' Albert had been rash enough to declare one evening at dinner in Hall. Sir Norman was not dining that night, but in a small college a wise man behaves as if the whole society were present on all occasions. The elderly fellows who had felt in doubt about electing a man who had not been an undergraduate of Oxford now saw their doubts bear fruit. Somehow the remark was disrespectful to the Deity as well as to Sir Norman Bunstone.

Now, as Albert watched the Professor chewing a ham sandwich with an impressive air, he wanted to make amends. The Professor was too lofty to be flattered, but all the same the conversation was going well. It came to a friendly pause for a moment.

'My idea about pseudo-Wurmer–Klaus reactions. . . .'

In the lull both overheard Dibdin's phrase. Albert glanced up at the Professor with a grin.

'Pseudo-original research . . .'

'I beg your pardon Woods.' The Professor turned a burning uncomprehending glance down on him. 'That seems to me a very singular remark.'

Albert stammered. It was useless to say he had not meant it. As the Professor had no sense of humour it was equally useless to try and explain it. The best he could do was to turn the conversation on to serious scientific topics.

Dibdin, who had moved nearer to them, now turned to greet the Professor.

The Professor congratulated Dibdin as if he had had nothing whatsoever to do with Dibdin's election to the Royal Society. Dibdin looked up at him with a cheerful rosy face.

'Don't congratulate me, Prof,' he said. A guileful flicker shone from his eyes. 'Congratulate the real workers, those who really toil

66

in the vineyard.' And he turned blandly and affectionately to Albert. 'Here is one of them.'

A few moments later Albert, with a face almost purple, excused himself and left them. He felt that he needed a little fresh air.

Albert strode towards an open door beside the lecture bench. He turned through it so rapidly that he bumped into two undergraduates who were peeping at the spectacle in the lecture-theatre.

'I beg your pardon,' Albert said politely – he was always polite to the young.

The undergraduates stepped aside. Albert found himself in the middle of the corridor, inflamed with rage but with nothing to do. The undergraduates did not know what to do either. The first to recover was a youth, taller than Albert, with a pale handsome beaky face. His fair hair grew up in a quiff: his eyes were grey and piercing. He had a most unusual air of penetrating, relentless intelligence.

'Oo're all the nobs?' he said. His tone was of penetrating relentless disrespect, his accent was a mixture of Mancunian and Cockney.

In four years Albert had made great progress in eliminating the accent of his native region.

'Are you interested?' he said with perfect precision. 'Perhaps you'd like to go in.' He smiled. 'I don't think you need pay.'

'You mean somethink for nothink?' The youth turned to his companion. 'What're we waiting for? We're in!' With that he went through the door, his companion followed him, and Albert was left to survey their receding backs.

Albert's rage changed to indignation. 'Secondary-schoolboys!' he said aloud: 'What manners! . . .' He had of course forgotten that he was a secondary-schoolboy himself.

A few minutes later, when his indignation had faded, he went back to the party. He did not forget the pale handsome beaky face and the unusual stare although he did not speak to the undergraduates again that afternoon. He saw Dibdin beckoning him.

'My dear Bowls, in a few minutes' – Dibdin glanced at the clock on the wall – 'I have a surprise for you. Some more visitors. . . .'

'Who, Dr Dibdin?'

'You can't guess, Bowls.' Dibdin's high spirits had made him frankly playful. 'It's a reward for you, for getting up this party.' He looked Albert in the eye. 'My wife and daughter are going to look in.'

'I'm afraid the best cakes may be gone.'

'There's no need to worry about that. The distaff side won't be keen on cakes. It will be the people ...' He glanced round the room. 'I want them to see all the people who've come to this wonderful party you're giving me.' He turned back to Albert. 'I particularly want them to meet you, Bowls ... Just to prove to them that it isn't all beer and skittles in the vineyard.' He laughed happily for no reason that was obvious to Albert. Then suddenly he made a triumphant gesture towards the open doorway.

'There they are.'

As if they had been produced by a conjuring trick, there stood Mrs Dibdin and Margaret.

Mrs Dibdin was aristocratic. She was the younger daughter of a Lord. She was The Honourable Mrs Dibdin. Her forebears in Elizabethan times were notable, a fact which did not distinguish her from many another person, and traceable, a fact which did. Like most aristocrats she was especially preoccupied with traceability.

Mrs Dibdin was a year older than her husband – in 1928 she was forty-three. She was tall, strongly and stiffly built. She seemed by instinct rather than by training to hold her back straight. Though her hands and feet were not large, her wrists and ankles were thick. She was a vigorous active woman, ambitious, warm-hearted, deeply affectionate especially inside her family: also she was stubborn, obtuse, and for all her worldliness quite innocent.

The features of Mrs Dibdin's face were well-proportioned: she had a short blunt nose, dark brown eyes, greying dark hair and a fine skin. The characteristic expression in her eyes was a bold look – it was the look she would have expected people to notice. But much more frequently than she realized the look changed: the whites reddened and the dark brown irises shone more warmly – she was being touched by emotion.

Margaret Dibdin bore no obvious resemblance to either her mother or her father. She had a strong and comely body, rather more graceful and mature than is usual for a girl of nineteen. People thought Margaret's face, in contrast to her mother's, was aristocratic-looking: underneath the firm rounded flesh the bone structure was beautifully refined. She had a broad high forehead, narrow grey eyes and a fine slightly hooked nose: her lips were shapely and her chin balanced perfectly the rest of her face. She seemed shy and diffident, almost a shade sullen; and yet her eyes sparkled steadily. She was much cleverer than her mother, and she was as intelligent if not as shrewd as her father. She held her head up proudly, and even when she blushed there was still something imperious about her. She was an only child.

Mrs Dibdin and Margaret stood in the open doorway of the lecture-theatre and paused. Mrs Dibdin was wearing a handsome fur coat. She looked boldly round at the company.

Margaret gave a quick glance upwards at her mother – it was a natural daughterly gesture: she was clearly feeling nervous and dependent; and yet there was a faint touch of amusement as if she were saying to an invisible third member of the family: 'There's Mama behaving like a Vicereine again.'

Dibdin waved to them, and taking Albert by the elbow said, 'Come and be introduced!'

Dibdin kissed his wife and Margaret kissed him; they were an affectionate and demonstrative family.

Albert was introduced: he blushed. It was the first time he had ever met the daughter of a Lord. 'This is Dr Woods.'

'I always look forward,' said Mrs Dibdin, 'to meeting any of my husband's colleagues.'

Just as when he looked up to the crest of his college and was made aware of four hundred years of romantic history, so when he looked up at Mrs Dibdin's face, at the bold brown eyes, the blunt nose and fine skin, he was aware of four hundred years of a family's glory. 'What a wonderfully aristocratic face,' he was thinking.

Dibdin introduced Albert to Margaret. Albert met her clear sparkling glance with a slight shock. Then she too blushed. The soft rosiness of it spread from her neck into her rounded cheeks. With a nervous movement she pushed away a strand of fair hair that had fallen across the corner of her eye.

'I always look forward to a party,' she said enthusiastically. Albert heard with surprise the clear confident sharpness of her voice and the rather unusual drawl with which she spoke. To his ear it was the voice of the upper classes. And then with equally surprising diffidence she lowered her eyelids and smiled. His glance lingered on the line of her cheek and her mouth.

'And this is Dr Smith.'

Albert turned with frank irritation to see that Clinton had contrived to join the party. He took care to remain standing between Clinton and Margaret.

During the fresh hand-shaking Albert found himself compelled to look back at Mrs Dibdin. To his slight chagrin she appeared to have found Clinton the more interesting, or possibly the more important, of her husband's research assistants.

'I notice my husband presented you both as Dr not as Mr.' She smiled graciously at Clinton.

'That is correct,' said Clinton. He and Albert had some time ago been admitted to the degree of Doctor of Philosophy.

'Ah yes. But one isn't certain that with such a recent kind of degree you would want to make use of it.'

She was referring to the fact that Oxford University had invented the degree of Doctor of Philosophy about ten years ago in order to compete with the universities of America which were already in the habit of handing out doctorates on a lavish scale.

'You think it isn't old enough?' said Albert, under her spell.

'Exactly, Mr Woods.' She looked at him with approval.

Margaret interrupted. 'Mama, a degree isn't like a title.'

Mrs Dibdin looked at Albert again. 'Mr Woods agrees with me.'

'Mama!' Margaret put her arm round her mother's waist.

Albert watched them and was touched.

'I wonder if I can persuade you to have some tea, Mrs Dibdin,' he said. 'I'm afraid it will all be gone.'

Margaret gave him a sudden glance.

'I'm sure you'd like some,' Albert said to Margaret. He smiled friendlily. 'Then you can join in the party afterwards.'

'How very kind of you,' said Mrs Dibdin. 'I'd love to,' said Margaret. 'I'll lead the way,' said Dibdin. Clinton said nothing.

Albert suddenly felt he had been a social success. The atmosphere was easier and warm.

While they chatted over tea Albert's confidence began to bloom. He could scarcely believe that he, Albert Woods, was getting on with the daughter and the grand-daughter of a Lord. He felt sorry for Clinton, who was behaving stiffly, and tried to draw him into the conversation. Their party was joined by the Professor and other distinguished guests.

'I'm glad we arranged this party, aren't you?' Albert said to Clinton.

Clinton nodded curtly and grinned. His gold fillings flashed.

At that moment Albert noticed Dibdin watching them, overhearing their remarks. Dibdin's face was lit with a broad, mischievous, faintly speculative smile. 'It's a reward for you . . .' Albert recalled Dibdin's words earlier on. Almost against his will Albert found his glance being drawn round to Margaret. She was talking animatedly to the Professor. For a moment Albert could not take his eyes off her face. Surely, he thought, surely that could not be what Dibdin meant. The room seemed to spin as if he were intoxicated. He stood with his feet planted firmly apart, his body straight and his face gradually turning pink as he drank a cup of tea.

'Can you spare me a moment before you go, Bowls?' Dibdin whispered.

'It's a little matter in confidence. Just between you and me.' Dibdin glanced down the corridor. 'Just between these four walls.'

They were standing at the top of the stone staircase which led into the entrance. Mrs Dibdin and Margaret were standing in the outer doorway talking to some of Dibdin's colleagues. Albert and Dibdin were effectively alone.

'Yes,' said Albert, his eyes bulging hopefully behind his spectacles.

'I expect you know the university have decided that I'm one of the labourers who's worthy of his hire.'

'Yes.' They stared at each other. Albert presumed he had been told that he was to get the new chair of experimental chemistry.

Dibdin lowered his voice and gave Albert a guileful smile. 'It isn't all beer and skittles,' he said.

'No,' said Albert.

'There's another little idea I've got in mind.'

Albert waited.

'You mustn't build on it, Bowls.'

'I'll try not to,' said Albert.

Dibdin glanced at him sharply. 'Do you know what I'm talking about?'

'No,' said Albert.

Dibdin relaxed into a smile.

'I should like to know, Dr Dibdin, I mean, what you were referring to.'

Dibdin leaned a little closer to him, and said in a sensible tone of voice: 'If, all being well, I get my reward for honest toil – and you know what that is – there'll be a lectureship going.' He paused. 'Now do you understand what I'm referring to?'

Albert just managed to say 'I do.'

Dibdin was laughing happily. 'We must think it over,' he said. 'I think you'd do for the job, Bowls.'

That night Albert wrote in his diary that Woods was walking on air.

CHAPTER FOUR
WALKING ON AIR

The setting up of a chair of experimental chemistry was a certainty and the choice of F. R. Dibdin to be its first occupant next door to a certainty; and, both of these certainties having been fulfilled, the appointment of Albert Woods to a lectureship followed. No mention had been made of dates. The University, as was its wont, moved slowly – if you are a Hebdomadal Council you do not set up a new chair in a hurry: in even less of a hurry do you elect the candidate for it who happens to be nearest to hand. One of the maxims of academic politics is 'Before you make a decision, sleep on it!' Over the chair in experimental chemistry the maxim was triumphantly upheld, night after night. Albert Woods found himself walking on air, meanwhile, for over a year.

After the first few buoyant moments most men find air is a rather unsubstantial medium for walking on. Not so Albert Woods. 'Dr Dibdin has promised me a lectureship,' he told himself with juvenile confidence whenever the going underfoot left something to be desired. Albert was no fool, and in his sensible moments he was capable of assessing his chances of getting the lectureship. Whether he got it or not his position was more secure than it had ever been before. All the same he rashly let his juvenile confidence supervene, because walking on air was delightful. New stars lured him on.

There were two stars that lured Albert on. They were personified in Margaret Dibdin and her mother – the stars of romance and snobbism respectively. And in the early stages it was the star of snobbism that exercised the more compulsive lure on Albert.

Most Englishmen love a Lord. We should not have tolerated Lords and Ladies for so many hundreds of years if we had hated them, that is to say if we had felt their titles and privileges were a constant affront to our self-respect. Albert Woods was a man of strong self-respect. When he loved a Lord it was not because he had discarded the dignity of man, far from it. No: his self-respect was strong enough for him to feel that he could, if not by birth, then certainly by temperament, be a Lord himself. Albert Woods had been smiled upon by a Lady: in a little while he was beginning to see himself as a great gentleman.

It is a pleasing thought to speculate upon – why is the smile of an aristocrat so much more warming than that of a commoner? Why does it stir so many more emotions in the human breast, emotions of a genial uplifting kind? Why in fact does it make a little man like Albert Woods see himself magnified into a great gentleman? Is magnification catching – can it be picked up in a smile from a noble? Observation leads one to believe that it can. If so, let Lords and Ladies smile more on the rest of us, because magnification of any kind is a delightful thing, both for those to whom it happens and for those who behold it in others.

One of the first buoyant thoughts to enter Albert's mind the night Dibdin offered him a prospective lectureship was that his income was going to be substantially increased. With his fellowship and without very much teaching he would make £1000 a year. After coming to Oxford on £250 the increase seemed like an inflation. He imagined the look of combined awe and satisfaction that would come on his father's face when he told him; he knew what his father would say.

'You'll be earning four figures now, lad.'

To Albert as well as to his father the need when denoting his annual income in pounds to use four digits instead of three was symbolical of worldly success. Something happened between £999 and £1001. Nobody in the Woods family had ever got into four figures before.

Albert was no miser. To him an income of four figures did not stand for impressive savings: it stood for impressive expenditure. It is probable that the promise of money came simultaneously with his desire to cut a dash. It is probable that at any point in his life given the money Albert would have tried to cut a dash. It so happened that the promise of money came simultaneously with his desire to cut a dash in the eyes of Mrs Dibdin and Margaret. Within a week of meeting them he had ordered three new suits from the best tailor in Oxford and had put in hand the complete redecoration of his set of rooms in college. He did not have the money to pay for them, of course, but in those days the tradesmen of Oxford would allow a fellow of a college to run up unlimited bills.

The things that Albert bought with his soon-to-be-acquired wealth did him credit as far as taste went. A man's taste is often indicative of his temperament, and often it can be linked with the kind of body he has. Albert was basically sturdy and tough, but his body was both sleek and subject to delicate nervous control: it was made for a considerable refinement of healthy sensual taste. He was sensitive to the colour and texture of material objects, to the taste and smell of food: he was very fond of physical comfort. Though as yet he was uneducated in these matters his first adventures in them had agreeable results. His general impetuosity and lavishness did not lead him into anything outrageously vulgar, though it did lead him into acquiring property that gave off a glow of richness. But Albert liked richness, anyway: he liked it for itself, quite apart from whether it would ultimately impress someone else . . . Mrs Dibdin.

The common fashion of the time in interior decoration was a mixture of the austere and the bizarrely titillating – greyish-white walls and woodwork, zebra carpets, patches of bright red in unexpected places, white pianos and what was called functional furniture. Albert conceded to austerity by having the walls and woodwork coloured plainly cream. For curtains he chose velvet of a dark regal purple. He covered the nondescript college Wilton carpet with a handsome silky Persian rug that he bluffed a London dealer into letting him have on credit. He decided to keep most of the furniture the college had lent him. On the heavy mahogany writing-table he installed a pair of ornate gilt candlesticks. Cushions, there were cushions in profusion, covered with an assortment of variegated silks. For the bedroom he bought a new bed with the latest kind of spring mattresses: it was a double bed: he was very proud of that.

When the work was finished Albert surveyed it with warm emotion. For the first time in his life he could live in beautiful rooms. The living-room was a large one: it looked into the quad-rangle facing north-west, so that although it was dark for most of the day it was illumined by the evening sun. The cream-coloured walls were never dazzling but late in the day they glowed rosily.

The purple velvet, the gilt, the patches of golden brown in the Persian carpet, all gave an air of luxurious comfort. 'Rich but not gaudy . . .' There was not much resemblance between Polonius and Mr Woods, but that did not strike Albert as the phrase floated through his mind. As for Polonius's strictures about getting into debt – they were wafted away before they ever got near his mind.

The day came when Albert invited Mrs Dibdin and Margaret to take tea with him. He waited for them sitting in a window-seat looking over the quadrangle. It was a warm sunny day in May and he had the window wide open. A constant stirring of the air carried up the scent of wallflowers which grew in a bed outside the Warden's lodgings. A gardener was cutting the lawn with a heavy whirring mower. Albert was wearing one of his new suits – the darkness of the cloth and the subtlety of the cut were designed to conceal the fact that he had started to put on weight.

'Rich but not gaudy . . .' His glance strayed round the room. 'Everything in perfect taste.'

The visitors arrived. Albert's small round face was pink. The visitors paid no attention to the beauties of the room: they sat down and prepared to enjoy their tea.

'I hope you'll excuse us, Mr Woods,' Mrs Dibdin said, 'if we have to leave you very soon.'

Albert's face fell.

Mrs Dibdin's bold brown eyes were fixed on him. 'We're giving a dinner party this evening for my brother, who's staying with us.'

'Of course.' Albert curved his mouth into a false social smile. He fussed over making the tea.

'I didn't have tea sent up from the college kitchen as they can't make it properly,' he said. He went out of the room to empty the hot water with which he had warmed the tea-pot down the sink in the scout's room.

When he came back he said:

'I hope you'll like my tea.'

His exaggerated tone made Mrs Dibdin think it must be something special.

'What sort is it?' she asked.

'Ty-phoo tips,' said Albert.

'Ah,' said Mrs Dibdin: 'That must be Indian.'

'I hope you don't mind Indian tea, Mrs Dibdin.'

'I'm sure it will be delicious, for a change.'

Albert blushed. Everything was not in perfect taste. He said: 'What do you usually have?'

'We always have Earl Grey at home.'

'I prefer Indian tea.' It was the first remark from Margaret. Albert was startled, and so was her mother. Margaret was watching her mother. Her eyes were sparkling. She was wearing a pretty summer dress made of pale blue material with sprigs of flowers on it. She glanced at Albert to see if he was enjoying the fun. 'I know Earl Grey is supposed to be a refined taste, Mama. But don't you see it's become rather *bourgeois*?'

'Really, Margaret, I don't know what leads you to make such an extraordinary statement.' Mrs Dibdin gave Margaret an anxious look. Then she said to Albert with a reassuring smile. 'I expect you know that Margaret has been in Switzerland for the last two years, where she made a lot of extraordinary friends.'

'I'm afraid Mama means I picked up a lot of extraordinary ideas.'

'Indeed I don't, Margaret. No ideas are extraordinary to me – I pride myself on that I've always been used to them.' Mrs Dibdin's back was very straight: she was holding her tea-cup rather high. 'You'll be surprised, when we come to talk them over together, how we shall agree.'

'Yes, Mama.' Margaret's firm lips twitched with a smile, and she looked down at her lap.

There was a pause. The tea was enjoyable wherever its origin. Through the window came the scent of the wallflowers and the sound of the mower. The afternoon sun began to shine on one of the walls and a reflection glimmered from the gilt candlesticks.

'This is an uncommonly pleasant set of rooms you have, Mr Woods. So much lighter than my husband's.'

'They've just been painted,' said Albert hopefully.

'So I see. I was saying to the President only a few days ago – I think it's time the college did my husband's.'

'Oh I had these done myself.'

Mrs Dibdin looked at him with surprise. 'Indeed.'

Albert felt there was a difference between spending all his time in his rooms and spending, as Dibdin did, only one night per week. 'I wanted something a little more comfortable,' he said, 'than the college would have provided.' He smirked with satisfaction.

'Of course, you live here, don't you.'

'In my fashion.' Albert had recently been reading Dowson. He felt rather pleased with his reply. He turned to Margaret and offered her a plate of cakes.

Mrs Dibdin gave the room a glance of inspection.

'I see you have no pictures.'

Margaret interrupted. 'Mama, that's the fashion.'

'I want to hear what Mr Woods says.'

It was the moment Albert had anticipated. He had prepared his speech in advance, but he delivered it hesitantly all the same. 'I should like some pictures but I'm afraid I don't know anything about painting . . . I should very much like someone to help me choose some.' An eager look came into his bulging eyes. 'I wondered if perhaps sometime I might ask you to help me. I feel that your taste must be so perfect. . . .'

Mrs Dibdin turned to him. Not for nothing had her family been warding off social-climbers for centuries. She opened her eyes wider.

'I should love to, Mr Woods – it's so kind of you to ask me. But I know so little about painting myself. Why, I was saying to the President of the Royal Academy the other evening, I hardly know Picasso's rose period from his blue.' She smiled at Albert. 'I'm afraid you must ask someone a little more expert.'

'I'll help him.'

It was Margaret who spoke.

Albert turned to her. His face had reddened. 'Will you?' He stammered as he met Margaret's steady look. She too was blushing faintly. Albert thanked her profusely.

Mrs Dibdin had momentarily lost her hold on them.

'I really think, Margaret, if Mr Woods will excuse us, we must be going.' She uncrossed her knees as she leaned forward to put down her cup and saucer.

Margaret and Albert were looking into each other's eyes.

'Margaret.'

'Yes, Mama.'

Mrs Dibdin said: 'I hope Margaret can help you, Mr Woods. She's seen most of the fine paintings of Europe.'

Albert said: 'I'm afraid I can only afford a few reproductions.'

'Of course.' Mrs Dibdin stood up. She caught a glimpse of the expression on Albert's face. She had not intended to wound him. 'I expect Margaret will know where to buy them.'

'Come along, Mama,' said Margaret.

The two women walked slowly to the door. Mrs Dibdin began to thank Albert for his entertainment and for a moment he had a feeling that she was reluctant to go. Her dark eyes glowed uneasily. 'I hope the motor's waiting,' she said.

'I'll come down with you to the gate,' said Albert. 'Just in case.'

'Thank you, Mr Woods.'

In the quadrangle Mrs Dibdin walked between Albert and Margaret.

The motor car was waiting. It was a Rolls Royce – a wonderfully antiquated one.

Albert strolled back to his rooms, where his scout was clearing away the tea things. He went across to the telephone and asked for the college kitchens.

'I want the kitchen steward.'

The kitchen steward was found for him.

'You're in the habit,' Albert said, 'of sending me Indian tea. In the future I want China, Earl Grey. Do you have it?'

'Certainly, sir.'

'All right. Then be sure to send it.'

'Certainly sir.' The steward was thoroughly used to accepting such orders and carrying them out.

Albert was not satisfied. His voice was filled with authority.

'I want you to make a special note of it. Tell your people Dr Woods is always to be supplied in the future with Earl Grey tea. The best quality. I want a special note.'

'Certainly, sir.'

I said a little while ago that magnification is a delightful thing, and I stick to it. I expect most of us have known well somebody who was magnified – by whom we were then dropped. We were hurt. But is it fair for us to expect a laugh at someone's expense without paying for it? And let us put ourselves in the shoes of the magnified one – inflated, how could we bear to listen to the puncturing laughter of our old friends? Alas! there is nothing to be done about it: human behaviour is something that we can only accept. And what makes the human comedy human is its streak of sadness.

Albert's inflation was well under way: he was beginning to ascend. Like a balloon he was likely to get bigger the higher he went.

Thelma Mason – I have now to tell what happened to Thelma.

79

She was one of Albert's oldest friends as well as one of his longest loves. Albert was still driving home to see Thelma three weekends of the month. On the fourth Thelma came up to Oxford. But a new star had begun to shine in the firmament of Albert's sentimental fancy, Margaret Dibdin. Thelma had by no means lost her glow: the firmament of Albert's sentimental fancy rarely displayed an eclipse. The romantic hero or alternatively the saint turns his devotion to the particular lady or the particular expression of divine love that inspires him, renouncing all others. But Albert Woods was a little man, not a romantic hero or a saint; and the little man does not renounce one love until he has safely landed another – he has sometimes been known for earthbound safety to keep on two at once.

Albert's good-natured planning to bring interest and solace of a particular kind into Clinton Smith's life had been successful. The prospect of the first cosy dinner-party for four had occupied his spare time for a week: candle-light, wine, a special menu from the college kitchen, none of them had escaped his busy attention. At the same time he had encouraged Clinton to regret the habit of abstinence and look forward to the pleasures of bohemian life. It enhanced Albert's satisfaction to think of himself as the leader, the initiator, as well as the dispenser of warmth and comfort.

The girls had come up to Oxford very charmingly dressed for the occasion. Thelma was in high spirits, while Madge, though just as cool and distant and pretty, seemed excited. The dinner was excellent and they drank a lot of wine. Every now and then Albert glanced at Clinton to see how things were going. Clinton's brown face had a fixed amused smile: occasionally he gave Madge a piercing glance from under his heavy eyelids and in return she flicked her fine pencilled eyebrows like a puzzled film-star. With a hopeful thrill of delight Albert began to plan a romance between them.

After dinner Clinton and Madge sat on a sofa together while Albert sat on the arm of Thelma's chair and fondled her hand. Albert's eyes began to look a trifle hot and bulging, but the scene was essentially decorous. In due course Albert poured out some whisky, which they drank. Clinton stood up.

'I think we'll be getting back to Islip now, old boy,' he said. He took hold of Madge's hand and she stood up too.

Albert stared at them in stupefaction. Clinton's gold fillings glistened steadily, Madge's eyebrows were raised in an imperturbable smile. Albert had not heard them exchange a private word. He pulled himself together and politely showed them out of his rooms. But when he came back again his face was tinged with purple.

'To think!' he said to Thelma, who was settling herself on the sofa – it was before the days of the fine double bed – 'Until a few hours ago that man was a monk!'

His indignation startled even Thelma. She raised her head to look at him, and then burst into laughter.

'Albert,' she said, 'I think you're sweet. Come here!'

Albert was quick to recover from chagrin. After that evening he arranged regular parties. If Clinton's mother happened to be remaining in the cottage at Islip for the weekend Clinton stayed in college. They had dinner-parties, evenings on the river, they went to the theatre, to the Mitre and the Randolph. It seemed to Albert that Clinton was still missing romance, but the major gap in Clinton's existence had clearly been filled and Albert considered his duty done.

During the weeks in which Albert's rooms were being refurnished Thelma and Madge stayed at home and Albert and Clinton visited them there. Their first visit to Albert in his new grandeur took place the weekend after he had entertained Mrs Dibdin and Margaret to tea. Albert was uplifted by the thought of the impression his grandeur would make on them.

From the moment when he flung open the door and welcomed them in, Albert was disappointed. They were impressed, but somehow it was not in the way he had hoped. They walked a few paces towards the writing-table and stopped hesitantly. To their eyes the room was grand. Albert watched Thelma. She turned to him diffidently.

'I think it's terribly nice, Albert. I mean, I really do ... it's really ...' Her breath came in gasps between the phrases. She stammered and her homely accent was much more marked than usual. 'It's terribly nice.'

'Do you think so, Thelma?' Albert's eyes goggled compellingly.

Thelma giggled and made a gesture with her hand. 'Oh Albert, I don't know where to sit down.'

The room was too grand for Thelma.

Albert was disappointed, touched, irritated. 'Anywhere will do,' he said.

Madge was standing close to the writing-table. Albert had some time previously come to the conclusion that the unconcern of her manner was partly due to her being short-sighted and refusing to wear spectacles. She viewed the world with a bright distant impersonal interest partly because she could only see it indistinctly.

Madge touched one of the gilt candlesticks and then turned to Albert with a smile that showed she was doing her best to please.

'Sweet,' she said. And then she added: 'Posh.'

'Is that all?' Albert could not restrain himself. His voice now had a note almost of anguish. 'What about the rest?'

Madge turned what might be called her gaze round the rest of the room. 'That's sweet too,' she said. And then added: 'Posh.'

'You'd better sit down, Madge.'

The two girls sat down on the sofa.

'I'm sorry you're not more enthusiastic,' Albert said.

'But we are,' said Madge. 'Aren't we, Thel?'

Madge and Thelma looked at each other, into each other's eyes: it was the look Albert felt left out of.

The weekend had started badly and it never recovered. Even when Clinton came they never seemed to find their old form. For this celebratory occasion Albert had chosen for dinner the dishes the girls liked most – their tastes, though different, were eccentric. Yet something of their old freedom was lost. It was not so much in Madge – Albert did not mind a change in her anyway – it was in Thelma.

'Oh Albert, I don't know where to sit.' And her accent. Albert was touched, sympathetic. And yet he was hurt.

Albert wanted simply to impress Thelma and to rouse her wonderment. After all, one of the chief delights to be found in magnification is the envy of one's contemporaries who stay the same size: it is by the extent of their wonderment that we judge the extent of our magnification. If only Thelma had said, 'It's simply marvellous. I wish I lived here,' all would have been well . . . Or so Albert thought.

Albert was very fond of Thelma. He would have said that at the moment he threw open the door of his new rooms, his hopes of the future with Thelma – those sanguine dreams with which he instilled any of his activities, from scientific research to buying a new bicycle – were at their warmest and most flourishing. Thelma hurt them. His irritation at the time did not last, and yet when she had gone he could not prevent the thought crossing his mind: 'Why couldn't she have said she wished she lived here?'

It is not easy to say who dropped whom. With each meeting that followed, Albert and Thelma moved farther apart.

It was one day just after the end of the same term that Clinton Smith came into Albert's room – they now had separate laboratories – with an astonishing piece of news. It was not the sort of information that in the ordinary way Clinton would have confided to his rival. Astonishment and fury had temporarily got the better of his judgement.

Albert was writing at the time: he had finished his experiments for the term and was making some notes before he packed up and went away for his holidays. The department was quiet, for Albert was almost the last person left working in it. The laboratory stewards had all gone away and the workmen, due to do repairs, had not yet come in. Dibdin had taken his family touring along the Côte d'Azur.

Albert heard footsteps coming up the corridor and recognized them as Clinton's. The door of the room was open because it was a warm afternoon. Clinton came straight in.

'I thought I should find you here,' he said.

'Just a minute.' Albert finished a calculation he was doing before he looked up.

Instead of sitting down Clinton strode across to the window. It was open and he looked out at the façade of another laboratory a few yards away.

'Yes,' said Albert.

Clinton turned round. He was wearing a pair of flannels and an open-necked shirt with the sleeves rolled up.

'I've just heard something very amusing,' he said. Nobody but Clinton could make the word 'amusing' sound so menacing, brutal and unfunny. His teeth showed in a characteristic stiff smile. 'I just ran into Lewin in the High.'

Lewin was another senior research assistant in the experimental chemistry department.

'It's ruffled you,' Albert said. He surveyed Clinton easily and friendlily.

Clinton was silent for a moment. Then with an unexpected masterful movement he turned a chair round and sat on it.

'You're bound to hear this sooner or later,' he said.

Albert glanced at him. The tone was not that of a friend. Clinton sat compactly on the chair. In his youth he had been barrel-chested: he was now beginning to look like a barrel all the way down, a strong, muscular, meaty, powerful barrel. His hair was clipped very short. Apart from the intent light in his eyes his face was expressionless.

Albert waited cautiously.

Clinton said: 'It's about the reorganization of the department when F. R. gets his chair.' His lip curled faintly. 'I suppose he will get the chair.'

'Of course he will,' said Albert, loyal to Dibdin.

'The chair doesn't even exist yet, but for the moment that's beside the point. If and when it does, there'll be a lectureship going.'

'Quite,' said Albert.

'You might as well know F. R.'s offered it me.'

'What!'

'There's no need to look surprised. F. R.'s offered it me.'

By a tremendous effort Albert restrained himself from giving away that Dibdin had offered it to him as well.

'The amusing thing,' said Clinton in his earlier 'amusing' tone, 'is that Lewin says F. R.'s offered it him.'

'The ——!' The 'u' was shorter, lighter, more gentlemanly than ever before, but somehow the old indignation broke out recklessly.

Albert and Clinton stared at each other. Albert's expression did not change: only his face turned from pink to red to purple.

Clinton's eyelids remained motionlessly half-closed; then suddenly his teeth showed in a glitter as he laughed. 'Has he offered it you as well?'

'Yes.'

There was nothing for either of them to say. Clinton stood up and strode back to the window: his broad shoulders filled the lower half of it.

'We've got to do something about it,' said Albert.

'What?'

'Confront him with it.'

'He'll be in Nice by now.'

'Then we'll go to Nice. We'll follow him till we find him.'

There was another silence.

'We'd better wait till he comes back,' said Clinton.

'He'll probably have offered it to a fourth party by then.' Albert's spectacles flashed as he looked up at Clinton. 'He'll probably spend his holiday sending French telegrams to every member of the department in turn.'

Clinton acknowledged Albert's humour with his usual grimace of contempt. 'I don't think so.'

'It would be a simple way of pleasing everybody. I suppose that's what he wants to do.'

'I can't say that I'm interested in his motives.' Clinton's tone was harsh. 'I don't go in for psychoanalysis.'

'Look here, Clinton, I'm just as involved in this as you.'

'Then I advise you to keep to the point.'

'Then I advise you not to lose your temper with me.'

They paused.

'I've already made a suggestion,' said Albert, 'about what we ought to do.'

'We can't,' Clinton said angrily.

'I agree.'

'We've got to wait till he comes back.'

'And then we go to him together.'

'Agreed.'

'Do we take Lewin with us?'

'No. We'll leave him out of it.'

'I think you're right, Clinton.'

The tone of their conversation was forceful and unfriendly not because they were angry with each other, nor really at this moment because they were angry with Dibdin, but because they were angry with fate. They were both young men who were indiscriminately given to action on all occasions: not being able to act made them indiscriminately enraged.

During the hour or so in which they raged over Dibdin's escape to Nice it occurred to neither of them, and especially not to Albert, that the escape was possibly a lucky chance not only for Dibdin but for himself.

CHAPTER FIVE
MARGARET'S ROMANCE

The Dibdins were staying not in Nice but in Cap d'Antibes.
One might see photographs in society magazines of certain
independent members of the European aristocracy walking along
the Promenade des Anglais, apparently careless of the fact that
beside them walked proletarian holiday makers from Lyons: the
photographs of Eden Roc displayed only persons whom Mrs Dibdin
regarded as suitable to know.

Margaret preferred Nice. They kept driving through the town on
their way to visit some of her mother's friends who were staying in
Monte Carlo.

'I don't know what you see in Nice,' said Mrs Dibdin.

'It's a town,' said Margaret, 'not just a resort. Can't you see
they're real people, Mama? People who are earning their living and
having interesting lives.'

'I've no doubt they're earning their living, Margaret. But you
aren't likely to meet them, so I don't see why you want to be
among them all the time.'

'We might meet them.'

'Good gracious, Margaret.'

The antiquated Rolls Royce was speeding sweetly and comfortably along the lower Corniche in a cloud of dust. Mrs Dibdin
would have been wise to let the conversation lapse. Margaret's
father, who was driving, sucked his pipe meditatively.

'I should have thought,' Mrs Dibdin persisted, 'a girl of your age
would have thought Eden Roc was perfect. Other girls who are
staying there seem to make lots of friends.'

'I have,' said Margaret.

'But you don't seem to care for them, somehow.'

Margaret laughed. 'They're all right.'

Mrs Dibdin glanced at her with concern. 'It's something about your attitude,' she said.

Margaret looked through the window. Her eyes were hidden from her mother.

Mrs Dibdin's concern for Margaret was very strong and very simple. She wanted Margaret to find a suitable husband, and she was alarmed that Margaret showed no signs of encouraging suitable serious-intentioned young men. But deep as her concern was she was quite incapable of saying it directly. Sometimes when they were discussing the topic her eyes would redden with loving emotion, but the only words she could utter were 'It's something about your attitude, Margaret.'

'Eden Roc's only fashionable,' Margaret said. 'I think you're taken in by the people there.'

'I'm sure I'm not.' Mrs Dibdin was wounded. It seemed incredible to her that a girl who was only just twenty could observe her circle of acquaintances in such a way.

Margaret knew perfectly well what her mother was getting at. In years to come she would feel a mixture of irritation and pity: now she felt nothing because she was thinking about something else.

'Here we are.' It was Margaret's father who interrupted them by bringing the motor-car to a standstill.

They had just turned a bend in the road so as to come upon the first view of Villefranche. It was one of Margaret's favourite sights. The harbour was narrow and the rocky coast fell steeply to the water's edge. They got out of the motor-car and looked down. It was a dazzling afternoon. The sky was a pure soft blue, and in the creek it was reflected by waves in a shade twice as deep and twice as brilliant. Against the dusty rocks of the landscape the buildings sparkled in a jumble of distempered gable-ends that advertised *aperitifs* called Byrrh, Suze and Dubonnet. In the harbour lay a sleek slender French warship dressed with flags.

'It's lovely,' said Mrs Dibdin stalking to the edge of the road.

Dibdin lit his pipe and blew out a cloud of smoke. His mind happened to be on Wurmer–Klaus reactions.

There was a hazy shimmer over everything. Near to where Margaret stood was an oleander bush. She picked a flower and glanced at it. She was still preoccupied with what her mother had been saying. She was smiling.

Suddenly she brushed her fair hair from her forehead and looked up. She was thinking that she had fallen in love with Albert Woods.

When she had returned to England after two years in Switzerland, Margaret Dibdin felt as if the world were unfolding before her eyes like the petals of a rose in an accelerated film. Her twentieth birthday passed. She had become a beautiful young woman. Her body was showing its final shape, wide across the shoulders and the hips, with a smooth line along breast and waist that made men's eyes follow her when she walked across the terrace of an hotel. About her face, for all the clear delicate rosiness of her skin, there was a strength, almost a nobility of expression. It was beauty of an unusual kind. There were men who, seeing the steady sparkle in her grey eyes, found it slightly forbidding even when it was softened by youthful girlish nervousness.

Margaret was simple and direct and clever. She had strong simple emotions. Her mind was clear and powerful. Yet, although she often studied her face in the looking-glass, she could never be certain that she was beautiful, still less that she was desired by men. She never really identified the flicker in their expressions when they were put off by the penetrating look in her eyes or the harsh drawl in her voice: what she felt was a stronger desire to be at ease in their company, a stronger need for them to make her feel that she was loved. In her social life the kind of diffidence that made many a girl stay tremulously on the edge made Margaret plunge in. She loved parties. Even her mother had to admit that she was apparently popular among her friends and had many of them.

Now that she was going to live again in Oxford Margaret had to make up her mind whether she wanted to go up to Somerville. Her father appeared to expect, without any particular sign of thinking she was right or wrong, that she would. On the other hand her mother wanted her to be presented at Court next summer or the summer after. Margaret gave it a lot of thought: in this kind of thing she was unaware of being hampered by emotion.

Yet all the same Margaret wavered. She really was hampered by two things: one, she was well-connected, and the other, she was rich. Mrs Dibdin had brought a name as the chief part of her dowry: Dibdin was the son of a middle-class family who owned a large fortune made out of railways. When her father died Margaret was likely to come into a lot of money.

Margaret's connexions did not trouble her greatly. She went to stay with her mother's family from time to time, with her grandfather and her uncle. She got on well with them, but at heart their relations were purely the conventions of a family and she already had intuitions of their weakening and decline. No, it was Margaret's money that troubled her the more.

The early 'thirties was a period in the country's history when many young men and women were troubled, as Margaret was, by the thought of possessing money. The malady came to be known as the sick conscience of the rich. And a very tiresome malady it was to their friends. It led the rich to subdue the outward sign of their wealth – there is no record of any of them parting with it – and to take up some morally unexceptionable profession such as that of being a doctor or a civil servant. All well and good. Nobody minds rich young men becoming doctors or civil servants. What made the malady so tiresome was the song they made about it.

It took fifteen times as much fuss for a rich young man to decide to become a doctor as it did for a poor man. When one saw the bright face of a rich young man coming round the door for the eighty-eighth time to compel one's attention with the drama of his sick conscience, 'Should I or shouldn't I?' the temptation was very great to say under one's breath, 'As if it matters!' Often there are moments when only an effort of will prevents us seeing the struggles of someone else's conscience as a manifestation of unredeemed egocentricity.

Fortunately Margaret's case was not typical sick conscience of the rich, partly because she was not overwhelmingly egocentric and partly because she was a healthy young woman: she knew that she would marry. It was merely that being rich and having a whole social world opening for her made her feel that she owed it to her intelligence to sidestep both. In particular it made her feel that she owed it to her intelligence to sidestep her mother's plans for marrying her off.

It was in a mood of amused discontent that Margaret surveyed the young men whom her mother would have thought eligible, boys who were going to inherit estates and serve in the Brigade of Guards. It was in this mood that she met Albert Woods.

The temptation to try and find out about the lectureship before the following term began was too great for Albert to resist. A few days after agreeing to their plan of campaign with Clinton he was travelling down to Nice. To tell the whole story, I have to include the information that he had spent the few intervening days in quarrels with Thelma over another young man in whom she appeared to have discovered unexpected charms. He had no clear plan of campaign ready for when he got to Nice. He did not know where the Dibdins were staying: optimism plus faith in physical movement sustained him, apart from a list of grand hotels at which he intended to inquire for them.

As the Dibdins were not staying in Nice and never had stayed there, the list of hotels produced no results. Albert was stumped: he did not know the Dibdins' itinerary, or even whether they were travelling east or west along the coast.

Albert had never seen any part of the Côte d'Azur before. He was dazzled. His agitation over not getting the lectureship disappeared, and he gave himself up to enthusiasm for the scene. And having parted from Thelma in a huff, the next thing he did was to send her a telegram saying:

ALL FORGIVEN PLEASE JOIN ME AT ONCE

A few afternoons in the hot blinding sunshine and a few evenings drinking wine with his dinner and brandy later in the night had stirred Albert in a way that he took very seriously. Instead of wondering hotly whether he would meet Dibdin or not, he now spent his time wondering hotly whether Thelma would come or not. Of the two the latter, as no good could possibly come of his confronting Dibdin, was likely to do his career the less harm.

On the morning he got a telegram from Thelma saying she could not come – giving no reason why – Albert met Margaret Dibdin. It happened at about ten o'clock in the old port. If you think that as a consequence of Thelma's defection Albert was either struck with grief or ramping off to the nearest brothel you are mistaken. He was busily taking photographs with his little Kodak of the fishermen landing their catch. An entrancing spectacle it was. The sun glittered on the water and the scales of the fish. Black-headed little men with brown arms and stained white and blue striped jerseys were passionately exchanging selected parts of the verb *s'en foûtre* in a hideous *Niçois* accent. And an acrid stink rose up into the bright cerulean heavens. There were too many rocks, waves, boats, palms, cafés, nets, fish and bustling men for the little bay to hold.

'Good morning, Dr Woods.'

'Margaret – I mean Miss Dibdin.'

They stared at each other for a moment in delighted surprise, and then Albert took her hand. She looked radiant. She was wearing a diaphanous pink dress, and her bare legs and arms glowed with a light rosy tan – Albert's face was scarlet with sunburn. On her head was a cone-shaped flower-seller's straw hat.

'Don't look at that – it's to keep the sun off my face.'

'It looks' – Albert was stammering – 'superb.'

Margaret laughed. 'What are you doing here?'

As he replied Albert totally forgot about her father. 'I'm on holiday.' It was not a lie. A new wonderment was filling his heart and head, sweeping out everything else. 'What are you doing here?'

'I'm on holiday too.' She fixed her sparkling gaze on him. 'I suppose you're wondering why I'm alone?'

'Yes, where is your father?' For the first time it occurred to Albert that an encounter with Dibdin would have done no good.

'He and mama have gone to Menton. I was determined to stay in Nice by myself. Under protest they let me stay . . . I'm going to Monte Carlo by bus and then some friends are driving me on to Menton – '

Albert could not wait for the end of her speech. 'When? How long are you staying here?'

'Till tomorrow.'

They both paused. The little port overflowed its distracting vitality all round them with no effect on them whatsoever.

'Let's sit down in a café and talk,' Albert said.

Together they went to the nearest café, and sat under an awning.

'I should like a Cinzano,' said Margaret. 'It's a vermouth.'

The waiter was standing beside him. 'I'll have a Suze,' said Albert with equal knowingness. He had never tasted one.

They began to talk. It would have been difficult for either of them to recall afterwards what they said. What they never forgot was a fresh nervous animation that exalted every word, every thought, every look, every flicker.

Albert's Suze was a lesson to him. He found it was made from gentian.

Margaret burst into laughter when he took his first sip. 'What's the matter?' he said, blushing. He imagined he had concealed his distaste.

'Haven't you drunk it before?'

'Yes – I mean no.' He made an effort to look unconcerned and then he too laughed. 'It's revolting,' he said frankly and furiously.

The incident seemed extraordinarily funny to both of them.

'Try mine.'

To his astonishment Margaret was holding out her glass to him. The golden liquid glowed. 'You can drink out of the other side,' she said. Their fingers touched as the glass changed hands.

Albert tasted the Cinzano, speechless. It became his favourite, his only *apéritif*.

They sat and talked for the rest of the morning. The sun grew hotter, and there was no breeze under the awning. They were both in a trance.

'What a wonderful place this is,' Margaret said. She was watching the activity on the quay.

Albert followed her glance, his hand playing lightly with the strap of his camera-case. Margaret's hand was lying on the table about half an inch away.

'I should like to go to Monte Carlo,' he said.

Margaret glanced at him in surprise, not being used to such restlessness.

'This is much more fun,' she said.

Albert turned his bulging eyes to look at her.

'Monte Carlo,' Margaret said, 'is more *mondaine*. But this is more fun.'

Reflections of a similar kind had motivated Albert's desire to make Monte Carlo his next visiting place.

'Mama can understand people staying in Monte Carlo, but not here.'

'Ah, your mother,' said Albert.

Margaret was amused by him. 'She's made a great impression on you.'

'She's a superb woman.' Albert pursed his lips and put a very wise expression on his spectacled face.

Margaret laughed. There was a harsh note in her laughter, and yet there was a deeper indulgent note of affection.

'You made quite an impression on her,' said Margaret.

'Do you think so?' Albert was completely humble and naïf.

'She thought you were very ambitious.'

Albert was not exactly pleased. And yet any mark of attention from Mrs Dibdin was dear to him.

'I suppose you know,' he said, 'I only went to a grammar school?' Actually it was a secondary school. 'To a man like me your mother seems particularly wonderful.' His voice sank with warm gluey emotion.

Margaret was watching him with fascinated interest.

'So aristocratic.' Albert shook his head at the thought of it. 'Unbelievably aristocratic.'

'But Albert' – it was the first time Margaret had called him by his Christian name – 'she's a perfect *bourgeoise*. I know she thinks of herself as frightfully aristocratic by birth – she is. But her nature's that of a *bourgeoise* through and through. Don't you see she's a *bourgeoise*?'

Albert did not see. He was cross. He felt as if Margaret had caught him making a mistake for one thing, and he wanted to believe Mrs Dibdin was an aristocrat for another. His scarlet sunburnt face showed a momentary tinge of purple.

Instead of keeping quiet, Margaret said: 'Don't you see I'm right?'

'No, Margaret.'

They began to argue about the difference between an aristocrat and a *bourgeoise*, and though Margaret was eight years younger the argument was conducted on equal intellectual terms. Albert felt the impact of a strong independent personality. He became heated. Their voices rose.

The waiter, hearing them arguing, saw both romance and business disappearing: he came and asked them if they wanted another drink.

'Yes,' said Albert.

'You need a Suze now,' said Margaret. Albert glanced at her and they both laughed.

'You're an extraordinary girl.' Albert touched his hand against hers. 'Margaret.'

Margaret blushed. She looked down, and after a pause said: 'I think you're like mama – in thinking I have extraordinary ideas. I expect you wonder where I picked them up, as if they were measles or something.'

'I suppose you picked them up in Switzerland,' said Albert,

remembering Mrs Dibdin's observations about Margaret's extraordinary friends.

There was a pause.

Albert watched her. 'What were you doing in Switzerland?'

Margaret looked up. 'I went to a so-called finishing school there.' She met his glance. 'Also I had a short spell in a sanatorium. They thought I had T.B.'

Albert felt a spasm almost of pain. 'Had you?'

'I don't really know.' She smiled. 'I'm all right now, anyway.'

Albert smiled back at her. His mood had changed completely. 'I'm glad.' He no longer felt challenged by her. Sentiment almost prevented his repeating, 'I'm so glad, Margaret.'

The waiter brought their vermouth. They decided to have luncheon together.

After luncheon they decided to spend the afternoon together, and then the evening. At midnight Albert took her to the entrance of her hotel. She stood curiously still while he said good night. He wondered whether he might kiss her. His courage failed him: it was too soon, he thought.

And so next morning Margaret went away, and Albert was left alone to reflect. He felt his life had been transformed. Suddenly he saw his affair with Thelma in a completely different light. It was over. He wrote this at great length in his diary, and he wrote also about his new, great, wonderful, different feeling for Margaret. He had fallen in love with Margaret, and this was a love that made of him not only a great amorist – he saw now what a great amorist lacked – but a perfect knight as well.

He went to Monte Carlo after a couple of days, and thought of nothing but Margaret only fifteen kilometres farther along the coast.

And after two days of that he took a train to Menton.

CHAPTER SIX

SILVER SPOONS AND A PROPOSAL

The confrontation between Dibdin and his two senior research assistants took place at the beginning of the next term. By that time Albert's chief desire was to avoid rather than to have an angry scene. The thought had crossed his mind to marry Margaret. Clinton's insistence on making Dibdin declare his intentions was unchanged.

The nature of the scene, however, was settled by Dibdin.

Clinton opened it by demanding to know what Dibdin meant by offering the lectureship to Lewin.

Dibdin looked badgered and astonished. His glance shifted from one to the other of them. His answer took the wind out of their sails.

'Who's Lewin?'

Dibdin asked in such a guileless fluster that for a moment they thought he must be suffering from amnesia.

Tersely Clinton explained who Lewin was.

'Oh yes,' said Dibdin. 'Dr Lewin.' He now remembered triumphantly. 'The Dr Lewin who works in Room 23.'

'That's my room,' said Albert.

Dibdin turned to him. 'I thought you were sharing a room with Dr Lewin.'

'That was with me,' said Clinton. 'We've had rooms of our own for the last two years.'

'I'm very glad,' said Dibdin. 'I'm glad we've been able to make you comfortable.'

Clinton was exasperated.

'I want to know,' he said, 'if it's true you've offered a lectureship to Lewin.'

'Dr Smith, I haven't offered a lectureship, to my knowledge, to anyone.'

'To your knowledge!' Clinton burst out. 'You've offered it to me.'

'And me,' said Albert.

Dibdin glanced at the door: Clinton's body turned as if he were going to bar his way. A look of great alarm spread over Dibdin's flat face. His big round eyes fixed them unwaveringly.

'There must be some misunderstanding,' he said.

'That's precisely why we've come to see you,' said Clinton. 'We should like you to clear it up before it goes any farther.' He glanced at Albert for support.

Albert was doing his best to make it clear that the initiative was Clinton's. He said in a calculatedly emollient tone:

'We should like you to tell us, Dr Dibdin.'

'I wish I could,' said Dibdin. 'I should like to offer you a lectureship, Smith and you too, Bowls. You both deserve it.'

Clinton said: 'We can't both have it.'

Dibdin was silent. He was silent so long that their exasperation changed to puzzlement. His eyes now had a sad look, very definitely a sad look.

'I don't like to tell you this,' he began.

Immediately they both thought he was going to say he meant to give it to Lewin.

'What I wanted you both to understand,' Dibdin said, 'was that if there were a lectureship going, I should like you to be considered for it.'

'That's not good enough,' Clinton interrupted.

Dibdin went on, looking sadder than ever. 'If there were a lectureship going, Clinton, Albert . . .' He paused with emotion. 'But it isn't certain that there will be.'

Both Clinton and Albert exclaimed.

Dibdin said, with heavy-hearted mystery: 'I have my own worries.' He looked sideways at each of them in turn. 'You know what I mean.'

Clinton said: 'I'm afraid I don't.'

'You don't mean,' said Albert, 'there's a hitch in the professorship.'

Instantly Dibdin said: 'That's just what I do mean.' A glint had appeared in his eye: it vanished again. 'Thank you, Bowls.'

Although Albert had put the idea into words he could hardly believe it: Clinton frankly disbelieved it but he said nothing.

'I have my own worries,' Dibdin repeated quietly. 'And now you know what that means . . . You've been kind enough to say what I find it difficult to say myself. I hope you'll treat the matter as confidential, highly confidential.'

'Of course,' said Albert. Clinton nodded.

'And now, if you'll excuse me,' Dibdin said, 'I must be getting along to Mr Mackenzie's room. I promised to give him a hand with his experiment.' He smiled relievedly, and then broadly, 'I like to keep my hand in . . . I hope it won't ever lose its skill.'

And Dibdin went out of the room.

Albert and Clinton stared at each other.

'What's your opinion, Clinton?'

Clinton spoke almost without opening his mouth.

'We're foxed.'

Whether or not there was a hitch in Dibdin's getting the new chair at the time he said there was, Clinton and Albert never found out. Certainly there must have been a hitch later. By the following spring no official announcement of the appointment had been made. Dibdin was seen rather less frequently in the department, and he often had a hunted expression when there was no apparent cause for it.

The prospect of holding a lectureship had disturbed both Clinton and Albert, and each began to feel that if he did not get it he would think about applying for one in some other university. While they were considering it Lewin got a chair in a provincial university college: though neither of them had applied for it or even wanted it, their feeling of uneasiness increased.

In the meantime Albert's debts were mounting. He had started to live extravagantly and it was difficult to stop. Quite apart from trying to impress the Dibdins and others, he enjoyed it. His rooms were beginning to look sumptuous. He found that he was very fond of wine and had a delicate palate, so he took advantage of the college cellar to educate his taste. It all cost money.

Albert's state of financial solvency, such as it was, was not improved by his making the discovery which many another young man who took to the good life at that time made at Oxford – the only way to stop the tradespeople dunning one with bills was to run up more. Albert ran up more. Clothes, furniture, pictures, a new motor-car, food, entertainments and the rest; he soon learned to buy shrewdly, but he knew that he was buying too much. He did not restrain himself. His mode of living was being transformed, and the transformation was lavish. He had decided that if he was going to be debtor, he might as well be a great debtor. And of course there was always the hope of the lectureship.

Throughout the winter Albert was wooing Margaret Dibdin. She had evaded her mother's efforts to make her go up to London and finally be presented at Court. Instead she was reading economics at Somerville. The more Albert saw of her the greater hold she took on his imagination. Such was the illusion of love that he began to feel he loved her for her mind, her clear, direct, penetrating mind. Never before had he been so slow to make love to a girl who attracted him so much. He impressed himself with his own slowness. As for hoping to seduce her – a hope that had never been far from his mind with every other girl who had attracted him – such an idea now affronted his new-found susceptibilities. It was marriage he was hoping for. Would she, he asked himself, would she ever marry him?

As usual when he was contemplating a certain course of action for himself, Albert exhorted others to do the same. As before, Clinton was nearest to hand. Having previously exhorted Clinton to embark on the joys of a bohemian life, Albert was restrained by no inhibitions whatsoever from exhorting Clinton to abandon them and turn his attention to the more wonderful joys of matrimony.

'It's time you were married,' Albert said in a weighty tone, and delivered a powerful somewhat loosely-reasoned harangue which he deemed to justify the statement.

Clinton listened without a glimmer of facial expression. Even for Clinton it was an exaggerated absence of response and Albert was put out of his stride.

'Thanks, Albert,' said Clinton.

'What do you mean?'

'Thanks, Albert. Thanks for the advice.'

There was a pause. Albert felt cross. The pause went on longer. At last he could not help saying:

'Well, are you going to take it?'

Clinton stared at him. 'It was taken before given.'

'What?'

'I got engaged two days ago.'

Albert blushed with humiliation.

'Who to?' he managed to say.

'A girl called Sylvia Callandar.'

'Who's she?' The surname was very familiar.

'Daughter of Sir Alfred Callandar.'

'Of Callandars Chemical Company?' Albert could barely bring himself to utter the name, though he knew what Clinton would say. Clinton nodded.

Now although it did not enter into his calculations, I have to admit that Albert was well aware that one day Margaret Dibdin would be rich. On the other hand Sylvia Callandar, only daughter of Sir Alfred Callandar, head of Callandars, one of the best-known chemical companies in the country and the biggest privately-owned one, was likely to be five times, ten times richer than Margaret.

Chagrin turned Albert's blush deeper shinier red.

Clinton was watching Albert steadily.

'I thought you'd be amused to know,' he said. His teeth glinted.

It now becomes necessary for me to touch on certain matters about Albert that I have not mentioned before. I approach them with diffidence. They are delicate; also they are ludicrous; also they appear to be quite common. I refer to doubts about one's birth.

'Have you ever thought that you might not be the child of the persons you know as your mother and father, or that there is some mystery attached to your birth?'

To my way of thinking the only answer is: 'No. Don't be silly!' This only goes to show how far away I am from the experience of most of my fellows. How often does the question elicit an answer surprisingly different! For example, an acute serious glance and the words: 'Do you mean now I'm mature or when I was a child?' or a bright distant smiling look in the eye and the words 'Well . . . it's funny you should ask that.'

And then the speaker usually discloses modestly that the person he suspects of being his true parent is of distinctly higher social status than his legal parent. There is no mistaking the note of pride which one would not expect from someone who is confessing that he is a bastard. It would appear that although being the illegitimate child of a bus conductor is viewed with very proper universal disapprobation, being the illegitimate child of a peer is not – far from it.

During his childhood Albert had felt there was some mystery surrounding his origin: at the age of thirteen he saw how the mystery could, as one might say, take shape. Instinct now told him that Mr Woods was not his father, and, instinct being what it is, it told him he had for his father some other man who was much grander. He did not doubt that a secret was, as he expressed it to himself, lodged in his mother's breast. He longed to ask her, but never dared. In his fantasies he imagined a scene in which his father died suddenly, and his mother stirred to drama, disclosing the truth. Mr Woods was skinny but healthy, and Albert's adolescence ended without his father having even a minor illness.

Albert could only try to solve the mystery by his own imagination. There was one fact to go on. But this fact was so massive that he could never get away from it. For some years after her marriage his mother had remained in service with the Duke of ——. Albert secretly studied the history of the ducal family and sought pictures of its head in the society magazines he found at public reading-rooms. After discovering such pictures he would study for a long time in the looking-glass the reflection of his own physiognomy.

When his social aspirations began to blossom, Albert for a time overlooked their specific basis. It is possible that he would have gone on overlooking it had it not been for pure chance.

At the beginning of the Trinity term in 1930 the university at last announced officially the creation of a chair in experimental chemistry and the appointment of F. R. Dibdin as the first professor. For most of the members of the department it was something like an anticlimax: for Albert and Clinton it was not. And Dibdin happened to be out of Oxford for a few days.

Albert and Clinton could barely bring themselves to speak to each other, yet neither wanted to let the other out of his sight. They both found out privately the exact time of Dibdin's return.

To Albert's surprise Dibdin sent for him the moment he got back to the laboratory. Albert's hopes rose. When he entered Dibdin's room he found Clinton Smith already there. His hopes fell.

Dibdin looked extremely pleased with himself.

'Sit down, Woods. Sit down, Smith.' His eyes sparkled. 'This is an occasion to celebrate.'

'We're delighted with your success,' Albert said, trying to contort his anxious face into a polite enthusiastic smile.

'And I'm delighted too. Do you remember, Woods, the first time you came into this room, I told you the labourer was worthy of his hire? And I expect I said the same to Smith as well.' He paused.

He was sitting at his desk: he had taken his pipe from his mouth and placed it on a tin lid, whence the smoke rose in a wavering line. His broken shapeless nose was reddened from having been in the sunshine, and his light-coloured hair was curling up on the crown of his head. 'The time has come,' he said, with a special meaning smile.

'The lectureship?' Albert burst out.

'I'm happy to say the university has agreed to two lectureships.'

Albert and Clinton looked at each other, dumbfounded.

'It's what I always had in mind.' Dibdin was rebuking them for having mistrusted him. He appeared to have forgotten that with two lectureships instead of one he had still made three promises.

However no such thought restrained Albert and Clinton while they were expressing their satisfaction.

'It's a step,' Dibdin said. He sat back, looking at them triumphantly. 'One step enough for me.' He showed his teeth in a smile. 'Enough's as good as a feast.' He turned to Albert with a mysterious air. 'Which reminds me, Woods. I should like you to be my guest at our college feast at the end of this term.'

Albert bowed and thanked him profusely. They all shook hands.

Each of the two young men felt his appointment really was a step. And in each case the step led to the same result – a resolve to get married as soon as possible.

Albert began to wonder how soon he could propose to Margaret. He decided to do it at the end of term. He was not certain that she would accept him – and even less certain that her mother would agree. And yet his sanguine nature made him impatient for the day when he should try his luck. The particular occasion he had chosen for the purpose was a Commemoration Ball.

In the university of Oxford, Commemoration Week takes place in the middle of June. In those days there were concerts, theatrical performances, rowing races, cricket matches and parties, but above all there were the balls which were held in the colleges. They began about ten o'clock and went on till dawn: one dined in the long summer dusk beforehand and one posed for a group photograph in the grey light of day afterwards. In between, if one were a man of spirit, one got engaged at least.

Albert's party consisted of himself and Margaret, Clinton and Sylvia Callandar, Lewin and the girl he had just married, and a friend of Clinton's who was a Lord accompanied by a girl from

London called Bimbo. They dined in Albert's rooms, sumptuously – the quails had been flown over from France. Instead of going by motor-car they sauntered on foot to Clinton's college where the ball was to be held.

It was twilight. The sky was cloudy and the air warm. The perspective of the buildings had begun to disappear – the Sheldonian Theatre was shadowy and flat, like a serene classic stage-set: the trees in Balliol garden had a thick lacy look. The air stirred with the scent of over-blown syringa.

Everywhere there were young men and women in evening-dress, pale naked shoulders and white shirt-fronts and waistcoats. There was a thrilling hush about it all. As I have observed, many of them would be engaged to be married before the night was out. The young men were screwing up their courage and the girls were trying to recall what their mothers had told them. Youthful, joyous and comely, they were launched on one of the most lovely rituals of the English upper-class marriage-market. Voices rang across the lawns, young, fresh, enthusiastic – and frequently a trifle too loud from the habit of addressing foreign porters. Happiness was in their hearts.

Margaret linked her arm in Albert's and leaned across him as they strolled. She was wearing a white dress with a soft full skirt that drifted along the ground. Round her neck was a delicate necklace of diamonds, and she had twined in her hair a pink rose the colour of her cheeks. Her eyes sparkled. Albert suavely fitted into a handsome new suit of tails, felt himself swelling with hope, with pride and of course with impatience.

The source of Albert's pride was double. He was proud of his success in the world which had enabled him to give this party. But glowing deeply in his mind was another cause of pride which he could barely keep from coming to the surface. This was where pure chance had come into his private affairs. He had spent the previous weekend at home, and in his mother's house he had made a startling discovery. He was proud of his success which had enabled him to give this party, yes: at the same time he saw through a matter which had previously given him cause for wonderment – the perfect way he was able to carry such occasions off. In his mother's house he had found some antique silver spoons. The spoons were adorned with a certain crest.

In Clinton's college they drank some more champagne in Clinton's rooms and then they all went down to the college hall. A sprung dance floor had been laid over the Jacobean stone flags, and in its softly polished surface were reflected lights from candle-sconces on the panelled walls and patches of colour from flowers, pink and blue hydrangeas, that were massed in the corners and along the front of the low dais. Where the high table normally stood there was now installed a smart orchestra hired from a London hotel. Below the collection of portraits of distinguished members of the college from the sixteenth century on there was a row of gilt chairs, on which sat freshly-bathed undergraduates and scented young girls. To the high vaulted ceiling there rose the sound of saxophones, fiddles and drums, of sliding footsteps and gay chatter. The first people Albert noticed as he and Margaret crossed the threshold were Mr and Mrs Dibdin.

At first Albert wondered if the Dibdins, Mrs Dibdin anyway, had come to keep an eye on Margaret, who refused any hint of being chaperoned: but his suspicions melted before Mrs Dibdin's effusive greeting. After all Dibdin was a senior fellow of the college and it was not unusual for him to go to the college ball.

'I'm so glad you've come, Mr Woods,' said Mrs Dibdin, rather as if it were a private dance in her own house. 'We've been looking forward to seeing you.' She was standing rather stiffly, with her feet planted several inches apart. Her black dress with a big red rose on the shoulder looked as if it were ten years old. She turned a little to look at Margaret: her eye brightened.

'Now don't go away and dance all night, my dear,' she said. 'There are a number of people I want you to meet.'

'But I've come to dance, Mama.'

'Yes, I know.'

Margaret glanced at Albert. He smiled ingratiatingly at Mrs Dibdin.

'I'll bring her back to you from time to time,' he said, in a smooth polite tone.

'I should be glad if you would.'

Albert and Margaret went away to dance. Margaret laid her hand firmly on Albert's shoulder and danced close to him. It was a waltz.

'Who does your mother want you to meet?'

'Some rather dreary young men, I suppose.'

Albert leaned his head back to look at her. 'Do you want to meet them?'

Margaret did not answer his question. She laughed.

'You don't care for conventional people?' He began to smile at her. 'I'm very unconventional.'

Margaret did not say anything.

'As you will find out,' Albert said. He was still smiling at her steadily.

Margaret met his glance momentarily. The music carried them round another turn. They were in the corner of the room, passing a pyramid of hydrangeas and ferns. Then they came into the straight and the conversation went on.

Margaret said: 'Mama's ambition only goes as far as wanting me to marry some young man who *is* somebody.'

'Who do you want to marry?'

Margaret's eyes were bright and sparkling. 'Someone who's going to *become* somebody.'

They stared at each other, their thoughts completely in tune.

'*I'm* going to become somebody.'

Margaret's eyes flickered and she looked down. Albert's grasp tightened round her waist. The music seemed to play louder. Her smooth fair hair was close to his lips. The lights seemed dim and concealing. Albert kissed her on the temple, fleetingly and yet firmly. He glanced round to see if Mrs Dibdin was watching. She was not. Albert kissed Margaret again.

They went on dancing without speaking any more.

The ball went on. The young men and women congratulated themselves on being there, congratulated each other on being there, congratulated the committee on having arranged it so perfectly. The band was never allowed to grow sober, the flowers showed no sign of wilting, the supper was delicious. More and more champagne was drunk. The supper was served in a marquee in the garden, and even the night-sky now played its part: the veil of cloud withdrew and stars sparkled over clumps of elm trees: in the warm air stirred the scents of lilacs and roses and phlox. Fairy lights along the paths glowed on the girls' skirts as they strolled by.

From time to time Albert dutifully returned Margaret to her mother so that she might be introduced to some eligible young man and dance with him. On each occasion if appeared to him that Mrs Dibdin became more friendly.

'I see that you're not determined to monopolize Margaret,' she said. 'I disapprove of young men who monopolize their partners at a dance of this kind.'

Albert felt that had he been an earl Mrs Dibdin would not have found monopoly so reprehensible.

Mrs Dibdin smiled at him in a way that was both knowing and naïve. She had not realized that Albert Woods had more than his share of native cunning.

While Margaret was dancing with rather ordinary young men who were well connected and were hoping to go into Parliament or the Diplomatic Service, Albert turned his attention to the rest of the party. He first made a set at Sylvia Callandar though really she did not attract him greatly. She was a pretty girl with auburn hair and a pink skin. She had a beautiful white dress that was embroidered with green and yellow and gold flowers after a most costly fashion. Her figure was slighter than Margaret's. But it was her temperament that made the sharpest impression on him. She had very bright brown eyes, which without her knowing it followed every personable man who crossed her range of vision: and her laugh was cool and self-centred. Albert somehow felt he was making no impression on her.

Clinton's aristocratic friend was named Lord Charles Fitz-clarence. He was a tall handsome young man who looked like a first-class tennis player, and he was in the Navy. His girl, the girl from London named Bimbo, for all her long black hair and over-plucked eyebrows kept reminding Albert of Thelma. When she and Lord Charles went to Clinton's rooms after supper and locked themselves in the bedroom the recollection was strengthened.

'What a charming young man,' said Mrs Dibdin when Lord Charles came back to the dance looking brighter in the eye and redder in the cheek. 'You can see he's enjoying himself.'

Mrs Dibdin had drunk a fair amount of champagne.

'I can see you're enjoying yourself,' said Albert, leaning a little closer to her.

Her brown eyes stared boldly into his and then flickered.

Albert seized the opportunity to say: 'Let us sit out this dance. May I get you another glass of champagne?' Out of the corner of his eye he had noticed Margaret going towards the hall with one of her mother's candidates for matrimony.

Mrs Dibdin had noticed the same thing. 'That is kind of you, Mr Woods.'

They went to a small common room that had been opened for guests who wanted a few moments' quietness. It was a small panelled room with easy chairs, heavily decorated with a glass chandelier and vases of red roses. Albert brought a bottle of champagne and a couple of glasses. He sat down beside Mrs Dibdin on a low cushiony sofa. There was nobody else in the room. It was the first time Albert had been alone with Mrs Dibdin: it was his first *tête-à-tête* with a Lady.

'What an interesting man Lord Charles Fitzclarence is,' he said sycophantically.

'I'm glad you agree,' Mrs Dibdin drank a large gulp of champagne – she had a robust liking for drink. 'He has a very distinguished career ahead of him. Of course I know his mother very well. And his father too. There's an interesting man for you. Have you ever met him?' She glanced at Albert. 'Oh no, of course you can't have.'

'Not yet. . . .'

They were both silent.

'I think I've had a lot of champagne,' said Mrs Dibdin. She giggled. 'I suddenly felt it. You know.' She touched her forehead with the back of her fingers.

'I've had quite a lot, too,' said Albert.

He lifted his glass to her. 'Come on.'

They both emptied their glasses. Albert reached for the bottle.

'You must meet Charles Fitzclarence's father, Mr Woods. At my house.'

Albert's drunken mood was suffused with joy. 'Oh thank you, Mrs Dibdin.' Never had he felt drawn to her so strongly. He wanted to be worthy of her. He wanted to confide in her.

'I'm interested in the great families of England,' Albert said.

'Indeed,' said Mrs Dibdin.

'Very interested indeed.' Albert's voice dropped. His face was red from champagne. His eyes were a trifle glassy. 'Very interested indeed.' His voice dropped still lower. 'I have reason to be.'

Mrs Dibdin caught a look in his eye of such concentration that she was startled into saying: 'I take it you haven't any connections, have you?'

Albert gave a long pause. Then he said: 'Yes.' And great emotion was released in the single word. 'Yes,' he repeated. 'I believe I have.'

'Please tell me, Mr Woods.'

Albert leaned very close to her. 'You're the only person I could tell. You're the only person I know who understands these things.'

In spite of being drunk, Mrs Dibdin leaned back a little. It was at this moment that Margaret, having escaped from her partner in search of Albert, appeared in the doorway. Neither Albert nor her mother looked up. She saw the glasses of champagne in their hands and she heard the intimate tone in their voices. She went away again.

Albert confided the story of his discovery. The antique silver spoons, far too valuable for his mother ever to have bought. The crest, the crest of the Duke of ——. His mother's secret.

Mrs Dibdin caught the idea immediately. 'But servants always take something when they leave,' she said.

'You're speaking of my mother.'

'Oh, I beg your pardon, Mr Woods. I do so beg your pardon.'

'They must have been a present,' said Albert. 'A very, very, very lavish present.'

'I see,' said Mrs Dibdin slowly. 'I see what you mean.'

Albert nodded his head. 'The Duke of ——.' His voice was awed.

There was a long pause. Then Mrs Dibdin said:

'Have you any other evidence?'

'Yes.'

'What is it?'

Albert gave her a long look. 'My face.'

'Your face?'

'There's a certain resemblance.'

His face was too close for her to focus it properly. 'Indeed,' she said, and tilted her head backwards a little. 'I could judge better with my spectacles.'

'There's no need, Mrs Dibdin, I know. I'm convinced of it. I've studied the portraits.'

Mrs Dibdin, moving her head from side to side, studied as far as she was able Albert's physiognomy.

And in the meantime Albert filled up their glasses again with champagne.

It was nearly an hour later that Albert and Mrs Dibdin returned to the dance. Margaret was nowhere to be seen. Already the early dawn was beginning to lighten the sky over the garden. In the hall far fewer couples were dancing. In some of the windows round the quadrangle lights were shining behind drawn curtains. Albert raced round the college looking for Margaret. He felt violent alarm. He met Lewin and his wife but they had not seen her. Charles Fitzclarence and his girl were sitting in the marquee drinking champagne – they were a little drunk. Clinton and Sylvia were in Clinton's rooms, talking quietly.

Albert did another round of the garden. On a bench that was nearly hidden by shrubbery Albert found Margaret. She was alone.

'My dear.' Albert sat down beside her.

Margaret did not speak. The tender light fell on her unmoving face. Her cloak was drawn across her shoulders. The rose glimmered in her hair.

'Aren't you cold, Margaret?' He put his arm round her.

She shook her head.

'What are you doing here?'

'What do you think?' Her voice was lifeless.

'I'm sorry.'

There was a long pause. A faint gust of wind blew, and there was a rustling of branches in the elms.

'Where were you?' Margaret roused herself.

'With your mother.'

'With my mother? All this time?'

'Yes.' He hesitated. 'We missed the time.'

'Oh Albert!'

'I'm sorry, Margaret. I've said I'm sorry.' He kissed her cheek.

Margaret turned to him.

'Don't you want me to be friendly with your mother?' He tried to smile at her. 'I've made great headway tonight.' He could not keep enthusiasm out of his voice.

Suddenly Margaret spoke loudly with great emotion: 'I should have thought you'd have wanted to be with me!'

Albert put both his arms round her immediately. She was warm. Her hair brushed his cheek.

'I love you, Margaret.'

He kissed her on the mouth.

'Do you really?' Her tone was softer. She was trying to look into his eyes. He said:

'I love you. I want you to marry me. Margaret, will you marry me?'

'Oh yes.'

The wind rustled the trees again impetuously. The stars seemed to vanish in the pale sky. Albert and Margaret clasped each other in a long, in a long, long embrace.

PART THREE

Rivals All

CHAPTER ONE
TALK AFTER A WEDDING

It took Albert Woods more than another six months to marry Margaret. I doubt if by the end of that time, although she had given in to the marriage, Margaret's mother realized just what she was up against. It was the first time Albert brought the full weight of his mature personality to bear against opposition. The weight, as other people began to notice later on, was formidable. Mrs Dibdin was not aware of it.

'I don't know what you *see* in him,' was the theme of her constant remonstrances with Margaret.

Margaret was willing to marry Albert immediately, on any terms. Actually the terms were not bad, even at the start, because Dibdin had no real objection. For Albert the terms were not good enough.

'I'm going to have your mother's consent,' he said.

Margaret glanced at him. There was a smile on his lips.

'What for?' said Margaret.

'I want it.' He paused: his voice filled with feeling. 'I need it.'

Margaret was mystified.

'You don't understand' – Albert tried to express himself perfectly – 'that your mother has a deep hold on my imagination.'

Margaret did not understand. Yet Albert was expressing himself well. Perhaps it was as well that Margaret did not understand. She might not have liked the idea of her prospective husband falling in love with her through devotion to the glamour of her mother's social position.

'I want your mother to welcome me into the family,' he said. And he could not help adding: 'What a family!'

Margaret, in a flash of detachment, laughed.

Albert quelled her immediately. 'I know that we couldn't be happy being married if your mother were unhappy about it.'

At the thought of his concern for her happiness tears came into Margaret's eyes.

'But what are we to do, Albert?'

'Give me time.'

Margaret was thoughtful.

She said: 'I wish papa were more use to us.'

Margaret loved her father. Albert smiled. 'I admit he's being a trifle evasive.'

'It isn't that.'

Albert interrupted her. 'I understand why he's evasive. He's on our side really, but he wants to be loyal to your mother. It's his loyalty that makes him evasive.'

'Do you think so?' Her instinct for loyalty was deeply rooted.

'Of course. It's admirable.'

This conversation took place in the early days of their unofficial engagement. Dibdin was evasive to the point of being for most of the time absent. Meanwhile Mrs Dibdin refused even to listen to Albert's plea.

'Margaret, I don't know what you see in him.'

The concept of 'seeing' things in a man was so integral a part of Mrs Dibdin's cosmos that she hypnotized other people into incorporating it in their own. No matter how sensible, realistic or detached one's observations of one's fellow human beings, one was not long in conversation with Mrs Dibdin before one found oneself seeing – or, of course, not seeing – things in them.

When first Margaret said she wanted to marry Albert Woods Mrs Dibdin said she did not believe Margaret could mean it.

Margaret said she did mean it.

'You amaze me,' said Mrs Dibdin.

Margaret had no observation to make on that.

Then came the classic observation, with tremendous long-drawn-out emphasis on the word 'see'.

Margaret explained what she saw in Albert, patiently, inflexibly, and with a streak of her mother's obtuseness. She ended up, saying:

'I see an extraordinary man.'

'You really do amaze me, Margaret. Now I see a nobody. Really a nobody.' She had taken Margaret's speech very seriously and the whites of her eyes reddened with emotion. 'Surely Margaret you must see he's a nobody. I mean, who is he? We'd never heard of him, not even a whisper from anyone, until he came to work with your father.'

'I don't see that that's of the slightest importance. And surely that hasn't got anything to do with what you see in him?'

She gave her mother a sharp glance. 'There are hosts of people you've heard of whom you don't see anything in.' She paused. 'And vice versa.'

'I don't agree with the vice versa. I really don't, Margaret.'

Margaret put her hand to her forehead impatiently. Her voice drawled.

'What did you see in papa when you married him?'

Mrs Dibdin opened her mouth to speak but no sound came out. Her eyes flickered as she looked over Margaret's shoulder. What had she seen? She could not quite recall – and what she had seen during the last twenty years was so different, not to say so variegated, that it put her off.

'At least your father had been to Eton,' she said, grasping at a solid detail of fact.

'And he was rich,' said Margaret. 'Didn't you see that in him?'

Mrs Dibdin was affronted. Never before had anyone suggested point-blank that what one might see in a man was pounds sterling.

'I don't think there's anything more to be said, Margaret.'

Mrs Dibdin and Margaret stared at each other. The conversation about what they saw in Albert Woods was closed – until the following day.

Albert's tactics were different from Margaret's.

During the following Michaelmas term he made an impression on Oxford. His parties were attended by Clinton Smith's friend, Lord Charles Fitzclarence, who in turn brought along some of his well-connected friends. The idea that the highly-born refuse to accept free entertainment from the lowly-born is not borne out by fact. The highly-born only refuse to accept inferior free entertainment, but then who would not? Albert found that the higher the quality of his parties the higher the quality of the persons who would consent to attend them.

One evening Lord Charles glanced at the spoon with which he was eating a *soufflé*. It was one of a certain set of silver spoons that were crested.

'I recognize this, Albert,' he said, and looked across the table: a slight grin made creases in his long handsome face.

'Yes.' Albert waved his hand through the air – it was now adorned, a plump white hand, with a chaste-looking signet ring. 'Just a bit of family property.'

Nobody else smiled. I have to say that the company had not been selected for their sharp mischievous wit, and of course they were young.

Albert took care that his movements in society were reported in full to Mrs Dibdin, not that she could have missed the signs of elevation when she met him. His dress was becoming truly elegant. And his accent was most gentlemanly in the Edwardian Oxford style: though he occasionally let slip 'bath' with a short 'a', he never failed to say for example, 'lawst' for 'lost'. And a new social smile hovered over all he said: it curled the corners of his mouth in a peculiarly silky, soapy expression. As a result of eating so many splendid dinners he was getting fat.

On the whole Albert did not press Mrs Dibdin to attend many of his entertainments. Sometimes he flattered her by asking her advice on matters of etiquette. Sometimes he expressed a regret that on certain occasions she had not been present.

Mrs Dibdin did not know what to make of him. She did not always recognize a formidable man when she saw one. She did not recognize the formidableness of a clever man whose will is both strong and fluid, a man who is determined to get his own way not by forcing you against your inclinations but by subtly, easily, powerfully bowling you along with him.

'You must find it very expensive, Mr Woods,' she said, as a protest.

'I'm positively bankrupt.' Albert smiled his social smile.

'Really?'

'I'm so bankrupt,' Albert said, 'I'm going to Cannes for Christmas – with Charles Fitzclarence. We're going to spend every moment in the Casino. If we don't win we shall have no alternative other than to blow our brains out.'

'That's just a romantic story, Mr Woods. I've never known anyone who did it. The only people who do that sort of thing are the French.'

'We shall see.' Albert was heavily in debt. What he was saying convinced Mrs Dibdin that he was not.

When he returned from Cannes Albert promptly invited Mr and Mrs Dibdin to his grandest dinner-party of all.

'I want you to meet my little circle of friends,' he said to Mrs Dibdin confidentially. He paused, while he thought of them. His mouth curled. 'I think I can say they'll all be members of the Bullingdon.' He uttered the word 'Bullingdon' with reverence. 'Every one of them.'

Mrs Dibdin's brown eyes glowed uncertainly.

'Will you come?'

She gave in. 'Thank you, Mr Woods. We shall be delighted.'

That evening Albert said to Margaret:

'Your mother and I understand each other.'

Mrs Dibdin never really welcomed Albert Woods as a son-in-law. She was very stubborn: Albert and Margaret had been married for twenty years before she finally let go her dream of Margaret's having married a diplomat or a lordling in the Brigade of Guards. On the other hand she was willing to see in Albert the future career which Margaret saw and which Dibdin told her was quite possible: it was a consolation.

'I find it so difficult to make him see *why* I don't think he's . . . suitable.' She looked at her husband in a kind of piteous accusation. 'One would have thought he'd see *why* without being told. But he doesn't.'

Mrs Dibdin felt it was unjust that not being a gentleman should have any advantages whatsoever.

Albert got his way. Mrs Dibdin finally allowed him to kiss her on the cheek and then with a great effort of will she called him Albert for the first time.

Margaret was radiant. Dibdin was readily available for consultation in the laboratory once more.

Mrs Dibdin was next preoccupied with the wedding. She could not see how to avoid meeting Albert's family. A big wedding in Oxford was out of the question. Margaret threatened to get married in a Register Office. After weeks of worrying Mrs Dibdin swallowed her pride and was immediately rewarded by inspiration. The little Norman church at Daunton, the two families and people from the village – 'a quiet little country wedding'. After all Mrs Dibdin herself had been married there, in similar style, for not entirely dissimilar reasons.

Albert was quite satisfied. He had been presented once only to Lord Daunton, but now that the first effects of intimidation had worn off he was confident that he could enjoy perfect social relations with the elderly nobleman.

Albert was not satisfied about something else. He was certain Dibdin would make a settlement on Margaret. He was told nothing about it before the wedding. The omission was an error in tact and manners on the part of the Dibdins. Albert did not take it ill. He expected to be told after the wedding.

Albert and Margaret were married in the New Year. It was a brilliant winter's morning. The little church was built on a mound that overlooked Daunton House, not more than two hundred yards away. The sky was a very clear pale blue and there was a sprinkling of snow under the trees and in the shadow of the grey stone wall round the churchyard. The two families walked across from the house and entered by their private gate. The Dauntons comported themselves with careless grandeur, the Woodses with awkward quietness. The villagers behaved as they had done on such occasions during the last three hundred years: they were looking forward to the cider-cup.

Albert had forgotten the settlement on Margaret until Dibdin took him aside at the reception.

'Yes, F. R.?' Albert said.

Dibdin put his fingers to his lips. 'Let us get away from the crowd for a moment.'

Albert was proud to be a member of such a crowd, but he agreed to be borne away from it by his father-in-law. They left the spacious series of rooms where the guests were drinking champagne and went along a wide corridor with windows on one side and portraits on the opposite wall: the corridor was icy.

Dibdin was padding along fatly in front of Albert. Suddenly he turned and said over his shoulder:

'We're going to my father-in-law's study.' And there was an unmistakable conspiratorial wink in his big light brown eye. Albert felt that he was being recruited, in the event of a contest Daunton versus Dibdin, definitely for the Dibdin side. He smiled with surprise, gratification and secret triumph.

Lord Daunton's study was a small lofty room with bookshelves covering all the walls except the one in which a single tall window opened directly on to the park. It was comfortable, almost cosy, and there was a fire burning brightly. Albert walked across to the window where a spray of winter jasmine in full bloom tapped lightly on the glass.

Albert noticed that Dibdin had carried away with him a box of cigars. Dibdin offered the box to Albert. They both took cigars and lit them. Dibdin crossed the room and stood with his ample beam turned to the fire. Albert sat down in a leather armchair, leaned his head back and blew out a cloud of smoke.

'Albert,' said Dibdin, 'there's no time like the present.'

'The present moment is the happiest in my life.'

'Exactly.' Dibdin put his hands in the pockets of his trousers and pulled the warm cloth of the seat tightly across his backside. 'Let me see, it will be a month before you'll be back in Oxford?'

Albert thought the question unnecessary.

'Then indeed, Albert, there's no time like the present . . . The time has come.'

The settlement, Albert thought, the settlement.

'I want to talk to you of cabbages and kings.'

Albert smoked luxuriously. A cigar in Lord Daunton's study on a sunny winter's afternoon – Albert did not mind how long his father-in-law took in coming to the point.

Dibdin's eyes were alight with mischievous pleasure.

'But not of sealing-wax and string . . . We don't want our apparatus to be made with makeshift materials – none of the Cavendish tradition for us.'

Albert thought Dibdin must have drunk too much champagne.

'I think we ought to lay the foundations of a quite different tradition.'

Albert nodded impatiently – the topic was not approaching the one he had in mind. 'Excellent,' he said, and waved his cigar through the air with a grandiose if off-hand gesture.

Dibdin fixed his eyes on Albert meditatively.

'We've got to come down from the ivory tower,' he said.

'What?'

'We chemists mustn't have our heads in the clouds all the time. We've got to get our feet on the earth.' At this Dibdin planted himself in an armchair opposite Albert.

'I've never had my head in the clouds, F. R. You know that. Starting where I did, I think you can take it I know what it is to have one's feet on the ground. Only too close to the ground. Without money one's feet are glued to the same spot.'

'You'll have money. Don't worry about that.'

'Oh!' cried Albert hopefully: 'Where from?'

'From the sweat of your brow.' Dibdin laughed. 'Just like the rest of us.'

Albert's face fell. Dibdin went on laughing.

'That's why I wanted to talk to you now.'

'Now?' Albert echoed. 'You want to talk to me about chemistry now?'

'There's no time like the present, Albert.'

Albert glanced round Lord Daunton's study. The bright sunshine was still glowing in the pale blue sky outside, the sprig of yellow jasmine was tapping on the window: it was his wedding-day.

'There's no time like the present. You're one of the family now.' Dibdin paused, and added cleverly: 'What's more you're going away for a month.' He took a puff at his cigar. 'Let's clear up all our business before you set off on pleasure.'

'Business?' Albert sat up.

'Affairs of state. Plans for the future. . . .'

Albert did his best to express eagerness for discussing the future. Dibdin looked away. 'The time has come for us to come down from the ivory tower. We scientists have got to play our part in the world.' He gave Albert a look of great and touching sincerity. 'Chemistry can do a great deal in the world. I want you to think of our research as the handmaid of society.'

Albert stared at his father-in-law.

Dibdin blew out a cloud of smoke.

'The handmaid of society,' Dibdin repeated, apparently pleased with the phrase.

Albert could not help laughing. Dibdin appeared to share the fun, but said nothing.

Albert said ruefully: 'I hoped I'd liberated myself from the . . . er . . . servant-class.'

'Ah,' said Dibdin: 'Even the handmaid is rewarded with her share of this world's goods.'

'You're telling me,' Albert cried. What's the share you're going to give me yourself? was what he wanted to cry. The settlement – what about the settlement?

'And this world's goods are not to be despised. I'll confess this to you, Albert' – Dibdin paused solemnly – 'I don't despise them myself.'

'No,' said Albert.

A footman came in: Mrs Dibdin wanted to know whether the conference was nearly over.

'Nearly,' Dibdin replied. He made no attempt to move from his chair. He picked up a leather-bound book from a little table beside him.

There was a pause. Albert was wondering what his father-in-law was getting at. He supposed that in due course he would be confronted with actions that would instantly make sense of the conversation but he would have liked to know now. His thoughts circulated round the idea of 'this world's goods' . . . An idea crossed his mind that was shrewd if nothing else – Albert wondered if his father-in-law had some scheme in mind for getting a larger endowment of this world's goods for the laboratory. Possibly from Sir Alfred Callandar.

'The first thing,' Dibdin said, 'is to put worldly thoughts out of our heads. Chemistry is what must always come first.' He put down the book – he had not opened it.

'I agree.'

'And then chemistry in the service of others second, a closer second than it has been.'

'I agree again.'

'That,' said Dibdin triumphantly, 'is what I mean by coming down out of the ivory tower. We must not forget to play our part in the service of others. In Oxford it's only too easy to forget.'

'I don't see what you mean by that.'

'Then think it over, my dear Albert.'

'Of course I will.'

Dibdin made a long speech about the relations between university research in chemistry and the uses to which it might be put in practical affairs.

Five minutes passed. The footman came back again. Albert wondered, now that he had no answer himself, what Mrs Dibdin thought her husband had taken him aside to say.

Dibdin stood up. Albert did the same. Albert was near the window, and Dibdin came and stood beside him. They looked at the bare glistening trees and the sprinkling of snow on the grass. Suddenly Dibdin put his arm round Albert's shoulder.

Albert turned to him. They confronted each other dramatically.

'Albert,' Dibdin said, 'I want to congratulate you. I really want to congratulate you.'

CHAPTER TWO

A FRUITFUL YEAR

Albert and Margaret went to Rome and thence to Taormina. Albert was exultant. The great amorist had been transformed by the tenderness of his passion into a great knight. Then he had married. You will not need to guess what he became next. A great husband of course. Not a week of the honeymoon had passed before Albert knew that being married was the most desirable state of all and was to be recommended to everybody without exception.

By the end of the month Albert was settled. In Taormina his natural exuberance had led to some excesses of which he was proud: Margaret, a strong healthy girl, was if anything more than qualified to cope with them, though Albert had not had time to notice that. He realized that he was a great husband. Margaret concurred.

Margaret had been lucky. Her instinct had led her to a successful choice of mate, yet it seems to me it might easily not have. Margaret was really too young to know what she was doing. To any other girl of her class Albert Woods would have looked small, absurd and not a gentleman. There was a great deal more to him, but Margaret at twenty could hardly have seen it.

Just as Margaret would not have been pleased to know how much Albert loved the idea of having a mother-in-law who was aristocratic, Albert would not have been pleased to know how much it meant to Margaret to marry someone her mother did not want her to. Her choice sprang from a sort of obtuseness, and I am afraid that no kind of obtuseness is a satisfactory guide to choosing a husband. Margaret was lucky: wilfully she happened to marry a good man.

In the first place Margaret was overwhelmed by physical delight.

'I was always afraid that I might not . . .'

'What?' Albert asked.

Margaret put her arms round his neck.

For all his exuberance Albert was affectionate and considerate. Also he loved initiating – initiating anyone into anything. There was a good deal of palaver. (A girl who is initiated by a great husband who is also something of a great teacher does not get away without a good deal of palaver.) All the same Margaret was enthralled. She fell deeply in love with her husband.

Albert found no difficulty at all in embracing his own fate. Being a great husband came to him easily, the reason being that it was really what he was cut out for. The vagaries of Albert's earlier days had been the expression of an uninhibited romantic imagination rather than of a peculiar sexual make-up. Sexually Albert Woods was really an ordinary man, and he was cut out for the rather ordinary married life that he subsequently led. It was not a mere trick of fate that he ended up as a great husband rather than a great rake.

About the great rake, though we are bound to deplore it, there is usually a streak of distinction – the distinction, if you like, of being odd, ruthless, even crazy: about the great husband, alas, there is something very ordinary indeed. (And about the ordinary husband, something more ordinary than that.)

All the same, it is a great advantage to a man who wants to get on in this world to have a sexual make-up that gives him no trouble. Albert, Clinton, Dibdin – not Charles Fitzclarence and Alfred Callandar – Eli Grevel, Redvers Jameson and several other successful men with whom Albert associated later were essentially ordinary in this respect. No trouble at all had they had.

Albert was happy. Margaret was happy. When they returned from Taormina Margaret had already conceived their first child. She was dreaming of her life with Albert.

And Albert? Albert, the great husband, was dreaming of his research. He had forgotten for the time being the important if mysterious concept that research had to play a part in the service of men – he was thinking about it just for itself, and he returned from his honeymoon in a state of simmering nervous excitement. While he had been occupied with other matters, his mind, too, had been fertilely at work. He was having ideas for new experiments. To anyone who has ever done research it is a state that is immediately recognizable. It is extraordinarily pleasurable. Albert was champing to get back to his laboratory.

It was now that a young chemist named Eli Grevel began to play a part in Albert's career. The part enthusiastically designed for him by Albert was that of research assistant and collaborator. The way in which Grevel played it was from the beginning unpredictable and unmanageable.

'Oo're all the nobs?'

Those were the first words, delivered in a curt rattle, that Albert Woods heard from the lips of Eli Grevel. They did not fall auspiciously on the ear of a man who aspired to be one of the world's greatest nobs.

'Are they makin' speeches or just eating?'

They were celebrating the election of F. R. Dibdin to the Royal Society and they were the *élite* of the Oxford chemical world.

Albert had a clear warning of what was in store for him if he got Eli Grevel to work with him. But he had no alternative. If he was in a hurry to dazzle the world with a monumental piece of research, Eli Grevel was his man. The pale handsome beaky youth with the relentlessly disrespectful air had turned out to be the most gifted undergraduate in the department of chemistry.

Albert had warning and he had no alternative. Yet that represents nowhere near the whole of the situation. Albert took a liking to Eli.

In physical appearance Eli was pleasing. He was of medium height, broad-shouldered, with a light strong frame that gave an impression of spareness and elegance. His head was finely massive, supported on a muscular neck. His face was distinguished and striking, partly for its beautiful proportions, its broad forehead, sharply-cut jaw and narrow eyes, but chiefly for its long thin nose which curved gracefully under at the end.

In manner Eli was less than pleasing. His narrow grey eyes persistently glittered with arrogance and contempt, his finely massive head was habitually thrust forward in a gesture of suspicion and rebellion. His cheeks were permanently creased from nose to mouth in his determination to express harsh judgements. On top of it all his fair quiff curled up like a symbol of ignorance. He was a Marxist.

Eli had come up to Oxford as an undergraduate of Clinton's college, so that Albert had seen little of him until the fourth year of the course, which was spent on research. Eli had gone to Clinton for his tutorials throughout, and Clinton was greatly impressed by

Eli's promise. In the examination at the end of his third year Eli had scored a record high mark.

'Grevel reminds me,' Clinton said to Albert, 'of the Professor.' And his tone was filled with the frank hero-worship that always appeared when he spoke of Sir Norman Bunstone.

'How do you get on with him, Clinton?'

'I find some of his ideas,' said Clinton, 'incomprehensible.'

Albert said: 'Does he want to attach himself to the Professor?'

'Attach himself?' Clinton snorted. 'That's amusing! I can't imagine Grevel wanting to attach himself to any of us.'

'Do you mind if I have a try with him?' They both made a slight pause, in deference to the principle that Eli might normally be expected to go on as one of Clinton's pupils.

Clinton yielded. 'All right.'

As soon as Albert got back from his honeymoon he sent a note to Eli asking him to call on him in his rooms in college.

It was at tea-time on a dark February afternoon when Eli arrived punctually. Albert's purple velvet curtains were drawn, and the walls flickered with the glow of a huge fire. The sheen in his Persian rug, the glisten of his silk cushion-covers, the sparkle from the gilt candlesticks on his writing-desk expressed the combination of refined taste and subdued opulence which he who stood in their midst deemed fitting. He stood at ease on the Persian rug, letting the heat of the fire warm his back.

Eli knocked and put his head round the door. 'Shall I come in?'

'By all means.' Albert switched on a small reading-lamp beside the fireplace.

Eli's pale handsome face rose from the collar of an overcoat that was threadbare and about four inches too long for him. 'Where shall I put my umbrella?' he said nervously.

'I'll take it.' Albert crossed the room and they shook hands. 'Please come and sit on the sofa in front of the fire. You must be cold.'

'I never feel cold, thanks.'

'I should like you to make yourself comfortable.' Albert smiled.

Eli went and sat on the edge of the sofa. He watched Albert dispose of his overcoat and umbrella. Albert came and settled himself in an easy chair.

They were both nervous. Eli ran his fingers over his hair to flatten down the quiff. Albert brought out his cigarette-case. At that moment Albert's scout brought in the tea: as he put down the teapot on the hearth Albert said to him:

'You did remember I wanted Indian today?'

Eli said: 'I should've thought you'd drink China, Dr Woods.'

'Would you,' said Albert: 'I thought you might prefer Indian.'

'Oh, I've had all sorts.'

Albert poured out two cups and invited Eli to help himself to muffins and jam. While they ate their tea they had an interesting conversation about books and politics. Albert discovered that Eli was trying to read Dostoievski's *Poor Folk* in Russian.

'Why not?' Eli said. 'I want to read Dostoievski and I want to learn Russian.' At that he shrugged his shoulders decisively.

After tea they sat back and smoked. The heat of the fire had made Albert's face red, but had had no effect on Eli's. Albert began to talk about his new plan of research.

Eli listened with his eyes narrow and bright. He had not lost his nervousness. From time to time he stroked his hair, unnecessarily flicked the ash off his cigarette, pulled up one of his socks. Albert was unaffected. The subject claimed so much of his heart and soul that Eli would have had to get up and walk out before he would have been affected.

Eli did not get up and walk out. Occasionally he made comments, but they were not of a specially distinguished or striking kind. Yet what you might call the intellectual temperature of the conversation went steadily up: a sort of excitement came into the air. Albert began to make subtler points and felt them go home. Though Eli was making no contribution Albert knew that sitting in the opposite chair was a man who was his equal.

'What do you think of it?' Albert wound up glowingly.

'What do *I* think of it?'

'Yes, you, Mr Grevel.' Albert made a gesture with his hand. 'I shall call you Eli, if I may.'

'What's my opinion worth?'

'A great deal.' Albert looked at him. 'I should be glad to have it.'

'I think,' said Eli, 'it sounds interesting.'

'Is that all?'

Eli tried to do better. 'Very interesting.'

'Then would you like to come in with me?'

Eli was clearly astounded. He put his hand on his chest. 'Me?'

'You've heard the outline of the scheme of research I'm just going to embark on.' Albert now spoke with some restraint and a good deal of politeness. 'I think I can find you a place in my lab if you're willing to join us. I should be glad to have you, Eli.' Albert gave him a friendly compelling stare. 'You're one of the first persons I should choose.'

'But this is research,' Eli said. 'Oo says I'm going to stay'n do research, anyway? Nobody knows yet?'

'Yet?'

'Not till the results are out at the end of the year.'

'Of course everybody knows you're going to stay and do research.'

'I don't. 'Ow do I know I'm going to get a first?'

'Of course you are. We all know. You've as good as got one already on your examination results alone.'

'I may make a hash of my research problem. There's another term and a half to go.'

'Of course you won't. You're doing splendidly.'

''Ow do you know? You haven't even seen my notes.'

'Dr Smith has and he's satisfied.'

'Well I'm not.' Eli corrected himself. 'Not satisfied enough to rely on it. You can't blame me for making alternative plans.'

'What alternative plans?'

'I'm going to be a schoolmaster.' Eli stared at Albert with a hard provocative look in his eye. 'I've applied for some jobs already.'

Albert raised his eyebrows. 'With success?'

'No.'

There was a pause. Albert shook his head. 'I'm sorry.' In 1931 it was not easy to get a job as a schoolmaster. 'The alternative seems to be rather . . . shall we say disappointing?'

Eli flicked his cigarette ash on the carpet.

Suddenly Albert's expression changed. He leaned forward a little. His voice was warm and kindly and he spoke as if he had not heard the tone of Eli's last remarks.

'You must allow me to reassure you, Eli,' he said. 'It means my breaking a confidence.' He paused. 'I can tell you that we've already decided, in the department, that you're the first on our list of men to be recommended for research grants at the end of the year. We've already made up our minds. You're the first on the list.'

'What about Baker?'

For a moment Albert could not think who Baker was.

'Baker's going to get a first, isn't he?'

'I expect so. But that doesn't alter our list of preference.'

'I should've thought you'd've put Baker before me. You ought to.'

Baker was likely to get a first-class degree, but in the opinion of Albert and Clinton he had no originality of mind whatsoever. 'Why?' Albert asked, his patience beginning to run out.

"E's got somethink I haven't got. D'yer know what that is?" Eli looked at Albert with a harsh light in his eyes.

'Frankly I don't.'

'*Self-discipline*.'

Albert's eyes remained wide-open, bulging behind his spectacles. A smile twitched at the corners of his mouth, as if stirred by the long-forgotten memory of an entry in a diary – 'He will give Woods the discipline he needs.' Albert did not remember, but his impatience disappeared completely.

Eli waited for Albert to say something.

Albert did not say anything.

The disclosure made, Eli's face gradually changed. It looked youthful and as if he too were about to smile.

Albert stood up to show him it was time to go. He handed Eli his umbrella and the overcoat that must have belonged to his grandfather.

'I hope you'll think over my offer,' Albert said. 'It's a handsome one, I expect you know.'

'I can see that.'

'I hope you'll take it. For all our sakes.'

'What's that mean?'

Albert held out his hand. 'You can give us some of your highly original ideas.'

Eli took his hand. 'Yes.'

'And we may be able to give you a little self-discipline. You haven't got much, have you?'

Eli let go his hand. 'What'yer taking all this trouble over me for?'

Albert ignored the question. 'There's no need to give your answer till the end of the year, but I should like to know as soon as possible.'

'O.K.'

Albert opened the door and Eli went out.

Albert went over to his writing-desk and switched on the lamp as he sat down. There was a confident smile on his face, also a look of friendliness and amusement. He was certain that Eli would come to work in his laboratory in June. Of what would happen after that he was far from certain. As he had ceased to keep a diary he missed the chance to write 'Woods must wait and see.'

Albert began to inflate on a new scale.

'Woods is at the height of his powers.' That was what he thought when he returned from his honeymoon. Ideas came spinning through his mind. Some of them he could only unashamedly acclaim as brilliant, others as superb and others as inspired. He spent the spring months collecting together his apparatus and assistants. 'Woods is at the height of his powers' he thought again in the summer, and this time they seemed a little higher.

In June Eli Grevel came to work in his laboratory, just as he had surmised. But just as he had not surmised Eli, instead of undertaking a series of experiments that were part of Albert's master-plan, produced an independent scheme of research that had nothing at all to do with Albert's masterplan. Albert was in much too fine a state of self-confidence to be upset by that – Woods could afford to wait for a long time and see. Also Eli's scheme of research was so original that even Albert could not expect him to give it up.

'Grevel's got ideas – that's the important thing,' Albert said to Clinton, just to make sure that Clinton did not think Eli's independence had put him out of countenance.

Dibdin smiled approvingly and paternally upon them all.

In the autumn Albert launched into work. The height of his powers was put to the test and found to be as high as he could possibly wish. He had no doubt now that his research was going to be the main achievement of the experimental chemistry department. He had known for some time that he was a better man than his stable-mates, Smith and Lewin. Now there seemed to be nothing to stop him outstripping his teacher and master.

Dibdin continued to smile approvingly and paternally. Albert was too engrossed to wonder why. The bustle and palaver with which he invested the launching of his own research made it apparent that he looked upon it as superseding everybody else's research, Dibdin's included.

Eli Grevel christened him 'The Little Boss.'

In September Albert became a father. The child was a girl.

Certain persons in Oxford saw fit to commiserate with him on not becoming the father of a son. 'The virility of a race is judged by its capacity for producing girls,' he said huffily. Woods's powers of any kind were not easily to be impugned.

At the end of the year something happened that Albert had not foreseen, which added at first sight even more to his inflation. Dibdin said he intended to give up his extra-mural research for Callandars and offered the contract to Albert.

'The labourer is worthy of his hire,' Dibdin said. His approving paternal smile was guileful and confident, not at all the smile of an old man who is stripping himself in favour of the one who is to supersede him.

Albert was blushing with satisfaction on being the recipient of so much generosity.

'One has to give up some things,' Dibdin added: 'one can't keep an indefinite number of balls in the air at once.' And he began to act as if he were juggling.

Albert was alert. His blush disappeared. 'What else are you taking on?' he said.

Dibdin's glance flickered away from him.

'Another job?' Albert said.

Dibdin's smile came back broad direct and triumphant. 'I've been asked to sit,' he said, 'on the Production Executive Committee in Whitehall.'

Albert went home that evening in a state of minor, temporary but unambiguous deflation. He admitted Dibdin's triumph. The Production Executive Committee was the most important committee of which a scientist might hope to become a member. Dibdin's interpretation of science being the handmaid of society stood revealed: it was characteristically simple.

As he turned into New Cross Road, where the Dibdins had bought him and Margaret a house next door to their own, Albert's feet did not exactly trail at the ankles, but they looked looser than they had done throughout the whole of that year. Just when 'The Little Boss' was about to overtake 'The Big Boss,' 'The Big Boss' had become bigger.

It was a bitterly cold night and Albert hurried towards the lighted windows of his cosy little home. He wanted reassurance from Margaret.

By the time he came into the room where Margaret was, Albert was beginning to hang back from asking for reassurance. Something told him Margaret might try to reassure him by telling him Dibdin's triumphs were undesirable – that was not what he wanted at all. He did his best to behave as if nothing had happened to disturb him.

'You're just in time, darling.' Margaret looked up for him to kiss her. She was getting the baby ready to put her to bed. Albert, now transmogrified into a great father, always came home in time to watch the performance. The baby was lying naked across Margaret's knees while she powdered it. 'Isn't she pretty?' Margaret said. Albert knelt down beside her and kissed the baby's outstretched hand.

Margaret said to Albert: 'What's the matter?'

'Nothing.' Albert kissed the baby's buttock.

Margaret began to wind round the baby's middle a binder that was supposed to hold a penny in place over her navel. Margaret was not deft.

'Darling.' Albert touched the binder. 'Can I?'

Margaret smiled and held the baby while Albert did the task. 'I'm not a great experimenter for nothing,' he said. His spirits were beginning to return.

When the baby had been put to bed they walked downstairs together into the sitting-room. Albert's arm was round Margaret's waist.

'Now are you going to tell me?' Margaret said.

Albert said: 'When I've poured you a glass of sherry.'

He poured two glasses and they sat down on the sofa.

Albert told Margaret first of all about the contract with Callandars.

Margaret's face lit up with a smile.

'Your father's very generous,' Albert said.

Margaret could not permit herself to reply. It was just what she wanted to hear Albert say. She glanced down at Albert's hand, which was holding hers. Then she said:

'Do you want to do research for industry?'

'If it doesn't take up too much attention. This won't.' Albert grinned at her sideways. 'As a matter of fact, this is money for jam.' He was thinking, 'Trust F.R. for that.'

Margaret said seriously: 'It won't interfere with your real research, will it?'

'No.'

Albert was discouraged from going on to his second piece of news.

Margaret said: 'Why is Papa giving it up?'

Albert told her. The enthusiasm returned to his voice.

Margaret listened dutifully. At the end of it she said: 'But do you think Papa's wise?' There was a faint drawl in her voice.

'Of course,' Albert said, with great enough conviction to show that he did not think Dibdin's new triumph was in the least undesirable. He followed up with a long speech about research as the handmaid of society and about the duty of great and successful scientists to descend from their ivory tower. Margaret tried to interrupt to tell him that she had heard it before, but he swept on to the end.

The sparkle had come back to Margaret's eyes. Her hand tightened round Albert's thumb. 'I know that's what everybody says, so it must be right. I wasn't questioning that. I was only questioning whether Papa was really ... right for that sort of thing.'

'Oh!' said Albert, with a look of surprise on his face.

'What did you think I meant?'

Relief and encouragement flooded back into Albert. His eyes bulged and his voice became breathy as he leaned closer to her and said:

'Do you think I should be right for it?'

'I think you would, darling.'

'Do you think I could go *farther* on committees?'

There was a flicker of amusement in Margaret's steady look.

'Of course.'

Albert could not speak – there was no need. His minor deflation had been swept away. Inflation came back in a grander and more glorious form, inflation with the promise of super-inflation.

Suddenly Albert lifted his glass with the remainder of the sherry in it. Margaret lifted hers.

'To the future!' he said.

CHAPTER THREE

OVERSTEPPING THE MARK

During the next three years Albert was too preoccupied with his research to do anything about trying to outshine his father-in-law in the world of affairs. He did not forget his new ambition – his new goal lay before him radiant but unspecified, like heaven, the thought of it inspiriting him during his present struggles.

Albert's present struggles brought him into closer touch with the affairs of Callandars. He plunged into their research with enthusiasm.

'I think I'm going to make a friend,' he confided to Margaret, 'of Sir Alfred Callandar.'

Margaret nodded with approval.

'I think,' he went on, 'Sir Alfred Callandar prefers me to Clinton.'

Margaret's look of approval changed to one of amazement and amusement. 'What does that mean, darling?'

'I don't know, yet.'

Since Dibdin had handed over the contract to Albert, the experimental chemistry department's research for Callandars had made a thrust forward. Within a year the number of young research assistants working on it had been increased from two to five – by Albert. Sir Alfred Callandar was kept constantly informed about the course of their experiments – by Albert. Sir Alfred Callandar formed the opinion, as far as a gentleman could, that Callandars was getting greater value for its money than ever before. He began to invite Albert to visit him more frequently at the works.

Callandars' Chemical Company was a family firm. It had been founded in the middle of the nineteenth century by Sir Alfred's grandfather: it had passed from him to his father, and from him to Sir Alfred. Throughout it had been unfailingly prosperous. The policy of the firm had been laid down by Sir Alfred's grandfather: it was to stop the firm expanding whenever it showed signs of becoming too big to be held in the grasp of its chairman. The result was that Sir Alfred was not only wealthy but powerful. Instead of sitting importantly if impotently at the bottom of a board of directors of a huge cartel, he sat at the top of a small board of which he was undisputed boss.

The way in which Callandars had made a fortune while remaining small and independent was by marking out a limited piece of territory and exploiting what was inside it down to the last detail. So that when Sir Alfred Callandar kept a sharp eye on the experiments of his team in Professor F. R. Dibdin's department at Oxford, he had, in addition to an intellectual taste for such matters, a good business reason.

Sir Alfred Callandar did not look at first sight like an undisputed boss. He was a small man, wiry and active, with bright little eyes that sparkled from under long bushy eyebrows. He was shy and courteous – with strangers his manner was polite in a distinctly formal, old-fashioned style. He stooped a little and he was usually dressed in a black coat, and grey striped trousers. Sir Alfred was clever: he had an enthusiastic respect for what he chose to call 'the splendid intellects such as one finds in the older universities', yet his own was as good as many a one of theirs. He was peculiarly sweet-natured.

In spite of these gifts Sir Alfred Callandar had not led a happy married life: however, his wife was now dead. He had no sons and Sylvia was his only daughter. He spent his days inordinately busily. He worked over-long hours in the firm and devoted the rest of his time to hypochondria – his health was perfect.

Albert liked him. Sir Alfred's darting movements reminded him of a jacksharp, his formal politenesses were somewhat constraining, and yet his innate courteousness made him an attractive man. Also Albert had his share of Clinton-like hero-worship for a great industrialist.

Callandars' works were situated just outside Wigan. Not far from Wigan there is, contrary to what people who have never been there imagine, some pleasing countryside: Callandars was not situated in it.

A few days after the beginning of the Hilary term in 1935 Albert was on a visit to the works at Sir Alfred's invitation. Albert had been looking forward to it with undisguised enthusiasm. His research for

Callandars was going well and Sir Alfred knew all about it: there was nothing in the research going on at Wigan that it was necessary for him to go and see. The visit was one more beautiful incontrovertible sign of the personal friendship between him and Sir Alfred: Albert had a feeling that in some way that friendship had reached a point where it was going to bloom.

Albert did not think of going into industry. A great industrialist was one of the few things Albert Woods had never thought of becoming. He was not thinking that the flower of his friendship with Sir Alfred Callandar would take the shape of an offer of a job in the firm. (In any case Albert was ready enough to see that in due course Clinton was bound to go into the firm to direct Callandars' research and probably to succeed Sir Alfred when he retired.) No. In Albert's mind the flower of his friendship with Sir Alfred had for a long time remained mysterious – it had only recently begun to take a somewhat vague though alluring shape.

For some months it had seemed to Albert that Sir Alfred was meditating a closer collaboration between his firm and the department of experimental chemistry. That was the meaning of his and Sir Alfred's drawing closer together as personal friends.

There is one way in which all scientists in universities are used to interpreting such a closer collaboration. Albert was not the first man to whom it had occurred, far from it – after all those who had gone before him he must have proved himself half-witted, let alone not devoted to scientific research, if he had failed to see closer collaboration between a firm and a laboratory in any terms other than an endowment of the laboratory by the firm.

When the time came for him actually to set off for Wigan, Albert's enthusiasm was damped by some news of a quite different kind. He had heard that for the second time he had failed to be elected to the Royal Society. There was nothing remarkable about that. Clinton had failed as well. Dibdin had warned them at the start that they were not likely to get in till the fourth or fifth time. All the same it would have taken a sterner and colder man than Albert not to be upset. The elections would not be formally announced till March but in Albert's case the result was already certain. Dibdin told him the Professor had refused to sign his certificates.

Albert's *amour-propre* was injured. Woods was not getting his just recognition. And though it was quite irrational, Albert somehow held his father-in-law, who had put him up for the society, responsible.

Being treated with great respect at Wigan restored Albert's feelings a little. He and Sir Alfred spent the morning in the laboratories. For all his self-abasement before 'the splendid intellects such as one finds in the older universities', Sir Alfred never retired modestly when such intellects got to work. He stayed at Albert's side throughout all his technical conversations with Callandars' research men: his little grey eyes were bright with interest under eyebrows that stuck out sensitively like a prawn's: and he occasionally joined in with courteous aplomb. Albert was never certain whether Sir Alfred understood what it was all about or not: on the other hand Sir Alfred had a liking for clarity in expression which led him to put his finger on something that Albert and his colleagues were not clear about themselves.

At one o'clock Sir Alfred asked Albert if he would join him for luncheon. The first time this had happened Albert had imagined a sumptuous repast in the oak-panelled board room. He now knew that Sir Alfred was offering him sandwiches in his office. They went to the office where Sir Alfred sat down at his desk and rang the bell for his secretary.

A pretty young woman brought in a tray with two bottles of milk and two glasses on it.

'Excellent,' said Sir Alfred, his face lighting up at the sight of the milk.

Albert was sitting in an arm-chair beside the desk. Sir Alfred began to undo a packet of sandwiches wrapped in a white starched table-napkin. Albert's eyes glanced round the walls: on one was a large steel engraving in a gilt frame, a portrait of the founder of the firm; on another was a portrait in oils of Sir Alfred's father. Their faces were distinctly less intelligent than Sir Alfred's, but somehow more impressive.

'I told my housekeeper to put something up especially for you, Albert.'

Albert saw the sandwiches in the napkin being handed to him. Though Sir Alfred was much too concerned with his personal routine – he normally ate the sandwiches and milk while working at his desk – to give Albert a good luncheon, his old fashioned manners led him to have sandwiches made that would be more likely to appeal to Albert's taste than those prepared in accordance with his hypochondriac's diet-chart.

'I won't offer you a bikky,' he said, with a glint in his eye. A 'bikky' was a biscuit made of presumedly health-giving soya flour which he knew Albert particularly disliked.

'Thank you, Sir Alfred,' said Albert, choosing one of the sandwiches made for him with thick slices of boiled ham.

They drank their glasses of milk while talking of the firm's research.

'It's coming on by leaps and bounds,' Sir Alfred said. 'During the last two years we've seen quite a remarkable advance.'

'I agree,' said Albert, with pleasing absence of modesty.

'I've no doubt said it to you before, my dear Albert' – as a shy man who found it hard to call another by his Christian name, Sir Alfred, once he had made a start, overdid it – 'I feel the change is due to your remarkable gift for inspiring research.' (Sir Alfred was much too shrewd and truthful to pretend Albert had done the research himself.) He smiled at Albert. 'I'm being neither indiscreet nor likely to give offence to anyone else if I say that in public, am I?'

'No,' said Albert. 'Not if you think so.'

'But I do think so!' Sir Alfred's voice sounded with enthusiasm. He opened a drawer. 'Have one of these bananas, my dear Albert. They're in excellent condition.'

Albert took a banana.

'It gives me great pleasure to express my high opinion of you.' Sir Alfred said.

His tone changed. 'I feel it was a great piece of good fortune for my firm when we decided to ask Professor Dibdin and his colleagues to do extra-mural research for us.'

Albert assented.

Sir Alfred said simply: 'It was my own idea.'

Albert congratulated him.

'I've been giving some thought to how we can take our . . . partnership still farther.'

At that Sir Alfred paused. It was a remark he had made on several previous occasions.

Albert was certain he knew what was in Sir Alfred's mind. But how to put it into words?

'I'm afraid,' said Sir Alfred, not without a touch of triumph, 'that inspiration has deserted me.'

'Oh, but it needn't,' cried Albert.

'I'm happy to hear it.' Sir Alfred cocked his head on one side expectantly.

'Other great industrialists have had the inspiration – '

Sir Alfred's attention, appeared to wander.

'It isn't at all unusual,' Albert went on.

'What isn't unusual?' said Sir Alfred, seeking clarity.

'It isn't unusual,' said Albert, 'for a great industrialist to endow a lab in which he's personally interested.'

'Endow a laboratory,' said Sir Alfred.

'Yes,' said Albert, suddenly bursting with moral fervour. 'Other great industrialists have endowed labs. Why don't you, Sir Alfred?'

The call to duty rang round the room. 'Why don't you, Sir Alfred?'

Sir Alfred looked more bright-eyed than ever.

'It's an interesting suggestion,' he said. 'Now have you any other suggestions, Albert?'

Albert shook his head, unable to speak. Why don't you, Sir Alfred?

Sir Alfred closed the drawer in which the bananas had been, and leapt up from his chair:

'Why! We shall miss our little after-luncheon trot.'

Sir Alfred put on his overcoat and Albert did the same. They went out of the office and down to the road that ran through the works. Sir Alfred set off at a quick pace towards one of the exits and Albert kept beside him. They went up a hill. Albert was soon breathless: Sir Alfred was not.

Sir Alfred did not start a train of conversation. His routine of health took precedence over everything. Albert waited.

It was a cold but balmy January day. The sun shone from a cloudless sky, drawing from the ground a thick milky haze. In the fields the cows stood vague and motionless. At one place in the hedgerow there was a holly bush with bright red berries shining on the topmost branches. A few sparrows chirped.

'There,' said Sir Alfred. They had reached the top of the hill, and he turned about. They paused and looked down. Shrouded in soft opal light Callandars' Chemical Works for the first time presented itself as a thing of exquisite beauty. Albert, thinking of endowments and laboratories, was filled with emotion as if Satan had taken him up into a high place. The works buildings, now flat walls and roofs of soft grey and fawn, receded in glimmering planes one behind the other, while three slender chimneys pointed upwards into a radiant haze. Callandars called to him – like a star, like a woman, like a knighthood.

Sir Alfred spoke.

'Do you think if I considered endowing your laboratory, the suggestion would be well received?'

Albert turned to him.

'It would be accepted with open hands,' he cried.

Sir Alfred smiled. They were standing close together. 'You don't foresee,' said Sir Alfred, 'the slightest objection from Professor Dibdin?'

Albert's breath was taken right away. 'You mean,' he said, 'you might endow a lab for *me*?'

Sir Alfred did not reply.

Albert did not reply.

Albert thought 'It can't be true!' He looked into Sir Alfred's face. Sir Alfred had his steady bright-eyed smile which told Albert nothing. Albert thought 'It can be true!'

'You think,' Albert said, trying to keep his voice steady – he succeeded – 'there may be a case for endowing a lab that's more or less independent of the experimental chemistry department?'

'My dear Albert,' said Sir Alfred, 'I was asking a simple question. Before I take any step, you understand, I must try to cover all contingencies.'

'Of course,' said Albert. 'All contingencies,' he echoed. The contingency of Dibdin being wildly angry at Callandars endowing an independent laboratory for him, Albert.

Sir Alfred said: 'Time to trot back.'

Albert returned to Oxford not knowing whether he was on his head or his heels. Time after time he repeated to himself Sir Alfred's remarks. Had he misinterpreted them completely? Had Sir Alfred meant that Dibdin might object to the experimental chemistry department appearing to lose some of its independence, although there was no reason why it should, by accepting a large sum of money from an industrial firm? Sir Alfred was sufficiently unrealistic, in his excess of punctilio, to think so.

On the other hand, Albert kept repeating to himself, Sir Alfred could not have mistaken his, Albert's, meaning when he had said, 'You might endow a lab for *me*.'

A fatal objection appeared. Sir Alfred could not possibly endow a laboratory for Albert while Clinton was still in the department.

When he got back to Oxford Albert paid an immediate friendly call on Clinton, as he always did after a visit to Wigan. It was an evening when Clinton gave a tutorial in college. As Albert climbed the stairs he met the pupils coming down. He went directly into Clinton's rooms.

Clinton was standing, with his feet apart, in front of the fireplace. Albert saw immediately that there was a stiff look on his face.

'Whisky?'

'Thank you, Clinton. It's a cold night.'

Albert sat down. Clinton handed him a glass and said:

'You've heard the latest.'

'What? . . .' Albert paused with his glass in mid-air.

'About the Royal.'

Albert took a sip of whisky. 'I'm sorry, Clinton.'

'It's my third time.'

'Well, it's my second.'

Clinton did not speak. He had gone back to the fireplace. He lit a cigarette.

'I suppose,' said Albert, 'we shall have to put up with it for God-knows-how-many more years. Till the old gentlemen finally give in.'

'Has The Professor signed your certificates?'

'F. R. says not.'

'F. R.'s amusing.'

There was a long pause.

Clinton said:

'I'm going to get out.'

'What?'

'I'm going to get out of Oxford. I intend to move over to Callandars, straight away.'

'Do you mean you're going to cut your losses in academic research and – '

'Don't be a fool, man. I shall carry on my research there.'

Albert said: 'I think you're being rather hasty, aren't you?'

'That's my business.'

Albert took a long sip of his whisky.

'What's your advice?' said Clinton.

Albert smiled and shook his head. There was a long pause. Clinton sat down in a chair facing Albert.

'And now, about Callandars.'

Albert began to repeat his scientific conversations in Callandars' research laboratories. Clinton was going to leave Oxford: excitement seized Albert. He went on to describe his conversation with Sir Alfred. It was the first time he had ever confided in Clinton.

'Have another whisky.' Clinton poured double the original quantity into both their glasses and sat down again.

Albert did not confide everything, but Clinton took his main point.

'I don't know,' said Clinton, 'whether the old man thinks of endowing a lab for you or F. R. How can I?'

Albert shrugged his shoulders. 'Suppose the alternative does arise . . .'

'You want to know which side I'm on?'

'It would be a help to know.'

Clinton waited a long time before he said:

'I should decide which the firm would gain the more from.'

Albert suppressed a faint smile. Clinton saw it all the same. He took a gulp of whisky, and then glanced sideways at Albert.

'It's pretty obvious, isn't it?'

Albert stared at him with his eyes bulging. He was satisfied.

CHAPTER FOUR

THE FATE OF AN ENDOWMENT

A lbert ought not to have done it.
Whether the idea of Sir Alfred Callandar setting him up in a laboratory independent of Dibdin had originally sprung from a misunderstanding or not, Albert ought not to have acted on it. Instead he went ahead, full steam ahead.

During the next few months Albert travelled to and fro constantly between Oxford and Wigan, nominally in the course of his extramural research for Callandars. And Sir Alfred in turn came to Oxford – Albert arranged that these visits should coincide with Dibdin's absences in London. (This was not difficult to arrange as Dibdin was spending an average of two days a week in the environs of Whitehall.)

What Albert was doing was reprehensible. And what made matters worse, as it always does when a man behaves reprehensibly, was that he was bound to be found out. Albert was enjoying himself. It was his first taste of handling affairs and he found it delicious. He immersed himself totally.

Benefactors do not benefact, industrialists do not endow laboratories, rich men do not part with their money, in a hurry. Sir Alfred enjoyed himself too. They had protracted discussions in which he put questions galore to Albert. He wanted to consider all contingencies, and the project of a Callandar Laboratory in South Parks Road, as seen by Sir Alfred, was built on contingencies.

Among the contingencies was the attitude of Dibdin – Sir Alfred saw that clearly enough. Albert reassured him. Dibdin was frequently out of Oxford, he pointed out. Albert was lured into deeper reaches of reprehensibility: he was not above implying that his teacher and master was now preoccupied with affairs of state and *passé* as a scientist. It was deplorable.

On the other hand, if the project had arisen through a new

friendship between Sir Alfred and Dibdin, would Dibdin have offered Albert a share of the proceeds? Would he? Life is a sad thing and deplorable on all sides. It would have taken a man of a hyper-refined judgement to award the palm of virtue between Albert and Dibdin, or between either of them and hosts of their kin.

In what way, you may well ask, do men of the world differ from beasts of the wild? Please address your question elsewhere. I beg to be excused.

Perhaps we may draw comfort, however, from the fact that Sir Alfred Callandar behaved with probity throughout. The fruit of success seemed to Albert to be dangling before his eyes, but Sir Alfred was still a long way from being ready to let anyone pluck it. Sir Alfred had considered all the contingencies with Albert, and Albert was inclined to think that was the end of it. For Sir Alfred that was only the half of it. With his perfect probity and his old-fashioned manners he proceeded to another fascinating stretch of contingency-considering, with Dibdin.

Only a vulgar phrase does justice to what happened next. The fat was in the fire.

The heat of Dibdin's anger was such that he first of all threatened to have Albert turned out of Oxford altogether. (This, as Albert observed, he was not in a position to do.)

Next he broke off personal relations with his son-in-law. In the laboratory he and Albert began to send written memoranda to each other. The only connexion between the two adjacent *ménages* in New Cross Road was by the women telephoning.

Within a few hours the news of the rumpus, tasty meat for gossips of academic life, was all over Oxford. (It lingers still, transmogrified by the art of high-table conversation into a dramatic scene in which Sir Alfred Callandar was in the act of laying the foundation-stone of Woods's laboratory when Dibdin came up, seized the stone and carried it away in his Rolls Royce.)

Mrs Dibdin was alarmed and annoyed by the turn of events. Margaret was deeply concerned. After a week of her husband and her father being divided by anger, Margaret could bear it no longer. She decided to try and reconcile them.

With Albert, Margaret tried to conceal the depth of her feeling.

'I want you to meet Papa,' she said to him. 'It's positively absurd not to be on speaking terms.'

'I hardly know what you expect me to say to him, my dear,' Albert replied. 'I'm afraid I think his attitude to me is very unfair.'

'Albert!'

'In any case,' Albert said, 'the next word must come from Sir Alfred Callandar.'

'What next word?' Margaret asked.

'Whether he intends to go ahead with the endowment or not.'

Margaret suppressed the impulse to exclaim with surprise and incredulity. 'I want you to meet Papa,' she said firmly. 'Please will you meet Papa, Albert?'

Albert gave in.

With her father Margaret had less trouble.

'I welcome the opportunity,' he said. 'Thank you, my dear.'

'But surely it was you who started this absurd break?'

'Break in what?' Dibdin's hazel eyes shifted innocently.

Margaret kissed him on the forehead instead of trying to explain.

Albert agreed to his father-in-law and mother-in-law coming to dine the next evening.

The external circumstances of the dinner-party were auspicious. Margaret had taken great care over the food and drink. It was a hot summer evening and the sun was shining with a heavenly golden light. Margaret's dining-room was quite small but it was lofty and it had a tall french window opening on to the garden. She had the window open and the evening scent of flowers, of buddleia and of stock sometimes wafted into the room.

Albert and Dibdin spoke to each other. They were wearing their dinner-jackets. Dibdin came into the room. Albert gave him a silky smile and said:

'A glass of sherry, F. R.?'

And Dibdin said:

'Thank you, Albert.'

Dibdin accepted a glass of sherry from Albert's hand and did not throw it in his face. The sherry was pale and dry and not poisonous. Dibdin drank it.

Mrs Dibdin, who had been up to the nursery to look at the children – Albert and Margaret now had a second child, a son – came into the room and accepted some sherry. Holding their glasses with delicate formality they all moved, Margaret, her father, her mother and Albert, towards the doorway opening on the garden.

The shadow of some thick leafy trees on the west side of the garden fell across the lawn, just covering a bed from which sprang a standard rose bush; so that although the stem was in the shade the flowers, like a fountain, caught the slanting golden sunlight. They were crimson, dazzling with illumination.

'How I wish I were a painter!' said Mrs Dibdin. 'Don't you see?' She turned to her husband and Albert as if they were one person.

'Superb,' said Albert sycophantically.

Dibdin laughed to himself.

Mrs Dibdin gave them a glance out of the corner of her eye, and plunged confidently on. 'I always think we who have the eye of an artist, without having the talent to put down what we see, are most to be pitied.' She addressed herself to Albert. 'Don't you agree, Albert?'

Margaret interrupted. 'Mama, dinner's ready.'

They turned back to the dining-table and sat down.

'You know, Margaret,' said Mrs Dibdin as she unfolded her table-napkin, 'I always think this is the most charming room in the house. Except the nursery, of course.' Her gaze passed round the walls hung with paper in dark green stripes, from the white marble chimneypiece, on which stood an urn filled with syringa, to a beautiful portrait in a gilt frame. It was a wedding-present from Daunton: it was of a woman in a violet riding-habit, painted by Romney. Something about her, the imperious set of the head and the bold yet appealing look in the eyes, instantly made one think of Mrs Dibdin herself.

'Yes, Mama.'

Mrs Dibdin leaned forward a little towards Margaret, and her brown eyes glowed with the excitement of their alliance. 'It's a great success, my dear.'

Margaret smiled at her mother. 'Thank you, Mama. . . .'

The men, although now on speaking terms, said nothing. There was nothing they could say. A servant came round the table with cups of *consommé* and everybody began to eat.

There was silence. Mrs Dibdin glanced at Margaret. Before the party Margaret had asked her mother to let her have the floor in conversation until the question of the endowment was settled. Now Margaret was struck with nervousness. Mrs Dibdin spoke.

'I wonder,' she said, 'how Dr Smith enjoyed his second visit to Germany.'

They all looked up.

Clinton Smith had conceived a great admiration for the leaders of the National-Socialist party. It dated from the previous summer, when he and Albert had been invited to visit I. G. Farben. They both accepted and the visit had produced opposite effects on them as far as politics were concerned. Albert, already stirred by events in Europe to revert to the radicalism of his boyhood, was now well on the way to becoming what in those days was called an anti-fascist. (You can take it that in a few more years he was to become a great anti-fascist.) The consequence of accepting the first invitation was that Albert turned down the second; and Clinton, his eyes alight with hero-worship, went alone.

'I believe Dr Smith,' Mrs Dibdin went on, 'is *persona grata* with the *régime* in that country.' Even though her father and grandfather had both taken their seats in the House of Lords as Liberals, even though personally she deplored the principles of National-Socialism, her voice did not conceal satisfaction at the thought of anybody she knew being *persona grata* with any *régime*.

'Too damned *grata*,' said Albert, dropping his silky tone.

'And so say all of us,' said Dibdin on the spur of the moment.

Margaret looked startled, Mrs Dibdin pleased. A servant brought in the next course, which consisted of salmon, without the flow of feeling being disturbed.

'I think it says a great deal for Dr Smith's personality,' Mrs Dibdin went on, 'that he can make such a strong impression on those men who – whatever else we may say about them – whom we have to admit have very strong personalities themselves. Very strong.'

In the ordinary way Albert would have adorned such an occasion with a few remarks about Jew-baiters. Instead he stood up and politely began to pour out the wine. As he leaned over his father-in-law, to fill his glass, Dibdin looked up at him.

'You know, friend Smith's last visit to I. G.' – he pronounced it in the German style 'Ee-Gay' – 'may pay some dividends.'

It was the first time in the evening that Dibdin had met Albert's glance directly.

'Dividends?' said Albert.

'Yes.' Dibdin tried his wine thoughtfully.

Albert sat down again in his place. 'He's picked up some interesting ideas?' Albert had not seen Clinton since his return.

'Who knows?' Dibdin was smiling.

Albert leaned forward. 'What are they, F. R.?' His tone was of undivided professional interest.

Mrs Dibdin smiled triumphantly at Margaret, as much as to say: 'Look, I've reconciled them for you!'

Instead of smiling back, Margaret's face was contorted in a frown, as much as to say: 'But it's no use till they've agreed about the endowment!'

Dibdin was replying to Albert. 'He hasn't told me exactly. I've only just picked up a few straws in the wind.' He glanced away and his eye seemed to brighten. 'Just a few straws in the wind.'

At the brightening in his father-in-law's eye Albert quailed: it crossed his mind that Dibdin was far from *passé* as a scientist. Intimations of the future assailed him, unfavourable intimations.

'We must have a little talk about them,' Dibdin said, expanding for them all to see.

Margaret caught her breath.

'I doubt if they'll be quite the thing for Smith to take up now he's gone to Callandars,' Dibdin went on. 'He might like you to take them up, here.'

Margaret said: 'In the new laboratory?'

Instantly there was a flicker of silence. Albert's knife scraped on his plate.

'Which laboratory, Margaret?' said Dibdin.

'The new one, that Sir Alfred Callandar's going to endow.'

'Is he?'

'Of course he is, F. R. If you give him a chance.' Albert's temper was stirring.

'Everyone will get their chance,' said Dibdin, laughingly.

'I'd like to see it.'

'Including Sir Alfred. If he wants to endow a lab, we'll give him his chance.' Dibdin paused. 'At the moment he's only examining contingencies.'

'Don't try and put us off,' said Albert.

'Albert!' said Mrs Dibdin.

'Mama!' said Margaret.

'What is the matter?' said Dibdin.

'You know what's the matter,' said Albert.

'Yes, Papa,' said Margaret. 'You do.' Her cheeks had reddened, and she suddenly spoke with strong emotion. 'Listen, Papa, we must talk about the endowment. You know, and Albert knows, why we're all here tonight. This can't go on. You can't go on not being on speaking terms.'

'No.' Dibdin looked at her with wide eyes for a moment: then he dropped his gaze, as if he were grieved by it all.

'I don't see why not,' Albert said. His cheeks, too, had reddened – with anger.

Margaret turned to him. 'It's positively absurd. It's childish.'

'It suits F. R. and me.'

Mrs Dibdin said: 'It isn't becoming. To either of you.'

'That's not the point,' said Margaret.

'What is the point?' said Dibdin.

'The point is that you've got to be reconciled,' said Margaret. 'You can't possibly hope to keep up not speaking to each other – that's too childish and too absurd. But you *can* keep up not being reconciled. That's what's the terrifying thing.'

'My dear, you're making too much of it,' said her father.

'Am I?' said Margaret, her voice trembling.

'Yes, is she?' said Albert.

Dibdin found them all looking at him. He tried to look unconcerned. He took a sip of wine.

'Am I?' Margaret repeated.

'No – I mean, yes.'

'Oh, Papa!'

'Can't we go on with our dinner?'

'Can't you come to some compromise?'

Margaret and her father looked at each other. Suddenly Margaret changed. 'If you intend to go on in this way,' she said in a different tone, 'I think you owe it to Mama and me to say why.'

Dibdin shifted uncomfortably in his seat. Margaret glanced at Albert who promptly glanced down.

'I think you each ought to state your case,' Margaret said, 'here and now, in each other's presence, and in the presence of Mama and me.'

Silence from both men.

'Go on,' said Margaret.

'That's right,' said Mrs Dibdin.

'Papa, you first.'

Dibdin looked badgered instead of triumphant. 'I refuse.'

'Albert, you . . .'

'The new lab was entirely my idea. It's my creation. He' – Albert pointed at his father-in-law – 'would have got nothing. I worked for this lab and I claim I ought to get it.'

'I'm not preventing you from getting it,' said Dibdin.

'Yes you are.'

'I won't have an independent Callandar Laboratory in Oxford. You can have it anywhere else you like.'

'So that's the idea. You can't throw me out of Oxford, so you're trying to make it so that I go myself. Well, I won't do it, F. R. I'm going to stay here!'

'Making the worst of both worlds!'

Albert's face was red as a turkey-cock's: Dibdin's jowl had a carmine sheen and his broken nose was purple.

Margaret cried: 'I won't have it!' And she rang the bell for the servant to bring in the next course.

The two men glowered silently at an ice-pudding made with raspberries.

'Now,' said Margaret, 'we've got to find a compromise.'

Dibdin and Albert began to eat.

'I see no possibility of us all being united again as long as you're hating each other because of this lab.' She paused. As if surprised at her own strength she glanced at her mother. 'There's only one thing to do. You must turn down the endowment altogether.'

'What?' Dibdin looked up, startled.

'No lab at all?' Albert cried in anguish.

'That's what I mean.'

They saw the serious expression on her bright youthful face. She meant it.

Dibdin and Albert glanced at each other. They recovered themselves.

'We must never look a gift-horse in the mouth, my dear.'

Albert's anger waned so far that he was able to purse his lips in a smile. 'It's an absurd idea, darling. Oh, quite absurd. . . .'

'Please explain to me why!'

'It's obvious,' said Albert.

'I don't see.' Margaret's voice rose again.

'You can't do research without labs.'

'You can't do research without labs,' said Dibdin. 'No discoveries without bricks and mortar.'

'You mean you're not going to give up the idea?' Margaret looked at them in turn. Tears suddenly sprang to her eyes.

They shook their heads.

Margaret impulsively ran out of the room.

She went up to her bedroom and sat down on the bed. Tears rolled from her eyes. Furious with herself she tried to stop them. She began to sob.

Mrs Dibdin came into the room.

'My dear . . .'

Margaret did not speak.

Mrs Dibdin sat beside her. 'What are you crying for, Margaret darling?'

'It's no use.'

'It is some use. Oh, my dear, you did splendidly.'

'Splendidly.' Margaret stared at her, momentarily sullen and tearless.

'Of course.' Mrs Dibdin, who found it so easy to be demonstrative in public, raised her arms awkwardly and diffidently. 'Of course, Margaret, darling. It's going to be all right. I'm sure it's all right.'

'But how?'

'We shall see.'

'But they're still quarrelling.'

'What do you expect? You mustn't expect them to shake hands and say it's all over.' Mrs Dibdin's eyes reddened as she smiled at Margaret. 'My dear, men don't do that.'

'I should.'

Mrs Dibdin kissed her gently on the cheek. Suddenly Margaret flung her arms round her mother.

They were silent for a little while.

Margaret knew her mother was looking at her. 'What's the matter?'

'You'll have to do your hair again before you go down.'

They both stood up. Margaret moved across to the dressing table, her mother to the window.

'Come and look.' Her mother beckoned.

They looked down in the garden. There, beside the rose bush, now in the shade, Albert and her father were strolling. Her father

150

was smoking his pipe and Albert had a cigarette. They were deep in conversation.

Margaret and her mother looked at each other.

'You see,' said Mrs Dibdin. 'Believe me, my dear ... It was a success.'

Margaret's lips trembled.

Mrs Dibdin went on looking at her. 'Margaret, I'm proud of the training I gave you.'

From now on Albert's conferences with Sir Alfred Callandar were attended by Dibdin, and Dibdin's by Albert. The upshot was never in doubt.

'We old hands,' said Dibdin to Sir Alfred, 'know how important it is to have these things on a formal footing.' A particularly shrewd and mysterious look came over his face. 'For the university, you know.'

A formal footing meant one thing – a formal endowment of the department of experimental chemistry.

And so at the end of the year the Callandar Laboratory, new home of the experimental chemistry department, began to rise among the trees of South Parks Road. Albert had a wing to himself, but his heart was heavy whenever he thought of what might have been. Dibdin's heart, judged from his demeanour, was unusually light.

'I thought something like this,' he said as he surveyed his new domain, 'was bound to come my way sooner or later.'

CHAPTER FIVE
OFF AGAIN!

Margaret was slow to be satisfied that she had truly reconciled Albert and her father. Superficially they were friendly enough, but she could not miss Albert's chagrin. She tried to comfort him with her own deep-flowing optimism.

Then she saw his chagrin change to restlessness. Having told her father nothing would induce him to leave Oxford, Albert suddenly proposed to Margaret that they should move to London. Margaret kept her head. (She was turning into a more strong-minded young woman than Albert had bargained for.) She persuaded Albert to accept the principle that the best thing he could do was to concentrate all his attention on his research. She ignored the fact that however involved in scientific research he was, Albert was a man who would always have some attention left that could only be occupied by meddling in human affairs. Yet she was neither disingenuous nor entirely unselfish in trying to keep him in Oxford – if they went to London she would see less and less of him.

It was with relief that Margaret heard him propose next that they should go to Australia – even Albert's restlessness could not make him do anything so silly. She knew he must be going to stay where he was.

A year passed. And, so inscrutable are the ways of one human being with another, time brought about the change Margaret had tried to bring about herself – Albert and her father made friends again of their own accord. She could doubt no longer. There was a bustling intimacy about their comings-and-goings which told her they were back on their old footing. And yet, was it the change Margaret had tried to bring about herself? Was it the old footing she loved so much? That is where time showed its own brand of inscrutability. Their quarrel had been made up by Dibdin's taking Albert into his confidence over his career in Whitehall.

Margaret was able to say that she had foreseen from the beginning what was bound to happen. Her father apparently did not foresee.

Dibdin was beginning to be a successful man of affairs. Physically he was quite a big man in the first place: he was beginning to look bigger. His shoulders were heavier and his waist longer: he trod more weightily. His light hair was greyer though no less thick and curly, his big hazel eyes gleamed constantly, and his heavy jowl had a permanent sheen of well-being. The Production Executive Committee and the Callandar Laboratory – he was entitled to regard them as large and showy feathers in his cap. He comported himself as men do when they know their headgear is impressive.

Albert was getting fatter.

Their bustling intimacy now focused on the Production Executive Committee.

The Production Executive Committee was worthy of their focusing. It was unlike most of the committees, commissions and councils before which scientists were wont to be asked to give evidence: when it came to a decision, it did not make a recommendation, it ordered action. It was composed chiefly of high civil servants and senior officers of the armed forces. It had the brisk, hearty, slightly brutal air common to most bodies that have executive power. The members were loyal to each other but did not hesitate to judge each other. Its reputation in the eyes of men whose concern was affairs-of-state was justly high.

Dibdin kept Albert *au fait* with the committee's doings. In a way the footing of their intimacy was unchanged. It was Dibdin's habit, when he came back from London, to tell Albert what he had said at that meeting and to 'throw out a few ideas' about what he might say at the next. Albert's rôle was to pick out those ideas in which the element of reason was present. It was not long, naturally, before Albert thought he could do better on the committee than his father-in-law.

The committee met frequently and regularly. When Dibdin was unable to attend he gave Albert the privilege of deputizing for him.

On his first appearance Albert made a discovery. Dibdin's seat was not on the Production Executive Committee but on its Chemistry Sub-Committee. A little mistake in nomenclature had never troubled Dibdin, and it did not worry Albert greatly. The Chemistry Sub-Committee was wonderful enough for him.

There was a feature of the Chemistry Sub-Committee which might have troubled Albert, which would certainly have troubled many men who stood outside it. The Chemistry Sub Committee of the Production Executive was occupied with making use of chemistry to enable the country to defend itself and to make war. It was ironical that Dibdin and Albert, both, whatever their failings, among the most humane of men, should have been called into affairs to take part in the production of explosives and poison-gases. Though they may have been deplorably ready to do anyone out of his job, the last thing they wanted was to do anyone out of his life.

Yet there they sat at meetings, their eyes alight with interest and their hearts curiously untouched. To anyone outside it may look strange, but in life it is quite common. Many human activities, when looked at from outside, are scarcely laudable: if they have got to be done it is perhaps a saving grace in human nature that men have an instinct to professionalize and domesticate them. That is what Dibdin, Albert and the other members of the committee – all decent men, after their fashion – did.

Albert was fascinated by affairs-of-state. For him there was a special glamour about the scientific problems that Dibdin brought back to Oxford from Whitehall. To begin with Albert felt a special pride in his deputy-appearances at the committee. It was Margaret who saw, while Albert's modesty still supervened, that deputizing would not remain enough.

One night at the end of a Michaelmas term, Dibdin was recounting his doings in Whitehall to Albert. He was satisfied with the part he had played in the most recent deliberations of the Production Executive Sub-Committee. The War Department was proposing to subsidize the setting up of a plant to make a certain variant of lewisite, and Dibdin had been asked a question about the process. The question was a straightforward one and Dibdin had given the answer that any knowledgeable chemist would have given.

Albert listened. It occurred to him that there might be another answer.

That is all there is to it. It happens. One hears someone give a conventional, apparently satisfactory answer, and suddenly one suspects that there may be another answer. One's mind fixes on the suspicion: it refuses to let one go. And then one sets to work.

Albert said nothing at the time. The suspicion germinated. He went to see Eli. If Albert was right, the work involved a short theoretical investigation related to the research Eli was doing at the time.

But that was not Albert's sole reason for going to Eli. He always went to Eli whenever he had a problem that he thought was likely to stir Eli's eccentric and independent imagination. He was still wooing Eli.

It was one of Albert's strong traits to want his friends, his colleagues, even his enemies, to live with him in a warm enclosed little world of intimacy, and Eli still stood too far outside it for him to be happy. As Albert declared himself with greater volume and greater frequency as a great anti-fascist, Eli appeared to permit himself a feeble jerky flow of empathy in Albert's direction. But that was not enough for Albert. The warm little world of intimacy was to encompass not only empathy, friendship even: it would never be complete without the joy of collaboration in research.

Albert had no special hopes of the particular problem he brought to Eli now. He was under the impression that Eli was far too arrogant – Eli's research was as remarkable as his academic performance – to be specially interested because it offered a chance of proving that Dibdin had made a mistake. Nor did he think he was bringing it at a moment in Eli's existence that was particularly opportune.

Eli listened. At the end he said:

'What're we going to do about it?'

It took Albert's breath away. He goggled, recovered himself, and said in a stately tone: 'The ideal would be for you to do the preliminary theory – nobody else could do it so rapidly and with so little trouble ... And then for me to do the experiments. I'm willing.' He paused. 'In that way we could clear the whole thing up in a fortnight. That's if we're right.'

Eli had not said he thought Albert was right. He said: 'That's if we're lucky.'

Albert smiled at him. 'I think we could be lucky if we joined forces.'

There was a long pause. Eli showed no signs of speaking. Albert could not bear it any longer. 'Well, are we, or aren't we?'

Eli did not answer the question. There was a faint glint of a smile in his hard grey eyes. He said to Albert:

'Why do you bring these things to me? I've noticed you're always bringing me odd problems. Interesting ones. You know. Tit-bits.'

'I hadn't thought of them as such, Eli.'

Eli made a derisive sound, but it was friendly.

'It makes me think about things I wouldn't think about otherwise,' he said.

It was Albert's turn not to reply. He presumed that Eli was relating the idea, in some crazily idiosyncratic way that passed Albert's comprehension, to the concept of self-discipline. Albert was not put off. He felt that if a man's intelligence was high enough it could begin to redeem his maddening flaws of temperament; and Eli's was high enough.

Their conversation was taking place on the last day of the term. Eli said:

'I was going home tomorrow. I don't mind sticking it for another week. If that suits you.'

Albert never learnt what made Eli decide to do it. Nor did he trouble himself with speculation. He settled down to work with Eli immediately, and for the next ten days they were absorbed.

It was one of the happiest weeks of research Albert had ever spent. Contact with Eli was exciting, thrilling. Albert had always believed that as scientists they were complementary to each other – one the theoretician, the other the experimenter. The speed and the perfection with which they did their task told him it was so. Also – the culminating joy of a beautiful partnership – they proved that Albert was right.

Albert went immediately to Dibdin with results.

Dibdin looked at Albert's and Eli's results and admitted they were correct. It meant that at the next committee meeting he had got to give a different answer or risk his mistake being brought to light in a costly fashion when the pilot plant got under way.

Three days before the next meeting Dibdin went down with laryngitis. He retired to bed with a high temperature and no voice. Albert went to see him.

Dibdin was sitting up in bed wearing soiled flannel pyjamas and looking unshaven.

'Pass me a grape,' he said soundlessly as Albert came close to him. 'I'm worried about the committee meeting.'

Albert sat down. Dibdin ate a couple of grapes and put the pips in a saucer on the bedside table.

'I want you to go in my place, Albert.'

'Do you want me to tell them about the work Eli and I have done?'

'What do you think?'

Dibdin's round bright eyes were fixed on him. Suddenly Dibdin turned away and helped himself to another grape.

'What do I think?' Albert said. He thought Dibdin must be losing his grip.

Dibdin ate his grape solemnly.

'I couldn't *not* tell them,' Albert said. 'Honestly, F. R., I don't see what else I could do.'

Dibdin laughed. He said, soundlessly again: 'Nor do I.'

Albert paused. 'I wish it could be postponed till you can go yourself.'

Dibdin shook his head. 'I should like you to go.'

There was a long pause.

A contented, omniscient look came into Dibdin's eye. He said:

'It's time you tasted some of the sweets that are going to be yours in the future.'

Albert sat at the wheel of his Rolls Royce motor-car. It was a freezing December day, sleet blew against the windscreen, he could hardly see across the road as he turned out of Whitehall into Trafalgar Square, but his face was glowing. The meeting was just over. Beside him sat the chairman of the committee, Redvers Jameson. They were going to have luncheon at Jameson's club, The Athenaeum. During the meeting, *after* Albert had delivered his speech, Jameson had passed him a note of invitation. To Albert the document was as historic as Magna Carta.

'Will you lunch with me at the Club? R. J.'

Underneath, Albert wrote: 'Thank you. I shall be delighted. A. W.'

Albert's face glowed with happiness while he drove into Cockspur Street with Jameson at his side, and his mouth curled in the smile of a man who is aware of his pomp.

Jameson took Albert straight in to luncheon. He had reserved a separate table.

'I wanted us to have a little *tête-à-tête*,' he said. 'I wonder if you'd like to try our claret. It's really quite drinkable, more than drinkable in fact.'

Jameson spoke with theatrical emphasis, and the effect was pleasing and cosy. He had a narrow pink face and bright transparent blue eyes: his hair and his eyebrows were an elegant silver-grey. His expression was mobile and lively, and his voice was resonant. He loved gossip. There was something about him of a lively small animal – he might well have had pointed ears.

Although he had arranged a cosy little *tête-à-tête*, Jameson began to gossip cordially about everything but private matters. He talked about Dibdin and Sir Alfred Callandar, about Albert's research and his future plans. He told a few anecdotes about Mr Lloyd George and Mr Stanley Baldwin, and finally settled down to entertaining speculations about affairs in Russia.

Jameson was a senior official in the Lord President's office. He was becoming an important figure in affairs. His chief characteristics were his ability and his cordiality – the second masked the first. No man in London could have been more cordial than Redvers Jameson, and there were not many who were more able. He was a happy man, and a successful one: he thoroughly enjoyed his official life. He might never reach the highest position of all, but he was happy to go as far as he went.

It was not until after luncheon, when they were smoking beside a window which overlooked Pall Mall, that Jameson came down to business. He sipped his coffee. Then he took off one pair of spectacles and put on another.

'Before we part after this most enjoyable meeting, Dr Woods, and you return to Oxford – by the way, I expect you are returning immediately to Oxford?'

'Yes.'

'How I envy you!'

'Thank you.'

'Before we part there is a little matter on which I should like to sound you. I'm bearing in mind that Professor Dibdin is your father-in-law. You are probably closer to him than anyone else.'

Albert had no idea what was coming next.

'I wonder,' said Jameson, 'if you have any idea how your father-in-law would regard an invitation to sit on the main committee instead of our little sub-committee.'

Albert stammered.

'One might call it,' said Jameson, 'translation to higher things.'

'I'm sure he'd like it,' said Albert.

'Do you think he'd be willing to shoulder even greater responsibility on our behalf? We realize what sacrifices we are asking, of time that would otherwise be spent on research.'

Albert presumed that by 'we' he meant himself and the Lord President. Albert's face, already rosy with drink, went rosier.

'I think such sacrifices are worth while,' he said. 'Superbly worth while.' He paused. 'We have got to make them.'

Jameson looked at him as if he were hanging on Albert's words, though he must have known exactly what Albert was going to say. 'I'm interested to hear you say that, Dr Woods.'

Albert said it again, this time in even fuller, weightier voice.

'Of course, we shall always be more than grateful for what Professor Dibdin has done for us already.'

Albert glanced at him. Was there a trace of irony in his voice? Was the last thing Dibdin had done for them a blunder that might have cost them thousands of pounds? Albert pursed his lips in his social smile.

'I'm sure you can rely on him for more,' said Albert. Somehow the surroundings, the atmosphere of the Athenaeum, the sight of other substantial men of affairs sitting in twos and threes, also arranging jobs, seemed to inspire him.

'Of course,' said Jameson, 'the members of the main committee are exceptionally distinguished men, so distinguished' – there was no mistaking now the slyness in his tone – 'that we can't expect them to meet as often as we might like.'

With a great effort Albert maintained his social smile.

'Naturally.'

'I'm glad you agree with me.'

They sat looking at each other. They were both smoking cigars. Albert leaned his head back. Jameson leaned his forward. He said:

'Between ourselves one doesn't want distinguished advice too often.' For an instant he looked as if the pleasure of indiscretion made his eyes bluer and his ears more pointed.

Albert held up his plump white hand and contemplated it. He now knew what must be coming next.

'If Professor Dibdin does find it possible to accept even further responsibility, it will leave a gap on our little Chemistry Sub-Committee, our little working committee, as I call it.'

'Naturally,' said Albert again. He felt faintly as if the room were swimming round him, the windows, the clouds of cigar smoke and the men in twos and threes.

There was a pause. Albert had the impression Jameson was pausing out of sheer mischievousness.

'Personally, my dear Woods, I should feel almost reconciled to the loss if we could see a little more of *you*.'

Albert listened to the words as if they were borne not on clouds of smoke but on angel's wings. To hold his tongue was impossible any longer – Jameson held up his hand.

'Don't reply now, my dear Woods. Don't reply now! I want you to think it over. All this is in the future, you know.'

Albert let out his breath in a strangled gasp, and managed to recover his smile once more.

The conversation went on. I do not need to record more. Albert left the Athenaeum in a daze of happiness.

As he drove back to Oxford, fast through the snow, the daze began to clear. It seemed to Albert that Redvers Jameson was the most Machiavellian man he had ever met. The plot was devastatingly simple – Dibdin was to be kicked upstairs and Albert was to take his place.

Albert began to feel triumph as he had never felt it before.

In spite of his having displayed that he was exceptionally gifted in research, in spite of his having dared to rival his teacher and master, Albert had never been completely confident in his success. Always he had been haunted by the expectation that one morning he would wake up and find he had been lured by the world into a gigantic hoax. (Perhaps the inability to believe completely in one's success, however great, is what characterizes the little man.) Now Albert's triumph was fact. He was up and Dibdin was down, by appointment of Redvers Jameson.

Albert tried to explain it all to himself in terms of common-sense. Why was he preferred to Dibdin? Because Dibdin's muddled flashes of inspiration and inaccuracy were not what a committee of matter-of-fact men of affairs wanted? For the first time it occurred to Albert that this present mistake might not have been Dibdin's first.

Snowflakes piled up on the windscreen and Albert stopped to clean them off. And when he started again he drove slowly and carefully. The glorious golden future in Whitehall dazzled him, but not to such an extent that he could overlook the fact that he must preserve his neck to enjoy it.

It was dark when the lights of Oxford glimmered before him. Never had they looked so dear and so entrancing. He was preferred to Dibdin.

'Onward, Woods! Onward and upward!'

I have said that Albert Woods was not a typical scientist: nor was he a typical man of affairs. His Rolls Royce drew up before his house in New Cross Road, and he paused a moment before he jumped out. With his soul inflated like a wonderful balloon, the fat little man paused for a moment. He shook his head with a sharp unexpected pang of regret, and he spoke aloud.

'Poor old Dibdin!' he said.

And then he added in his native dialect: 'Poor ——!'

PART FOUR

The Peak

CHAPTER ONE
THE PEARLY CITY

The autumn of 1937 saw Albert permanently installed in London, and his new friend and sponsor, Redvers Jameson, knighted.

Albert had been elected to a chair of chemistry at one of the colleges of London university. He was a professor – he had not yet been elected to the Royal Society, but one step was enough. 'Professor A. Woods.' Albert liked the look of it: it was just.

And Albert's friend and sponsor liked the look of 'Sir Redvers Jameson, K.B.E.'

Jameson had moved up in the world. Dibdin was now on the main committee of the Production Executive, Albert on the Chemistry Sub-Committee: Jameson had become chairman of the main committee and its three sub-committees as well. He was a sponsor worth having.

Jameson remained bland, shrewd and cordial, and in his new appointments he met with unusually little envy. Jameson's chief gift was not to arouse envy. He knew how to please and how to efface himself; but above all he had developed a technique for diverting attention elsewhere, by constantly acting with utmost deference towards his present minister. No one could envy a man who was so clearly the cat's-paw of another.

So that Jameson might fulfil his new task with the appearance as well as the fact of impartiality – the committees were given to rivalries between the service departments and the departments of supply – he had resigned from the civil service, but he still kept his office in the same place. He continued to speak with utmost deference towards his former minister.

Albert thought at first that there must be a connexion between Jameson's appointments and his becoming a Sir. There was no connexion. Albert began to study such matters carefully.

In his own affairs Albert began a run of luck as soon as he arrived in London.

The first thing Albert did was to persuade Eli to come and work with him. He got the college to create a special lectureship for Eli.

Eli said it was bribery, and accepted the bribe. Then he announced that he was going to get married.

Albert's congratulations came from the heart. This was before he had seen Eli's choice of mate.

You might expect that Eli would choose for his wife some typical Marxist drab whom no man could want to go to bed with except to prove his political solidarity. You would have been in for a surprise.

Eli's girl was the daughter of a wealthy mill-owner in Bradford. Her name was Rachel and she professed the faith of her forefathers in the wilderness. She went to Young Conservative dances. She was nineteen and she had just left the sort of girls' school where nobody was expected to take matriculation anyway. She was dark-eyed, plump and high-coloured – in a word, succulent.

'Isn't she terribly ordinary?' Margaret drawled.

Albert, taken aback in more ways than one, goggled. Then the loyalty of a great husband supervened.

'Really, what an unsuitable choice!' he said. 'She'll *never* make a professor's wife.'

Eli was not thinking about the girl's future in academic society. He married her and came to London. Albert was delighted by how docile Eli could be.

Albert's next stroke of luck came at the end of the year.

Dibdin, up in London for a meeting of the Production Executive Committee, asked Albert to dine with him at the Athenaeum.

They met in the small room where members were drinking sherry. Albert arrived in time to find Dibdin and Sir Redvers Jameson already in conversation. It was clear that Dibdin was in the highest of spirits. His round eyes were shining and his broad flat face was ruddy with amusement.

Albert caught a conspiratorial glance between his father-in-law and Jameson. The two men stood up. Jameson said he must leave and shook hands cordially with Albert and Dibdin. When he had gone Albert looked into his father-in-law's face.

'What is it?' he said in an eager whisper.

Dibdin put his finger to his lips and glanced round the room.

'Let us go into the hall.' He put his arm round Albert's shoulder. In the hall they waited for two gaitered clergymen to disappear behind the pillars.

Dibdin said:

'The Professor's signed your certificates for the Royal.'

Albert's face turned crimson.

Dibdin laughed: 'All's well that ends well.'

Albert opened his mouth to speak but no sound came out.

'Now let us go across and dine.'

They walked across to the dining-room, which was unusually empty. Instead of going to one of the long tables in the middle of the room Dibdin chose a table for two.

'I'm glad there's no one to overhear us,' he said. He paused as he saw the waiter approaching.

'Tonight's a night to celebrate,' he whispered.

Albert, recovering from his satisfaction and delight, looked at his father-in-law more closely. Dibdin's eyes looked brighter and wider than ever. There was a perceptible tone of mystery in his voice.

'I'm very happy,' Albert said. At the same time he had a strong suspicion that there was more in the wind than his father-in-law had told him.

'This is a night for the family to celebrate,' Dibdin said.

Albert became more puzzled. Margaret was going to have another child, but that could be nothing to do with it.

The waiter came with their *hors d'oeuvres*. Immediately Dibdin made a great show of remaining silent till he had gone away again.

Albert said: 'What have you got up your sleeve, F. R.? Not something more about me getting into the Royal?'

'You're bound to get into the Royal now, Albert . . . I think you can say it's in the bag.'

Albert said: 'Then what else have you got up your sleeve?'

'I've got something in the bag myself. Just a little bag, you know, but worth having.'

'What is it?'

'Can't you guess?'

Albert could not guess. Dibdin had just completed for the committee a survey of all the explosive-making and poison-gas-making establishments in the country. Albert wondered if it had something to do with that.

Dibdin said: 'Then you'll have to wait till you open your *Times* on New Year's Day. . . .'

For the second time within half an hour Albert's face turned crimson and he was unable to speak. He was astounded.

'I'm not supposed to tell anyone,' Dibdin said.

'Is it' – Albert stammered – 'going to be a κ?'

Dibdin clowningly went through the motions of giving himself the accolade.

'Rise, Sir Rowland,' he said.

Albert's crimson colour deepened, partly with pleasure, partly with chagrin.

'For my services to the committee,' Dibdin said triumphantly if inaccurately.

They spent a bibulous evening.

'Kicked upstairs,' Albert kept thinking every time he looked at his father-in-law, and realized that he still had a lot to learn about affairs.

But as he drove back to his new home in Hampstead that night, Albert forgot the chagrin of having mistakenly imagined his father-in-law's career was over. He contemplated his own career, and his spirit swelled. Professor A. Woods, F.R.S. What could sound better than that? It was a cold clear night and the traffic lights glittered ahead of him. What could sound better than Professor A. Woods, F.R.S.?

Professor Sir Albert Woods, F.R.S.

On New Year's Day Albert had luncheon at the Athenaeum with his father-in-law.

Somehow those members of the club whose names had appeared in the Honours List happened to drop in for luncheon that day: somehow they happened to be standing modestly near the doorway as their friends, not to mention their rivals, came in. It was a happy scene. There was no discordant air due to the presence of members who had hoped for honours and had not received them: somehow they appeared to have gone elsewhere for luncheon.

Albert was entirely at his ease. A hint from one of the members of the council of the society had finally set his mind at rest about his election to the Royal Society. He was able to feel unalloyed delight in his father-in-law's triumph. And his name was down for election to membership of the Athenaeum, proposed by Dibdin and seconded by Jameson.

Albert and Dibdin met Jameson inside the small room, standing sipping a glass of sherry a considerable distance from the doorway as if to show that he had been a Sir for a long time. His pink face beamed, his silver-grey hair shone, his bright eyes darted from face to face.

'A million congratulations!' he said to Dibdin, as if no one had the slightest idea it was he who was chiefly responsible for Dibdin's being honoured.

While they were shaking hands the Principal of Albert's university college came in with a dazzling pompous smile. He had been knighted, too. He kept throwing back his head and bowing. He bowed to Jameson.

Jameson bowed cordially back and turned to Albert.

'I haven't seen the list,' he said, lying gloriously, 'but they tell me your Principal got a plain K and was hoping for K.B.E.' He paused. 'They say he's an ambitious man. What do you think?'

'It's not ambition.' Albert threw back his head and mimicked the Principal's favourite phrase. 'It's illumination.' Somehow Albert contrived fleetingly to look like the Principal.

Jameson could not resist such an occasion to be indiscreet.

'Between ourselves,' he said, 'the only sound thing he ever did was to appoint you professor of chemistry.'

'I thought I had you to thank for that,' Albert said.

Jameson smiled at Dibdin. 'In that case I think an O.B.E. would have been sufficient for him, don't you?' He made the remark quietly lest it should be heard by a passing member who had just got an O.B.E. and was smirking like the rest.

At that moment the whole company was hushed. It was for the entry of a member of the central organization of a political party who had just become a Lord.

Dibdin and his friends drank their sherry and went to the dining-room. As they were crossing the hall a porter came out of his office and spoke to Albert.

'A gentleman's just been trying to get in touch with you on the telephone, sir. A Dr Callandar-Smith.'

'Callandar-Smith?' said Albert.

'That's the name he gave, sir.'

Suddenly Albert laughed and turned to Dibdin. 'Clinton's changed his name.'

Clinton wanted Albert to dine with him that night at the Oxford and Cambridge Club.

'I think Callandar-Smith is an improvement,' said Dibdin mischievously, as they went on their way.

A faint look of irritation passed over the surface of Albert's smile. 'We ought to have realized Clinton's one of those men who can't let his name alone. I wonder if he'll drop the Smith altogether.'

'To be or not to be,' said Dibdin. 'There are so many names to choose from. What's in a name?'

Albert shook his head. He wondered what on earth Clinton wanted him for.

Although Margaret was expecting him to spend the rest of New Year's day with her, Albert hurried along Pall Mall that evening to the Oxford and Cambridge Club. As he entered he saw Clinton waiting for him at the top of the steps.

Clinton was wearing a very handsome dark suit and a light blue shirt. Although he was now forty-two he had put on no more weight. Barrel-torsoed and vigorous, he stepped lightly down to shake hands with Albert. His hair was turning grey and was still cropped close to his rounded skull. His eyes kept their full hooded look, and his gold fillings glittered and his beak gave him a touch of the eagle.

Albert, fat and slightly out of breath, smiled spontaneously with old friendship.

'I was delighted to hear from you, Clinton.' Albert stopped his spectacles slipping down his nose and looked closely at Clinton. 'I'm looking forward to having a talk with you.'

They were now at the top of the stairs. Suddenly Clinton faced Albert and gave him his piercing unchanging stare.

'There's going to be another war.'

Albert's nice flow of social feeling was brought to a sudden stop. He did not speak.

Clinton led him first to the lavatory. While they were washing their hands Albert looked at Clinton through the looking-glass over the wash-basins.

'I imagine you didn't bring me here just to tell me there was going to be a war.'

It was Clinton's turn not to speak. He gave Albert in return a characteristic stare.

They left the lavatory. Clinton said: 'I'm going into the dining-room straight away. Where we can be alone.'

They went into the dining-room and Clinton insisted on taking a table in the corner which had been reserved for someone else. As he sat down he glanced round to judge whether any of the members near by might be within earshot. He ordered martinis to be brought while they were waiting for their soup.

Albert behaved with an easy unhurried manner. Clinton said:

'You know when I was over at I.G., I had some stimulating talks with Schraeder?' A slight humourless smile momentarily drew down the corners of his mouth. 'We won't go into how much of his work was inspiration and how much Teutonic method.' The smile was a good-tempered gibe at one of their past tiffs, in which Albert had claimed impartially that Clinton's research was an example of Teutonic method and his own an example of inspiration.

Albert could not resist showing off his knowledge of Callandars' trade-secret affairs.

'Of course, Clinton. That's how your insecticide division came to be following its present line. I should like to congratulate you on it, if I may.'

Clinton was silent. Suddenly he said:

'How much more do you know?'

'I know you decided to play about with phosphonium compounds – among others – that have asymmetric side-chains. Instead of being like everybody else and doing the symmetrical ones first.' He looked at Clinton. 'I should think it was a useful plan.' He smiled. 'I can see from your face it was a useful plan. Have you come across one that makes a really first-class insecticide?'

Clinton glanced round as if he expected to find a spy at his elbow. He saw the waiter bringing their soup. They paused till the man had gone, lifted their spoons and did not eat. Clinton gave Albert a compelling stare, so that Albert knew it was something compared with which his own guess was trivial.

'Last week one of our men who was messing about in the lab' – Clinton's tone was stiff with emphasis – 'began to see double.'

'Good Lord!' Albert burst into a laugh that stopped short.

They stared at each other. It was the longest stare of their lives.

What Clinton meant was this. The compound which was intended to affect the central nervous system of an insect was powerful enough to affect that of a man.

Both Clinton and Albert thought there was going to be a war.

What was passing through their minds is obvious.

Albert spoke only what was on the periphery of his thoughts: 'Who is he?'

'You don't know him – we only took him on a week ago. He's just an assistant, I tell you.' Clinton drew in his breath impatiently. 'He didn't even know what it meant. He went and asked the First Aid people if he'd got migraine.'

'Does it make *you* see double?'

Clinton nodded.

'Are Schraeder's people likely to have got it?' Albert said.

'They can't have missed it.'

'I wonder how long ago.'

'Your guess is as good as mine.'

There was a long pause. The waiter came near, seeing that they were not eating. Their plates were still half full. He went away again. Albert said to Clinton:

'Why are you telling me all this?'

'I want to know,' said Clinton, 'if you're willing to take the thing over.' He made a curt gesture with his hand. 'Wait!'

'It's out of the – '

'Wait, I said. You must take my word for it that it's beyond the scope of Callandars. The incident happened only a few days ago. We're not even certain what it was that caused the man's diplopia. But I've got a hunch I'd bet on. You see?'

'Why don't you do it yourself?'

'Do you think I haven't thought of that? I'm the only man in the firm who could.'

'Of course you are, Clinton.'

Clinton said: 'It needs the full time of somebody who's first class – more than first-class. I just can't do it and run the firm's research as well.'

'I'm sorry.' Albert shook his head and picked up some food.

'What are you sorry about?'

'That you've got to look elsewhere.'

'Look here, Woods, you've got to do it.'

'Don't try and bully me, Clinton. I'm not going to be bullied by anyone. Least of all by you.'

Clinton gave a snort of anger. He waved to the waiter. 'Why don't you bring the next course? Can't you see we're waiting for it?' He began to pour out some wine into Albert's glass, remembered he had not tasted the small quantity in his own glass, tried it, and then went on pouring.

'I gathered,' Clinton said, 'you're just about to embark on a new line of research – '

'How did you know that?'

' – Why not make it this?' Clinton ignored the interruption. 'It's something new. It's going to be damned fundamental.'

'I can see that for myself.'

'And you've got Grevel, haven't you?'

Albert's face reddened. 'I don't like the tone of that, Smith. I beg your pardon, Callandar-Smith.'

'Sorry.' Clinton picked up his glass. 'Try some of this. It's not bad.'

Albert tasted the wine. He tasted it again. His face changed its expression as he rolled the wine round his palate.

'It tastes like a Lafite,' he said. 'I should say . . . 1920.'

Clinton grinned.

Albert said. 'I won't be bullied. And I'm damned if I'll be wooed with a bottle of wine, even Lafite 1920.'

'Actually it's 1924.'

'Near enough.'

'Agreed.

They began to eat.

After a time Clinton returned to the charge.

'I know you don't want to take this thing on. But I think you've got to.'

'Why don't you ask someone else?'

'Because you're the best man in the country. I shall only ask someone else if you turn it down. If you do turn it down' – Clinton spoke slowly – 'you're taking on a grave responsibility.'

'It's bloody grave if I take it up!' Albert spoke freely with emotion. 'Don't you see it's bound to be repugnant to me, Clinton?'

'So's war.'

'You're half soldier anyway. I'm not.'

'You could be.' Clinton glanced at him and made a joke. 'Think of Napoleon.'

'Think of Napoleon yourself! We're both small.'

'Agreed,' said Clinton, and filled the glasses again.

'I hope,' Clinton said, 'you won't be rash enough to turn down my offer out of hand.'

Albert did not reply.

'Think it over, Albert.'

There was a long pause.

CHAPTER TWO

WAS HE MAD-HEADED OR DISHONEST?

A lbert took the plunge.
        The first thing Albert did when he went to Wigan and saw the results of the experiments was to harangue Clinton on his lack of enthusiasm.

Then Albert looked at the results a little more closely; and something told him that the organic compound, which did undoubtedly affect the central nervous system of about fifty per cent of a population of mice exposed to it, was probably not a single compound at all but a mixture of two compounds of very similar structure. While still at Wigan he suggested a method for separating them and waited to see it carried out. It was a success. One of the two substances had a seventy per cent higher lethality than the other.

Albert went back to London and asked Dibdin to come and see him. He was certain he was going to have a shot at the problem but he wanted Dibdin to advise him to do so. Dibdin did not advise him to do so. Dibdin listened with interest, made a number of suggestions for experiments, and refused to give the slightest hint of whether he would risk his money on success.

Albert next sent for Eli.

Eli listened with interest and suspicion. Albert would have preferred the interest without the suspicion.

Eli said: 'I want to think it over.'

'Of course.' Albert was most gracious. He had not expected Eli to agree on the spot. 'By all means.'

Two days later Eli came back with his answer.

'I can't do it.'

Albert's graciousness forsook him this time. In a bullying tone he said:

'Why not?'

'I don't know enough biochemistry.'

It was the last thing Albert had expected. 'My dear Eli!'

Eli stared at him. There was a slightly burning look in his eye. 'It's true. You know it's true.'

'I know it's completely false. You know as much biochemistry as . . .' Albert spluttered. 'As all the old men in this university.' He fixed Eli with a bulging eye. 'And anyway you can learn it.'

They launched into a long argument in which Albert got nowhere in the direction of proving to Eli that he was sufficiently well equipped to do the research. But willy-nilly they came round to discussing the research itself. And Eli duly brought forth a most ingenious theoretical reason why one of the two similar compounds should be so much more potent than the other. Albert was beside himself with rage, excitement and frustration.

'Don't you see that's enough reason for being confident?' he almost shouted.

'It's enough reason for setting up as a charlatan, if that's what you mean.'

'*This is the opportunity of a lifetime!*'

Eli looked down. After a pause he said: 'I'll think it over again.'

Next morning he came to Albert as near to shame-faced as it was possible for him to be.

'O. K. Woods, you win.'

'Win what?' said Albert.

'The argument we had yesterday.'

'You're going to do it?'

'Yes.'

Albert's face had a look of simmering delight and satisfaction. His spectacles flashed as he glanced at Eli. 'You do agree, it's a fascinating problem, don't you?'

Eli had the nerve to reply: 'I told you that, didn't I?'

They made their plans on the spot.

The gist of their programme was not difficult to understand. It was this. They wanted to make a series of organic compounds of the same type, believing that the farther up the series they went the more active the compound would be. (By active they meant capable of affecting the central nervous system of animals.) The substance which had been brought to light at Callandars was the second member of the series: as yet the others did not exist – they had to be synthesized.

It was a task familiar enough to organic chemists, it is true, of building up organic compounds which the Maker had not seen fit to include in His repertoire. In this case Albert and Eli were taking on a task which the Maker might well have turned down. It was not going to be easy. Yet neither of these two things had the slightest effect of diminishing the excitement they felt at the prospect. Once they had decided to embark on the research their imaginations flared up. They began to buzz like bees.

The problem was mainly a chemical one, and Albert was lucky in having at hand a supply of cheap labour in the shape of three mediocre M.Sc. students. Their biological assays were to be carried out at Callandars.

Eli said: 'I suppose when we show Sir Alfred Callandar how to synthesize the stuff he'll manufacture it and make a fortune.'

'I expect so,' Albert said easily. 'You don't want us to go in for manufacture, do you?'

'I don't believe in Callandar making a fortune out of me.'

'I shouldn't worry about the fortune. I think you can take it that we shall get all the credit we want.'

Eli glanced at him sharply and then grinned. 'Now I wonder what you would be wanting, Professor Woods?' he said.

Albert did not answer for a moment. And then he said with Dibdinesque innocence: 'I suppose it will soon be time we were putting you up for the Royal. . . .'

Into Eli's pale lined face there came the sudden glow of a blush.

Albert and Eli worked with tremendous concentration throughout the spring and summer. At first, when they were planning methods and designing apparatus, it was Albert who was to the fore. But when they got under way it was soon apparent to both of them that it was Eli who was making the running. Albert did not mind – he had always prided himself on his gifts as a catalyst in human affairs. He buzzed round Eli confidently and proprietorially, as much as to say: 'Of course Eli wouldn't be anything without me' – in fact I cannot guarantee that he did not actually say it.

At the same time things were not going so well with Eli. There was nothing wrong with his work – that was going forward with beautiful timing. Eli seemed to be coming into a phase of greater nervous strain. The burning look in his eye appeared more often and Albert suspected that he was not sleeping well. As there

177

appeared to be nothing wrong with Eli's marriage, Albert assumed that he was becoming increasingly worried about European affairs.

Eli synthesized the third compound of the series. It was August 1938.

They collected enough for Callandars to test and sent it to Wigan. They felt exhausted with the tension of waiting for the results – it was no use their having synthesized the third compound if Eli's deduction about its relatively greater activity turned out to be incorrect.

The report from Callandars arrived by an afternoon post. It was a hot airless afternoon and all the windows were wide open. Albert took the letter sealed to Eli's room and opened it in his presence. His hands were trembling. Eli came and looked over his shoulder. The foolscap sheets unfolded.

Eli's deduction had been correct. Complete paralysis of the nervous system had made its appearance.

'What d'yer think of that?' Eli's voice was filled with exultation.

Albert looked at him with glowing eyes and red cheeks. 'It's brilliant.'

There was a pause while they stared at each other.

'We may win a war with this, Eli.'

Eli made no reply at all. At first Albert thought he was going to tear up the sheets of paper in his hand. Instead he sat down to study them again.

Through the open window they heard a news-boy calling a special edition.

'Damnation!' Albert stood hesitant. Then he bustled out and bought a paper.

When he came back his expression had changed. He handed Eli the paper without speaking. Eli read the headlines and swore aloud. They stared at each other again: their exultation was momentarily eclipsed.

Eli said: 'I think you can assume our work's going to be unnecessary.'

'Unnecessary?' Albert cried. 'More necessary than ever!'

'Why?'

'I don't know, but it is.' He moved to Eli's side. 'Let me see these results again.'

He looked at them closely. A new idea had come to him.

Eli watched him with interest. 'What's biting you now, Prof?'

Albert said: 'Eli, I'm not convinced this is good enough. I don't think we can stop here at all.' Eli knew what he was going to say, but he said it all the same. 'I think, to make sure, we've got to go to number four.'

Eli said: 'So you think we've got to go to the fourth, eh?'

'I'm sure of it. You see, Eli – '

Eli interrupted him. 'There's no need to harangue me.'

Albert stopped, crossly. 'Why not?'

'Because I agree.' He tried to mimic Albert. 'To make sure.'

'Then what are you going to do about it?'

Suddenly Eli swept the newspaper off the bench on to the floor.

'Anything you say, Prof. Give the word and off we go!'

There was not a glimmer of a smile on Eli's face. His expression was fixed.

Albert had not been able to resist telling Redvers Jameson about his new experiments. Jameson saw the importance of them instantly. He was not a creative man but he was a first class impresario. He offered to get Albert assistance – the loan of some young scientists from one of the research establishments run by the Government, a grant of money from the Treasury. Albert refused for the simple reason that he did not need them.

'I've spoken to my minister,' Jameson said. 'A word in his ear is all that's necessary.'

'I hope we shall justify your confidence,' Albert said modestly.

'Of course you will,' Jameson said. 'We can hardly wait for it.'

As the months passed Jameson waited with excitement and impatience. There were no results. No one could say that Albert and Eli did not give their research every ounce of their attention. Albert's spirits began to follow the course of their experiments exactly. When things were going ill he was morose: when they were going well he was exultant. Nothing else mattered.

Margaret now knew what Albert was doing. She made no comment. She had been less happy ever since they came to London. She now had another child – it was a second boy. Albert congratulated himself on his wisdom in having filled her life for her, so that he could be free.

There was a reason for Jameson's impatience, apart from his desire to see his *protégé* launched. Interest was focusing on several different scientific projects which might be of use in war. There was secret talk among radio scientists of detecting aeroplanes by the reflection of very short radio waves: it was known that someone had broken the nucleus of an atom into two equal halves instead of merely knocking a bit off it, and the physicists were haunted by a dream of making a fantastically powerful explosion. Scientist-impresarios for these projects, Jameson himself among them, were waiting on defence committees: the Treasury was beginning to hand out money.

Jameson had an immense respect for academic prestige but little respect for academic methods of speeding up research. He wanted to move Albert and Eli out of their small university laboratory and to set them up in research establishments of their own. The sooner they staked their claim the better.

Late in the following summer, just a year after their first success, they had their second. Eli succeeded in making the fourth compound in the series.

They went up to Callandars themselves to see the first biological tests being made, although this time they had no doubts about the results.

The war was imminent. Clinton, as a Territorial, had been called up. Callandars were working overtime manufacturing lewisite: Albert and Eli spent their days of waiting studying the plant. In the distance hot sunshine shimmered over the roofs of Wigan and fighter aeroplanes rushed to and fro.

The first results came in. Albert and Eli were satisfied. Their new compound could be used as a military weapon. They returned to London in great haste. Arrangements were being made to transport different departments of the university college to other universities far from London. In London they found householders being instructed on how to darken their windows at night. There were notices about the distribution to civilians of gas-masks.

Albert and Eli were satisfied. The new substance was a potential military weapon of greater power than any other known lethal gas. Albert saw battalions being put out of action at once, provided the substance could be made in sufficient quantity. He was inflated with hope. He needed to be – their experiments were a great success in that they had achieved a very difficult synthesis, but the success was not complete. Eli's method of synthesis produced a minutely small yield: it could not possibly be multiplied up to produce the substance on a large enough scale to be of any use in war.

Albert reported his success to Redvers Jameson, who was jubilant.

It is only fair to Albert to say that he probably did his best to make it clear to Jameson that the synthesis was successful from an academic but not a practical point of view, but there is no doubt that Jameson did not immediately take the point. Jameson was not a scientist, and he was not familiar with the bane of the organic synthesizer's life – being able to make something but not enough of it for the making to be a practical proposition.

'We can make it. A million congratulations!'

In his joy Albert felt that Jameson was looking at him speculatively, as much as to say 'What reward can be great enough?'

'We can make it,' Albert echoed, truthfully.

It was at this point that Jameson laid before Albert his plan in its full glory – a small secret research establishment in the depths of the country, the cream of the country's young chemists to assist him, all the apparatus he needed. The terms of reference of the research: one, to bring the present method of synthesis up to the pilot-plant stage; two, to try and synthesize more active compounds still.

It was now that Albert should have said Eli's method of synthesis could not be brought up to the pilot-plant stage.

The moment passed without Albert saying anything. Albert was spending it wondering if the successful director of such an establishment would automatically be rewarded with a knighthood – and why not?

'It's important that we should bring this to pass as quickly as possible,' Jameson was saying. 'It's important for you' – he stressed the word 'you' with a cordial meaningful look. 'We've got to sell your nerve-gas to the Chiefs-of-Staff.' He was rather proud of his Americanisms.

Albert's eyes bulged at the thought of the Chiefs-of-Staff thinking he was wonderful.

'I'll start work immediately,' Jameson said.

The prospect was irresistible. 'What steps do you advise me to take?' Albert asked.

Jameson advised a secret memorandum to the Production

Executive Committee, outlining the nature of the discovery, its practical uses, and the probable immediate cost of developing it.

'Am I to take it that a suitable place for us to work will be found?'

'My dear fellow, everybody's being found them. In a few months' time there won't be a country mansion or a boarding school left empty. I won't mention the name of a distinguished scientist who at this very moment is biting my minister's ear, for the purpose of getting himself installed in – ' Even Jameson's indiscretions had their limits and he did not say where.

'I should like my estimate to be modest,' Albert said.

'I congratulate you on that decision. I always said to my minister that we could rely on you for that.' Jameson leaned his shining head a little closer to Albert's. 'But not too modest, I hope. Remember we've got to sell you to the Chiefs-of-Staff.'

Albert went back to his laboratory to think it over.

He found his dilemma heart-rending. How could he estimate his needs for developing the multiplication of a process that was too costly for the purpose and next door to unmultipliable anyway? (Remember that the war was only just beginning and the fashion for going ahead on the minimum basis at astronomical expense had not yet come in.) How? Albert asked himself.

There was, of course, an answer. By instinct.

Now you must not be too ready to laugh. Still less must you prepare to judge what Albert did as something between the foolish and the criminal. Instinct tells a scientist his job half the time.

Instinct told Albert that he and Eli could modify their method of synthesis to be satisfactory as a practical proposition.

'We've got to sell your nerve-gas to the Chiefs-of-Staff . . .' The prospect alone made his spirit swell, while the idea of his work not being sold to the Chiefs-of-Staff made his spirit trail its feet.

That Albert did not discuss what he was thinking with Eli or Margaret was symptomatic of what he was going to do. In a trance of glory and fright he cast the die.

It was not the first time a scientist had confidently said he had done some experiments when he had not. Albert was convinced they could be done after the event if they had not been done before. How could he lead the country to victory through chemistry if he failed to carry the day at this point?

And so the event was defined: it was the writing of a memorandum addressed to the Production Executive Committee. Impelled by a passionate belief that there was a kind of truth that superseded factual verity, Albert incorporated in his memorandum a summary of some experiments that had not been performed.

Albert dispatched his memorandum to Jameson in a fit of exultation.

Albert was summoned to appear at a meeting of the committee to be held at once. He was told he could then expect a summons from an even greater, even higher committee forthwith.

CHAPTER THREE
CRISIS

Albert returned triumphantly from the second committee meeting to his laboratory. He found Eli there. Eli was sitting with his back to the door, reading some papers.

'I'm glad to find you here.' Albert strode across the room and hung up his hat and brief-case.

'I was waiting for you.' Eli looked up with a white face. Albert had a shock. He was a courageous man, but Eli's expression took all the courage out of him at one blow. 'Sit down, Perfessor Woods.'

Albert sat down.

Eli suddenly held up the papers. 'What yer got to say about this?'

The papers were a copy of Albert's memorandum.

Albert tried to take the memorandum from Eli's hand. Eli snatched it away.

'Where did you get it?' said Albert.

Eli let out a harsh laugh. 'If that isn't a prize answer to the queshun! You're a remarkable man, Perfessor Woods.'

'If one's been betrayed, Eli, the first thing one always asks is by whom.' Albert fixed Eli with a mild unblinking stare. The fact that he was in a weak moral position did not in the least deter him from trying to adopt a weighty moral tone.

'So you'd like to know where I got it, eh?'

'If you'll let me have a look at it, I might be able to tell. The copies are all numbered.' Albert paused.

'You're cool.'

'That's more than you appear to be, Eli.'

'Very cool.'

'As a matter of fact, I'm far from cool. I'm gravely alarmed.'

'So you recognize this thing's a fake.'

'I don't recognize anything of the kind. I recognize that you're in a mood to try and do me a grave injury.'

'Don't you think I'm justified?'

Albert said: 'One's rarely justified in doing a fellow human being a grave injury, Eli, whatever the apparent grounds.'

'Apparent?' Eli cried. 'Do you think this isn't real? Can't I read?'

'I'm sure you can read.'

'This document is a fake.'

There was a silence. The redness faded from Albert's cheeks.

'You . . . Perfessor Woods, are a phoney.'

Albert was silent.

'This memorandum proves you're a phoney.'

Albert said nothing.

Eli put the memorandum on the bench beside him, then changed his mind and threw it into Albert's lap. 'It's all right,' he said in a quiet menacing voice. 'I always knew you were a phoney.'

Albert was terrified. He thought Eli had only to give him away to Redvers Jameson for his career in affairs to be ruined.

'The question now is what other people will say when they know you're a phoney.'

'Have you told anyone?'

Eli turned a piercing neurotic look on him. 'You'd like to know.'

Albert said: 'I think I have a right to know. I have a right to know what I must defend myself against.' He put all his weight into the tone in which he said it, and again looked at Eli unwinkingly.

With a quick flicker of his eyelids Eli wavered. 'As a matter of fact I haven't made up my mind yet, who to tell first.'

'I see.' Albert was curt, but the colour flooded slowly back into his face.

'I don't want to go to prison,' Eli said.

Albert was startled.

Eli said: 'People go to prison for trying to get money by false pretences, don't they? You've asked for money from the government.'

'You must be out of your mind, Eli.' It crossed Albert's mind that he was speaking the literal truth about Eli.

'You've associated my name with this swindle, haven't you?'

Albert did not reply to him.

'Answer me.'

'The only answer is that money is entirely secondary, as you well know, Eli. If you don't, you're more unrealistic about life than ever I imagined. What matters is our scientific reputations.'

'Do you mean to say you really think about that? Do you realize this move will ruin my scientific reputation?'

Albert grew angry. 'Look here, Eli, I'm tired of this. If you can't conduct yourself above this childish level you'd better leave this affair to someone who can.'

'When I do leave, it's going to be the end of your prospects. And before I go, you're going to hear some home-truths about yourself, Mr Woods.'

'I think I know more about myself than you do. I understand myself perfectly. I doubt if you understand yourself. I doubt if you understand your motives in doing what you're just about to do.' He stopped Eli interrupting. 'Oh yes, I can see perfectly well what you're going to do – I could, even if I didn't understand you so well. You're going to ruin my career in affairs – not my career as a scientist' – Albert tapped the memorandum with his knuckles – 'There's nothing wrong with the research described here, that we've actually done – '

'As distinct from that described there that we actually haven't,' Eli shouted.

'It's enough to make our reputations, if we hadn't made them already. Yes, Eli, yes!' Albert's emotion grew. 'Think what you're throwing away, if you ruin our life's-work now.'

'What?' Eli looked astounded.

'This research is superb, Eli. You'd be the first to admit it.' Albert almost succeeded in smiling at him. 'After all you did it yourself. We did it jointly. It's superb.'

'I did it myself – we did it jointly! What's that mean?'

'Never mind,' Albert went on. 'I was telling you some of the things you ought to know – things you ought to know about yourself, your motives in doing what you're going to do.' The moral fervour in his voice swelled. 'You can't harm the research we've done together. You can only prevent it bearing fruit. To enable it to bear fruit I had to take a risk. And you're going to prevent that risk coming off. You want to ruin my career in affairs out of envy and pique – '

'Pique!' Eli screamed as if he were going to explode. 'Envy! Envy of you!'

'Yes,' said Albert. 'Envy of my power to carry it off.'

Eli was a very clever young man, but for the moment he simply did not know where to start arguing. Against this disorderly farrago of psychological sense and nonsense, a training in rabbinical disputation was entirely useless. What is more, at this particular juncture there was something in what Albert was saying. Eli said:

'You're hoping to try and carry it off in my name as well as your own. You've faked some results in my name. In my name!' His voice rose. 'You've put your own name on some of my work and my name on some that I haven't done, that nobody's done. You've stolen my true research, and you've faked my, my . . .'

'Future research.'

'You're just one big —— swindler!'

'There seem to be two things you've got against me, Eli. Let's take them in turn. It will be better for us to be orderly. You say I've stolen your research. That's what the junior partner in a collaboration always says of the senior. It's probably true – but it's the way of the world, Eli.' Albert paused for an instant. 'If you hadn't wanted to collaborate, you needn't have. It was only out of arrogance that you did, in the hope of becoming as good an experimenter as me. I think you have become as good an experimenter as me. After these last three years most people would put you in a class higher than they did before.'

Eli was staring down at the floor. His face was contorted with anger.

'As for the second charge, that I've put your name to work we haven't done yet . . . Are you going to give me a chance to defend myself?'

'Have you got no idea of scientific integrity?'

'A very strong one, Eli. Will you listen to why I decided to do this?'

'I suppose I've got to.'

Albert began his explanation. In the ears of a detached listener it would have seemed to score higher marks for opportunism than for integrity. That is beside the point. Albert's explanation was notable for a fair degree of honesty: certainly it was lacking neither in reason nor in conviction. He delivered it with enthusiasm.

'Now you see why I did it,' he ended up. His confidence had momentarily returned under the influence of his own powers of exposition. He spoke to Eli in a fine, sweeping manner. 'One has to take some risks, my dear Eli.'

Eli looked up. 'Thanks,' he said, 'for a first-class lesson in chicanery.'

Albert was taken aback.

'But haven't I carried you with me?' he said, off his balance.

'Like hell you have!' Eli stood up. 'I've heard enough. If that's what it means to succeed in affairs, as you call them, then it's time I got out. Nothing you've said, Woods, has made the slightest difference.'

'Don't be a fool, man. With a major war beginning there's no time for high-minded integrity.'

There was a pause. Albert said:

'Look here, Eli, I'll make you an offer. Will you postpone the break between us if I ask Jameson to withdraw the memorandum?'

'Is this a bribe?' Eli turned on him with surprise.

Albert lowered his gaze. He remembered the time he had to withdraw an opinion given by Dibdin. It was an idiotic suggestion.

'Withdraw it indefinitely?' Eli said.

'No, no. Just put it into cold storage until we've done the experiments.' He made a powerful effort to sound persuasive. 'After all, the experiments can be done. I'm convinced you can do them.' He nodded his head for emphasis.

'That's what you think.'

Albert looked up quickly, very quickly indeed.

'I beg your pardon, Eli?'

'I said that's what you think. And that's what I mean.'

'But of course they can be done.' Albert's face began to redden. 'It's only a matter of time.'

'I'm glad to hear it. For your sake.'

'Why for my sake?'

'Because in that case you'll be able to get out of the hole you've got into.'

'I shall?' Albert almost stammered. 'But the point of the offer was that we should go on working together.'

'Working together!' Eli suddenly burst into a cackle of laughter. It was a frightening thing to hear. Albert even looked frightened. 'I don't intend to work with you again, even if I thought it was any use. In this case, my dear Perfessor, I know it isn't any use. I don't think the thing can be done.'

'What?' Albert's mouth opened and closed again. At last he managed to say, 'Have you been thinking about it?'

'What else do you think I've been thinking about ever since we got back from Callandars?' Eli paused. 'I'm glad you think it can be done, because frankly I don't know how.'

They stared at each other in rage, wonderment and a kind of deep frustration.

Albert said: 'Good God!'

Eli said each word separately: 'I . . . don't . . . know . . . how.' In Albert's ears it sounded like the four cracks of doom.

Eli was still standing up. Suddenly he swivelled away.

'I'm going,' he said, without looking back at Albert.

'Just a moment, Eli.'

'Yes?' Eli paused.

'Would it be asking too much to ask you what steps you propose to take about this?' Albert pointed to the memorandum.

'Oh that?' A flicker of contempt displaced the look of mingled hatred and unhappiness on Eli's face. 'Nothink.' Seeing that Albert did not comprehend – 'No steps at all.'

'I still don't understand, Eli.'

'Just to show you you don't know what you're talking about when you talk about envy and pique, I'm not going to ruin your little gamble for you.' Inexplicably he laughed. 'It'd be beneath my dignity.'

'Then what? . . .'

'Nothink, see? No steps at all. Walk out. *Fini.*'

Albert saw exactly what he meant.

Eli said: 'From now on, you're on your own. You can fabricate a whole organic chemistry of your own and sell it to the King of —— for fifty million pounds.' His tone became serious and bitter. 'You think this particular job can be done, in fact you've said we've done it.' He paused. 'Now do it.'

Albert was unable to reply.

Eli finished up: 'I shall keep my mouth shut. It won't need me to tell the world what sort of scientist you are.'

At that Eli walked out of the room.

'Onward and upward, Woods!' Albert saw nothing for it now but backward and downward. The dream of glory had suddenly changed to the prospect of public disgrace.

To try and withdraw the memorandum immediately would give the show away immediately. The memorandum not having been withdrawn, the show would give itself away, Albert calculated, in about three or four months' time. He had not sufficiently accounted for Redvers Jameson's enthusiasm in his calculation. The day after Eli's defection Jameson rang up.

'Our affairs are going swimmingly,' he announced. 'We've got the ear of none other than – ' he dropped his voice as he uttered the name.

Albert's heart dropped correspondingly.

'I thought you'd like to know.'

'I'm very grateful to you for letting me know.'

Jameson's cordiality was momentarily checked by Albert's formal tone, but only momentarily. 'I think,' he said, 'we shall get our little estimate through much more quickly than we'd imagined.'

Albert felt as if his tongue were sticking to the roof of his mouth. He saw three or four months going down to one or two. 'How quickly?' he cried. 'How quickly?'

'We shall very soon know.' Jameson was too cautious to give a date. 'But you shall be relieved of your anxiety at the first possible moment, my dear Woods. Be assured of that.'

'Yes, I'm very sure of that.'

'You can be certain that things couldn't be going better for you and your young colleague. By the way you have my permission, my encouragement, to tell Dr Grevel what I've just told you.'

Albert said: 'I'm going to tell him immediately. I know he'll be delighted.'

Satisfied, Jameson almost sang his goodbyes.

Eli had disappeared from the laboratory: Albert had no idea where he was.

I suppose this is where, were I a different man living in a different age, I should pause and draw a moral.

The little man had overreached himself. 'Vanity, vanity,' I should cry, 'All is vanity!' Or more properly, 'Megalomania, megalomania, all is megalomania!' All I can say is, try crying 'Megalomania, megalomania, all is megalomania!' yourself and see if you care as much as all that for what is more proper. You find it easier to get your tongue round the cry about vanity? Of course. And so you take the easier path. That is what Albert did.

The result of overreaching oneself through vanity or through megalomania is disaster and disgrace. No causal chain could be simpler than that. Everybody can understand it, so it must be extremely simple.

Unfortunately I cannot say that Albert understood it. The concept of simple causality ruled his scientific research of course: on the other hand it was singularly lacking in power over his private affairs. To have a strong sense of simple causality in one's private affairs one needs to have a clear idea of what one did in the past and what one is going to do in the future – one causes the other, so to speak. Albert Woods had an unusually feeble sense of both: he had a strong, a powerful and glorious sense of what he was doing in the present, instead. What he had done in the past – *autre temps, autre mœurs!* What he was going to do in the future – ah, the wonderful proliferating haze of it! But what he was doing in the present, the marvellous, ever-changing flux of the present moment, was a different matter altogether: it filled the whole of his existence.

Albert was not such a fool that he did not see that his over-developed sense of the present and his under-developed sense of the past and the future were likely to get him into trouble. That is why his life was a long struggle against what he thought of as his mad-headedness. Mad-headedness meant acting in the present, regardless of all else. But alas, if the only hold one has over an exuberant temperament is an intellectual hold, the prognosis is poor. One is likely to get into trouble, one does get into trouble, and one wishes afterwards that one had not got into trouble.

Sometimes Albert's mad-headedness got the better of him: sometimes he got the better of it. Yet even so I doubt if he saw the moral principle of his struggles as clearly as one would wish, both for the sake of his own eternal soul and of the example he might set to others. What he did see as clearly as anyone could was the expediency of struggling, and somehow nobody seems to find expediency half so edifying as moral principle.

So the fact of the matter is that for all his downfalls, Albert did not see that megalomania always leads to over-reaching oneself and that gambling always leads to losing one's shirt.

If it comes to that, do they?

Albert sat in his laboratory, abandoned to concentrated thought. He did not blame his own temperament for his disastrous straits. He blamed Eli. He did not see that he had failed to control himself. He thought Eli had gone mad.

Albert was convinced that Eli could save him. His gamble on the results of experiments not yet performed had not been made on the basis of a mixture of ambition with sheer irresponsibility. He would have backed his judgement on it, and for all his faults Albert's scientific judgement was both sound and sensible – if anything, sounder and more sensible than Eli's.

'I'd have backed my judgement on it,' Albert kept repeating obstinately to himself at regular intervals through the day and through the night. For he could not sleep. And what is more he had begun to have serious indigestion.

Eli had disappeared. Albert did not try to find him.

The trouble was that Eli's synthesis as it stood was just about on the limits of what Albert could grasp. He saw what Eli had done in a practical sense, but Eli's theoretical insight he had never really shared. Albert had boasted that Eli was nothing without him: he now had an opportunity to dwell on what he was without Eli. It was all very well to pride himself on being the catalyst: catalysts do not necessarily know what is going on in the rest of the reaction. Albert studied Eli's notes. He thought he would have to give up. He began to look pale and puffy. He was trailing his feet.

Albert did not tell Margaret what was the matter. They had been discussing whether she and the children ought to leave London for safety. Margaret did not want to go. Distracted and wretched Albert decided they must go. He wanted to be by himself.

Margaret agreed after long tiring arguments. They were constantly receiving invitations to go and live at Daunton, partly because Lord Daunton had a strong desire to preserve his great-grandchildren and partly because he did not want the house to be filled with strangers from the slums of Bristol.

There was a moment when Albert was afraid Margaret was going to weep. He was filled with compassion and embraced her tenderly.

'Perhaps it won't last long,' he said.

'Of course it will.' Even woe could not prevent Margaret from capably assessing the length of the war.

Albert said: 'My dear, we can't help it.'

Suddenly Margaret looked at him penetratingly. Her deep-running pride and loyalty were swamped by her longing for him. She struggled to prevent the tears welling into her eyes. All her unspoken accusations of the last two years passed between them at one glance. Of course she had been right about their coming to London, and this proved it. Not in her harshest drawl could she have said more clearly: 'You're sending me away because your life is full without me.'

Albert thinking of his own secret troubles, felt ill-judged.

'I love you, Albert,' she said. 'I love you.'

At this moment their elder boy came into the room. He had dark hair and bulging eyes like Albert's. A curious look of embarrassment came over his face as he saw them embracing, and they broke apart. Both Albert and Margaret turned to watch him, as they often did.

Margaret said in a flat voice: 'I'll write and tell D. we're coming. Mama will be pleased, anyway.'

And so a few days later Albert was left alone in London. It was now definite that the university college was going to be broken up and transported elsewhere, but he refused to have his laboratory touched. He did not know why he could not bear to have his laboratory disturbed, even though he was doing no good by merely sitting at his desk, hour after hour, interrupting his thoughts only to go out and buy newspapers which he merely glanced at. His deflation had reached its limit.

And then, somehow through sheer accumulation of physical energy his spirit began to perk up a little, he knew why he would not let them touch his laboratory. It was because he intended to have a shot at solving the problem himself.

It is difficult to try and convey to someone who has never done research what it is like to do it. Up to now I have just said that Albert or Eli or Dibdin did research and let it go at that. It seems a pity not to try and convey more.

At this crisis in his career Albert had everything against him that a man going in for research would try and avoid. Face to face with the unknown he had no option on which bit of it he must try and illuminate. Usually the beginning of a piece of research is when something strikes a spark on one's imagination: something one does not know seems a particularly fascinating thing to try and find out. Partly the thing itself seems important and fascinating in its own right, partly one has intimations that one can find it out. That is where the spark comes in – the intimation that one actually can find it out gives one a particular thrill that is irresistible. There is a flash, and as with love one knows that one is in it.

Now whether or not it is possible to put into words what one feels at the start, when the spark catches, when the thrill traps one completely, there is nowhere near as much difficulty about putting into words what happens next. One falls into a state to which psychologists give the label with so little provocation that they have made it sound absurd – obsessional.

The sort of research that Albert or Eli did was obsessional. It means that once you have started on it you cannot let it alone, that you could scream at the idea of having to think about anything else, that the only end you can see to it is when it is complete and perfect.

Albert had two things against him: the first, that he could not just lay himself open for something to strike a spark on him – he had got to strike a spark on it; the second, that his obsession could not take its natural course – completion and perfection had got to be reached in a couple of months if not earlier. That is what comes of overreaching yourself. And life is not made easier if you have to go to committees in the meantime where people congratulate you on having done the job.

Albert fell into the obsessional state. It was a relief that Margaret had gone away. It was almost a relief that circumstances prevented his discussing his research with anyone else. He had a bed made up in the laboratory so that he could stay and work through the night.

Albert's obsessional state was of the highest quality: one cannot say the same for the research he did in the earlier stages. He worked on the principle that any experiments are better than none. There were several standard approaches to the problem and Albert tried them all, though he was pretty certain that Eli had discarded them out of hand. He got nowhere, save that by following the paths Eli had rejected he came to understand how Eli had arrived at his theoretical judgement.

Curiously it pleased Albert: he felt a little proud of himself. He now understood perfectly how to synthesize the substance he wanted in quantities too small to be useful, but he was on equal terms with Eli. In fact the longer he thought about it the more he suspected that chance had played a greater part in Eli's discovery than Eli had calculated.

Also Albert saw something else, again not unfamiliar to organic chemists, that discovering a way of synthesizing a substance in large quantities could be a more difficult problem than synthesizing it at all in the first place. In fact it could be of a quite different order of difficulty. The more he thought of Eli's method the more certain he became that in this case Eli's was probably a minor discovery whereas what was required was something much more like a major one.

Albert quailed at the prospect. And yet, in spite of his fear, it roused in him a dreadful nervous excitement. He tried to be matter-of-fact with himself about it. Eli had said: 'It won't need me to tell the world what sort of a scientist you are!'

'If I succeed in this,' Albert framed his reply, 'I'll be a better scientist than you.'

The work went on. There is nothing much more that I can say to describe it. Days, weeks, passed. The lights in the laboratory came on and went off. Old sounds ceased, new ones started – pumps, condensers, fans, stirrers. Old chemical scents faded out, new ones wafted up – Albert's eyes had acquired a steady diplopia but it is doubtful if his nose was functioning at all. On the other hand his indigestion was much worse.

And so at last he came to the end of the crisis. His confidence for no apparent reason had been steadily rising.

Suddenly Albert found himself in the throes of the truly creative moment. He happened to be waiting for a kettle to boil to make himself a cup of tea.

His thoughts were far away, and suddenly inspiration blew through his mind like a strong sweet sound. It was utterly recognizable and utterly satisfying. He had suddenly seen the whole of his problem in a completely different way. Though the creative moment was not unfamiliar to him, he was astounded by it. He had seen something new. He had seen things that already existed from a different place.

'That's the way I'll do it,' he cried aloud.

Suppose you are looking down on a town from a range of hills and from where you are you see a higgledy-piggledy mass of towers and roof-tops. Suddenly you are swooped – the motion is important – to a different point whence you look down and see the streets and squares in all the beauty of an ordered pattern. Spellbound and triumphant are the only words I can think of.

Spellbound and triumphant Albert was watching his kettle boil.

'That's the way I'll do it!'

He made his tea. He was completely filled with elation. He took down his tin of stomach powder and unhesitatingly put a spoonful into his tea in place of sugar. It was joy that quite superseded any other experience he had ever had.

'That's the way I'll do it!' He *knew* that he was right. Before he lifted a finger to his apparatus, he knew that the job was done. It almost seemed unnecessary, even tiresome to do the experiments. The elation that permeated every fibre of his body told him that the experiments were done. *Woods's Synthesis* – that is how it would always be known. It was brilliant and it was entirely his.

Woods's Synthesis! Albert put a teaspoonful of sugar into a glass, added a little water and took it in place of stomach-powder.

Then in a dream, a methodical, energetic waking dream, Albert set to work. His new idea meant that he had to build new apparatus and begin all over again. Day after day the elation persisted, and at last he realized completely what had not been clear to him in the first instance, that his new idea was a universal one. Eli's synthesis had been an odd chance: Eli's key was one which opened one door only. Albert's was a master-key to hosts of doors: it would make a host of syntheses possible. *Woods's Synthesis* – the name of Woods would be known for ever.

At last he was ready to set the experiment going again. He waited. At last, at the end of his fantastic system of condensers and flasks, heaters and coolers, the liquid he wanted began to accumulate.

He was right.

CHAPTER FOUR

DIFFERENT RECONCILIATIONS

The first thing Albert felt compelled to do now was to boast. Unfortunately there was no one to whom he could boast without giving himself away. No one? There was one person. Eli.

Albert's experiments were by no means over. He did not have time to try and find Eli. But his obsession had relaxed. He began to wonder if he might not risk telling the whole story to his father-in-law or Clinton.

A few days later the temptation was put directly before him. Clinton rang him up in London.

They met as before for dinner at Clinton's club. Clinton was waiting for Albert at the top of the steps. And this time Clinton was dressed in the uniform of a Colonel. His brass buttons were glittering and he looked as if he had blown out his chest to catch more light on his ribbons from the last war. His hair was shorter and his moustache thicker. For an instant Albert felt his own glory in eclipse.

'I thought it was time we got together.' Clinton shook hands and gave him a fine brief military smile.

'I'm delighted to see you.' Albert was speaking no less than the truth.

Clinton dropped his eyelids with manly modesty. He must have thought Albert was impressed by his rank.

They went towards the cloak-room. Clinton glanced sideways at Albert and spoke in a low voice.

'I've got a damned interesting job.'

Albert waited.

Clinton looked over his shoulder. 'I'm being groomed to take over chemical warfare from the army side.' In spite of himself his voice swelled with pride.

'Oh,' said Albert silkily: 'Not a fighting job this time?'

Clinton's face went dark. 'The only fighting job worth having in this war will be in the air. I'm too old for that.'

'How old are you, Clinton?'

'Four years older than you.'

'You don't look it.' Albert felt inclined to please him. Clinton hated getting old.

'I'm not going to say whether you do or not.' They were striding down a corridor again, Albert moving fatly but still with a relic of his former bounce. Clinton glanced at him. Albert's dark silky hair had disappeared from his forehead, and though that made him look older the concentration of his features into a smaller part of his face made him still seem curiously youthful. At the moment he had a puffy seedy look.

'You look pretty shagged,' said Clinton. 'Work?'

Albert suddenly breathed deeply. There was a pause for a moment. And then he said:

'Of course.'

'What are you on at the moment?'

Albert said: 'The same thing, actually.'

'How's it going?'

Albert's cheeks lost their puffy seedy look as he blushed. 'Superbly.'

They went into the bar.

Albert said: 'Who's going to run Callandars while you're away?'

'I want to ask your advice on that.' Clinton ordered two dry martinis without asking Albert what he would like – Albert would have liked sherry. 'It isn't certain whether we'll be able to carry on with much original research.' Suddenly he looked at Albert. 'I'm wondering whether to offer it to Grevel.'

Albert caught the flicker of cunning in Clinton's expression. He thought 'Smith's trying it on.' Clinton caught the flicker of cunning in Albert's expression.

'Would he be tempted by Wigan?'

Clinton said: 'He seems to be satisfied with it at the moment.'

Albert's face went scarlet. 'At the moment?'

Clinton said: 'What's the matter?'

Albert spluttered into his glass as if the drink were choking him. He took out his handkerchief and wiped the lapels of his jacket.

Clinton was unusually solicitous in any kind of physical mishap.

'I'm sorry.' Albert now brought himself to face Clinton again. 'To return to our conversation . . .'

'Grevel.'

'Yes, Grevel.'

'Would you offer it Grevel, if you were me?'

'Considering the offers we've both made Grevel in the past,' Albert said, and a smile came into his eyes, 'I should say yes.'

'Yes?' Clinton looked as if he thought there was a catch in it.

'Yes.' Albert's smile broadened. 'I shan't quarrel with you over him. I have no offer to make him. If you have, make it. My advice oughtn't to carry any weight one way or the other.'

'Why not?'

'Because I've no idea what Grevel's reply would be.'

Clinton was silent. Suddenly he burst into his neighing laugh. 'That's damned amusing.'

Albert restrained himself. Two days later he was rewarded. Eli walked into the laboratory. He entered with a confident athletic stride, his head thrust forward and his eyes bright.

'I s'pose you didn't expect to see me?'

'I expected to see you some time, Eli, though I confess not now.' At a glance Albert saw that he was in a much less neurotic state.

Eli was carrying a brief-case. He put it down on one of the side-benches, took out a sheaf of papers and handed them to Albert.

'Perhaps these'll interest you. That's why I've come.' He laughed. 'A present for you, Perfessor.'

'Thank you.' Albert still did not know what they were, when his glance fell on the first page.

Eli had gone to Callandars and done the same piece of research as Albert.

Albert furled over the pages and a smile hovered round his lips.

'This is very interesting, Eli.' He looked up. 'Why are you presenting them to me?'

'To save your bacon for you, I suppose. I don't know why I should . . .'

Albert adjusted his spectacles and looked at Eli with grave interest – Eli was clearly put out by the scrutiny. 'It isn't difficult for me,' he said, 'to see why you should.' Albert now favoured him with a particularly fatherly expression. 'You wanted to show me that you could do it.'

'I told you it was impossible.' Eli sat down on a chair opposite Albert. 'I've done the impossible.'

'That indicates a certain changeableness of . . . what shall we say, opinion, Eli?'

There was a pause. Eli was waiting for the burst of Albert's applause and gratitude.

'I take it I'm not too late?' he said.

'What for?' said Albert, as if he did not know.

'To save your bacon.'

Albert paused deliberately. 'My dear Eli, I'm afraid you are too late.'

'What!' Eli jumped up. 'Damnation! I couldn't get it done any faster. I can't be too late . . . Do you mean to say you're not slick enough to carry it off now?'

Albert silently handed the papers back. Then he said: 'Thank you, Eli. I appreciate your efforts to help me.'

'But look at them, look at them!' Eli cried. 'Aren't you interested to see how I did it?'

Albert fairly licked his lips with satisfaction before he delivered his blow. 'My dear Eli, I know. As a matter of fact I did it myself.'

Eli looked as if he were going to speak, stopped incredulously, then thrust his face close to Albert's and stared into his eyes. 'Even you,' he said, 'are not as big a liar as that. O.K. I believe you. You must have done it.' He sat back again and meditated.

'So,' Eli said at last. 'I've made a fool of myself, eh?'

'Yes, Eli.'

Eli thought it over. 'Do I have to apologize? I suppose that's the rule, isn't it?'

'Don't do anything you don't feel like, Eli. We don't always keep to the rules.'

'I've noticed that.'

Albert was not too pleased with the remark.

'It was only luck,' Eli said, 'that you didn't make a colossal fool of yourself.'

'I took a perfectly legitimate risk that turned out to be justified.'

'O.K. Keep your 'air on.'

Albert involuntarily ran his hand over his head. He felt very little hair.

Eli burst into laughter, and Albert, after hesitating crossly, could not help joining in.

Eli suddenly stood up. 'Where's your records? I want to see them. If you please, Perfessor.'

'What for?'

'I believe you did it, but I want to see how.' He had lost his chastened tone. 'I bet you didn't do it as elegantly as I did.'

'I don't know about that.' All the same Albert reached for his notebooks.

'I do,' said Eli. 'I bet you.' He gave a knowing look and laid a finger against his beautifully curled-under nose. 'Believe me.'

Eli looked through Albert's notebooks while Albert read Eli's sheets of paper.

When they got to the end it was Eli who asked Albert's opinion.

'Superb,' said Albert.

'Elegant?' said Eli.

'Yes,' said Albert.

There was a long pause.

Albert said: 'We're the only two men in the country who could have done this.'

Eli said: 'I don't know about that' – meaning he doubted Albert's capacity.

'This time I do,' said Albert benignly. 'I was certain you could do it if you set about it, Eli. You probably don't realize just how much you've learnt from me.'

For the next few months Albert lived in a whirl of committees and personal meetings. He passionately believed that he had a scientific weapon which might one day win the war. Having convinced himself that he was a great scientist, he soon let Redvers Jameson convince him that he must be a great impresario too. His weapon must, in the up-to-date language of Jameson, be sold.

Albert sold it.

In the following year he was installed as the director of a secret research establishment. He had funds, he had staff; and he had the prospect of being able to acquire, if he wanted them, more funds and more staff.

The establishment was set up in a large boarding school for boys at a place called Ribblesfield, some thirty miles from Callandars. In the burning sunshine of the summer of 1940 Albert watched troops preparing the place for him to work in.

'How different from university methods,' Albert said, when Redvers Jameson paid him a flying visit.

In the park surrounding the school an encampment of huts had sprung up: round the periphery soldiers had strung up miles of barbed wire: there were sentries at all the openings.

Redvers Jameson made cordial assenting noises.

'I don't think,' Albert said, 'I shall ever be able to go back to academic life again.' And the present moment overwhelmed him.

'It was a matter of great regret on the part of my minister that we failed to persuade Grevel to join you.'

Albert was wrenched out of the present moment.

'Someone has got to carry on in the universities,' he said. 'I did not feel that we ought to press Grevel in the circumstances.'

Jameson nodded his head wisely.

When he left the university for Ribblesfield, Albert had got Eli appointed acting professor in his place.

'There's only one thing now that I want to make me completely content,' Albert said. He gave Jameson his social smile. 'That's to have my wife and family here with me.'

'Ah yes,' said Jameson. 'How well I understand that!'

Albert was speaking the truth. There was no doubt, when he sent Margaret to Daunton, that he had wanted to get rid of her. There was no doubt now that he just as passionately wanted her back again – more passionately, if it comes to that.

Albert was always too sudden for Margaret. By the time her stubbornness was borne down to the extent of permitting her to reconcile herself to Albert's actions, Albert reversed them. Poor Margaret! It meant that when he sent for her to come to Ribblesfield she could not bring herself to believe that he really wanted her.

It was about a year after their separation that Albert and Margaret were re-united. Albert, proud and happy, was brimming with emotion. He was slightly dashed to find the children were managing perfectly well, in their self-centred way, without him; but his instincts told him he could soon get them back. With Margaret it was different. There was something wrong.

Margaret appeared to be unwell. Albert, with hypochondria constantly in the offing nowadays, took it seriously, but ascribed it to fatigue from the journey. They discovered that she had a slight temperature. And at night he was frequently awakened by her coughing.

Next morning he questioned her and found that she had been coughing at night for some months.

'Have you called a doctor?'

Margaret shook her head.

'Why not?'

Margaret shook her head again. She glanced away, but not before Albert had caught a strange look in her eye. He was convinced she had meant to say it did not matter.

Albert felt a spurt of anger, as if she had done nothing about it on purpose to make life more difficult for him. He sent for a doctor immediately.

The doctor seemed to think there was nothing wrong with Margaret. Albert felt more than a spurt of anger, and only just remembered his own new eminence in society to the extent of waiting until the door closed behind the man before exclaiming: 'You stupid ———!' He had another doctor on the spot within an hour.

Margaret was taken into Manchester to have her lungs X-rayed. Albert insisted on being shown the plates himself. He recalled with extraordinary poignance a sparkling sunny day in Nice when he had touched her hand across the table and she had told him they suspected in Switzerland that she had tuberculosis. He had no doubt what the diagnosis would be now.

The disease was not as serious as Albert feared. The diagnosis was what was known as a shadow on the lung instead of a spot. The only way to treat it was for Margaret to go into a sanatorium immediately.

All restraint fell away. That night Margaret embraced Albert with fervour and abandon.

'I'm terribly, terribly sorry,' she kept saying.

Albert stroked her hair. 'Don't say that, my darling.'

'You were angry at first, weren't you? Weren't you, Albert?'

'What if I was?' His voice was full and kind.

She began to weep and he comforted her. 'I don't want to part from you,' she cried. 'I don't want to part from you ever.'

The morning came when Margaret had to leave Ribblesfield. She smiled at the children: her mother was coming to take them back to Daunton. Then Albert drove her away. She refused to let him take her all the way, and they parted where she changed into the doctor's motor-car for the second part of her journey. They had a moment together outside the doctor's house. It was a cool misty autumn morning. There was a rowan tree growing beside the gate, and bunches of scarlet berries dangled among the yellowing foliage. Albert noticed tiny drops of moisture condensed on Margaret's hair: he stroked them away. He embraced her.

Albert realized that she was strangely quiet. 'What's the matter?' Her face had a faintly distorted look.

Albert looked into her eyes. 'You must be at ease with yourself, if you want to get better quickly,' he said.

Margaret nodded and looked away.

There was a pause. Then Albert said impulsively:

'All this was very unnecessary . . . You know I really love you.'

Margaret looked at him again. The expression on her face changed. Her body leaned against his.

Albert went on looking into her eyes and smiling.

Margaret looked back. Tears came and she let them fall unashamedly.

CHAPTER FIVE
BANG GOES THE ACCOLADE

I expect that coming upon it so many years later you will already have perceived the irony of Albert's triumph. The second world war rolled by and neither side used gas.

Albert's predicament was a sad one. He was more relieved than anything else when it became obvious to him that his nerve-gas was not going to be made use of – but if it was not made use of, how could he get recognition for his discovery? He asked himself: he asked other people too. He did not want to have anything to do with killing inordinately large numbers of people, far, far from it. All he wanted to do was to become Sir Albert Woods.

And so he spent the war years in a gush of research and a frenzy of anxiety.

Albert's work at Ribblesfield was hugely successful. The Prime Minister followed its progress. Albert was visited by ministers of state, generals and distinguished scientists. In the establishment, Albert developed a truly Napoleonic touch. He inflated his staff with his exuberant confidence. He gave orders with grandeur from a great height, and if anyone disagreed with them he promptly got down on all-fours in a violent quarrel – in fact, with one scientist, whose temperament resembled Eli's, he got down on all-fours in physical combat. No one at Ribblesfield complained that life was dull or unsatisfactory. And the research they did there was remarkable.

By the beginning of 1944 Callandars were beginning to manufacture a nerve-gas that was not a laboratory specimen but a powerful weapon of war. Albert found it impossible to keep away from committees and meetings, anywhere where two or three people were gathered together who might overlook his claims. He paid a couple of flying visits to America. I repeat that he did not want his weapon to be used. But oh! how he wanted everybody to know about it.

In the spring of 1944 Albert was visited by inspiration. He did not want his weapon to be used against human beings, but there was nothing against having a secret full-scale demonstration with laboratory animals. It was arranged on a stretch of the North African desert in the presence of representatives of all the Allied Chiefs-of-Staff. The expense and the palaver were fabulous. The demonstration was, of course, satisfactory and impressive, and totally unnecessary.

Albert felt he had reached the peak of his career as far as making public appearances was concerned. He was overwhelmed by the success of his own showmanship. He thought he would be bound to get a knighthood when, at one of the celebrations after the demonstration, everybody else present happened to be a Sir.

'They *can't* pass over me now! . . .' It was a cry from the heart.

At last, just before the war ended, Albert had a hint from Redvers Jameson that an honour was bound to come his way. Albert had gained the favour of a minister of state before whose eminence Jameson was so deferential as to be abashed. The minister had said publicly that something must be done for Woods.

It could only be a knighthood, Albert was convinced. The anxiety which had formerly kept his inflation in check now lost its grip. He began to expect a letter to arrive at any moment asking him if he would accept. Gone were his pretensions to aristocratic birth and any of the advantages of gentlemanly breeding. He was right back at the start, a man of the people. What could be greater than a man of the people who had risen to dazzling heights? He began to see himself as having risen from lowlier people than was the case, and demoted his father from the comfortable petty *bourgeoisie* to the deepest proletariat. Albert Woods, the starving newspaper-boy who had become a Sir – it was a beautiful idea.

Albert was making his plans for when the war was over. He had decided to go back to academic research. Practically every scientist in the war who had come from a university was at that time threatening to go back at the earliest moment. Those who had been successful in their war jobs professed to have had enough of them: those who had been unsuccessful seemed to feel that such threats put up their price. Albert counted among the most successful: he had had more than enough of Ribblesfield: he saw greater glories ahead. What glories? He was only forty-five. He felt no diminution in his creative powers. He was going about in a constant state of nervous excitement which presaged the inspiration of a grandiose scheme of research. The thought had come to him that he might end up with a Nobel Prize.

And then, out of a blue sky the Gods saw fit to hurl a thunderbolt. It was only a small thunderbolt, and though it hit Albert Woods between the ears, one would have thought it hardly worth the trouble of hurling. But far be it from me to criticize Them. This is what happened.

A grand and distinguished entertainment was given at Daunton. Lord Daunton, now over eighty but revived by the thought of the war being over, decided to open the main part of the house again. The heir to the title and all his family were staying there; Sir Rowland and the Honourable Lady Dibdin, Margaret Woods and her three children; the son of one of the old Lord's lifelong friends who held an appointment in the Royal Household; and a distinguished historian of lowly origins whom they all treated as if he were a court jester.

There was a series of parties to which the owners of neighbouring big houses came, bringing their own guests. Albert arrived one evening when such a party was in progress. Margaret had told him that someone from another house was going to bring to this party the very minister of state to whom he would owe his coming honour.

It was a beautiful summer's night, and when Albert drove his Rolls Royce round a curve in the road and first came in sight of the house, he was startled. Under a dark blue sky, flickering with summer lightning, the house lay in its sheltering hollow with the small chapel beside it; and after six years of extinction, all the windows were lighted. The spectacle was startling in its beauty. Albert's spirit was suddenly illumined by the contrast between his first arrival at this house and his arrival now. He was coming from an important meeting in London: he was expecting his letter about a knighthood any day. The company was going to be distinguished: so was he.

And there, it may be, lay the cause of his downfall – in presumptuousness. How much better if he had gone to the party as he had gone to Daunton for the first time in his life, humbly and admiringly, on bended knee, to marry the grand-daughter of a Lord!

Margaret left the party to greet Albert.

'Has the minister come?' he asked.

Margaret nodded. She came up to their room and sat on the edge of the bed while he changed into evening-dress. A footman brought Albert a bottle of champagne with his Lordship's compliments. Albert drank a couple of glasses immediately.

'You look very beautiful tonight,' he said to Margaret.

Margaret was in good health again. Her hair glistened with a touch of brilliantine and her eyes were sharp and lively. She was wearing the diamond necklace she wore on the summer night Albert asked her to marry him.

'That's a beautiful dress.'

Margaret blushed.

Albert sat on the edge of the bed and put his arms round her.

'Albert, you must get dressed. You've simply got to put in an appearance straight away.'

Albert breathed heavily in her ear.

Margaret escaped from his arms and ran across to the window. Red-faced and puffing, Albert put on his trousers.

'Pour me some more of that champagne,' he said. He went to the dressing-table. 'It's perfectly delectable.' His voice assumed the silkiness which would bloom egregiously when he joined the social gathering downstairs. 'Perfectly delectable, my dear.' He glanced at himself in the looking-glass. 'Your grandfather knows how to choose champagne.'

When his toilet was finished Margaret came and stood beside him. He put his arm round her waist, which was substantial: Margaret did not attempt a similar move because Albert's waist was non-existent. In the looking-glass Margaret's diamonds sparkled and Albert's shirt-front made a bulging expanse of light. A handsome couple – who, seeing them, would not realize they were made to be Sir Albert and Lady Woods? They went to the nursery and looked at the children asleep, and then they went down to the party.

The big salon at Daunton was L-shaped, having been made from two rooms, one at a slightly higher level than the other, and it was still decorated in the mode which had smitten Lord Daunton's grandfather some century and a half earlier – the Chinese style of

Chippendale and his colleagues. The walls were hung with beautiful hand-painted Chinese paper in dull carmine and plum colour, and most of the woodwork was gilded; over the chimney-pieces and behind the light-sconces were faded looking-glasses in gilt frames that were fantastically scrolled, filigreed and adorned with stalactites and monkeys. But it was the furniture that was most wondrous – dark glowing pieces of mahogany that constantly reminded you of pagodas and yet could not possibly have been made anywhere but in England. The total effect was one of sumptuous ludicrous beauty.

Albert and Margaret entered the room and went directly to Lord Daunton, who was sitting near the doorway in his wheel-chair, resplendently dressed in tails that looked about thirty years old and a purple skull-cap. Every time someone fresh came in he got out of the wheel-chair perversely to demonstrate that he did not need it. He was very frail but his eyes still sparkled: it was from him that Margaret inherited her fine aquiline profile and her faintly sullen expression. No one, not even the most disaffected, dispossessed son of the people, could have denied Lord Daunton's great distinction.

There were many more people present than Albert had expected, and the company had the unusually glossy look that struck one when one saw for the first time after the war an assembly where all the men were in evening-dress. As soon as he had shaken hands with Lord Daunton and the gentleman from the Royal Household, Albert began trying to catch the minister's eye. He succeeded. Ah! ... He was able to concentrate on what he was saying to the aristocrats. A footman passed by with a tray of glasses of champagne: Albert took one and began to drink it.

'Life is very pleasant,' he said. He felt almost patronizing towards the bland faces round him, almost proprietorial towards the fabulous Chippendale *chinoiserie*. 'This champagne,' he said with lingering social silkiness, 'is perfectly delectable.'

In due course Albert moved along to the group, which included Dibdin, surrounding the minister. The minister turned a smile upon Albert and invited him into the circle.

For obvious reasons I cannot tell you the minister's name. He was a big handsome man, and he turned a smile upon everyone. The smile was quite fixed; it might have been painted on his handsome features, and it expressed a mixture of self-importance and self-satisfaction – rightly, for he was a very important minister indeed and he had every reason to be satisfied.

Albert received the minister's smile with satisfaction, and offered some remarks that were appropriately polite, inflated, and touched with sycophancy. He left the group feeling satisfied with his performance. He made his way fatly, with his pop-eyes bulging, with his purple cheeks and bald head shining, into the other half of the room.

In the other half of the room he hardly saw anyone he knew. The first half of the L seemed by chance to have contained most of the men, this one most of the women. He went towards the first group he came to because they were laughing at some joke or other. They made a place for him, and standing confidently with a glass of champagne in his hand Albert glanced round the circle. Two of the women were quite pretty, but his attention was flicked sharply by the third, to whom he took an instant dislike. Looking at the other two, he curled his lips in his social smile and said:

'May I share the joke?'

The two pretty women glanced at each other: the other one said boldly:

'It was a joke about the chosen race.'

'I beg your pardon.' Albert had to confront her directly. She was a big, healthy, shapeless, middle-aged woman, with dark hair turning grey and large brown eyes. It is not easy to explain why Albert took a dislike to her, unless you admit that one can decide at sight that another person is both stupid and compelling.

To avoid being too hard on Albert I must add that it is just possible to find physical reasons for his dislike. The woman was rather over-dressed, it is true, but then so was Cleopatra. On the other hand, what Cleopatra presumably had not were pink rims to her eyelids and a rather loud whinnying stylized laugh.

Albert did not realize at first what she meant. 'I beg your pardon. . . .'

'Come, you're not one of them yourself, but you must know who the chosen race are. The Jews, of course.' Her brown eyes seemed to brighten with fun – she was rather drunk – and she threw her head back to laugh again. It was a laugh she had copied from a celebrated actress of the time.

'I see,' said Albert. Whether she was joking or not, he was furious. It was a subject about which no decent humane person could possibly joke.

They both smiled at each other throughout the pause that followed.

'This is the first party I've been to for five years,' she said, 'where there isn't a single Jew, thank God!'

'Which is your God – Jehovah?'

'Thank God the war's over and we can say what we like about the Jews. I think Hitler was right. But perfectly right.'

'You must be mad.' Albert glared at her. 'Or drunk.'

'That's what you think.' She leaned towards him. 'If I had my way, little man, I'd load them all in Channel steamers and take the bung out of the bottom.'

'You stupid ———!'

Albert's shout sounded above the noise of conversation. Drunk though she was the woman was completely taken aback.

Albert, his pugnacity inflamed by champagne, lost his head altogether.

'Leave this house immediately!' he cried. 'You're not fit to be here, whoever you are. Go on! Leave!' His face was as red and purple as the Chinese wall-paper.

The big woman walked straight towards him and with a hefty arm pushed him backwards. 'Let me pass!'

She did pass. She went down the steps into the other half of the room and vanished. Albert, not to mention the other guests, watched in stupefaction.

Albert said to all and sundry. 'I'm glad I said that. She's a stupid ——.' He paused. 'Who is she?'

She was the wife of the minister.

It was a deplorable incident. Albert never found out exactly how near he had been to being offered a knighthood. In all probability he had thought he was much nearer than he really was. Anyway, the letter he had been awaiting never came.

During the next few weeks he felt certain Redvers Jameson was avoiding him. And then, when they did meet, something Jameson said about another acquaintance getting a knighthood, something in the coolness, almost the impartiality, of Jameson's tone, told Albert that he was out of the running.

Albert was deflated. The incident at the party had been deplorable, his behaviour absurd. Flown with wine and pride, you might say, he had put his foot in it. I cannot agree. The impulse that prompted his outburst was decent and humane, it was generous, pugnacious and thoroughly admirable. If only it had not been directed at the minister's wife!

I suppose none but a few can realize what misery the failure to achieve worldly honours may cause a man, a hopeful striving little man who wants honour among his fellows. All right, I will leave it at that. The Gods in Their wisdom had hurled a thunderbolt.

And this is where I come to the end of my story. Obviously it is not the end of the life-story of Albert Woods: I observed at the beginning that I am writing this in 1952, and he is still alive, or to put it more vulgarly, alive and kicking. Why then, end it now, with the hero deflated, with the little man just missing his heart's desire?

It seems to me that human vanity is such that none of us likes to see someone else having things all his own way. And so I have chosen to lose sight of Albert Woods when in our weakness we can feel regret at his momentary downfall instead of irritation at his being on top of the world.

I should like to lose sight of Albert himself through taking a cosmic view, through observing that in our country we have not only one Albert Woods but many. I am willing to bet that at any moment of our history there is an Albert Woods telling his ape-headed school-fellows that he is cut out for glory: I might even be willing to bet there is an Albert Woods strutting about with a Nobel Prize. And as for an Albert Woods being snubbed for his pains! . . . Look around you and you will see for yourself.

We have many of them, exuberantly being heroes to their mates, exuberantly making fools of themselves: struggling with their own temperaments – not to mention other people's – in a mixture of passionate endeavour and touching absurdity. Do not you agree? I thought as much. That is why I suggested you should look around. In fact you might not have to look far.

No distance at all, you say. May I remind you of what I said at the start? No distance at all.